Also by Ray Hobbs and published

G000097365

Published Elsewhere

UNKNOWN WARRIOR

RAY HOBBS

Wingspan Press

Published in the United States and the United Kingdom
by WingSpan Press, Livermore, CA

The WingSpan name, logo and colophon are the trademarks
of WingSpan Publishing.

ISBN 978-1-63683-020-9 (pbk.)
ISBN 978-1-63683-982-0 (ebook)

First edition 2021

Printed in the United States of America

www.wingspanpress.com

1 2 3 4 5 6 7 8 9 10

This book is dedicated to the memory of my late grandfather Harry Blamires, one of the first auxiliary firemen.

RH

'This is no war of chieftains or princes, of dynasties or national ambition; it is a war of peoples and of causes. There are vast numbers, not only in this island but in every land, who will render faithful service in this war, but whose names will never be known, whose deeds will never be recorded. This is a war of the unknown warriors; but let all strive without failing in faith or in duty, and the dark curse of Hitler will be lifted from our age.'

W.S. Churchill, July 1940.

Sources and Acknowledgements

Wilmoth, V. J., The Auxiliary Fireman (London, Lomax, Erskine & Co Ltd., 1939)

London County Council, *Fire Over London* (London, Hutchinson & Co, 1942. Republished London, Imperial War Museum, 1995)

Doyle, P., *ARP and Civil Defence in the Second World War* (Oxford, Shire Publications Ltd., 2010)

Leete, J., *Under Fire* (Stroud, Sutton Publishing, 2008)

Harris, C., *Blitz Diary* (Stroud, The History Press, 2010)

Gardiner, J., *The Blitz* (London, Harper Collins, 2010)

Baker, E. with Baker, H., *A City in Flames* (Beverley, Hutton Press Ltd., 1992)

Bellman, L. *et al*, *Nursing Through the Years* (Barnsley, Pen and Sword Books Ltd., 2018)

Winston, B., *"Fires Were Started"* (London, British Film Institute Publishing, 1999)

As always, I wish to acknowledge the invaluable assistance of my brother Chris in the planning of this book.

RH

Author's Note

I have tried, as far as the narrative allows, to offer some explanation of the technical terms used in the story, but I feel that a quick reference guide is always useful. I hope my readers will find it so.

Let's begin with the item most readily associated with the fire service, which is the fire engine, referred to by its crews as the **Appliance** or **Pump**. Only members of the public call them 'fire engines', but you are about to be admitted into an arcane and fascinating world.

A **Trailer Pump** was, as its name implies, towed by a motor vehicle, often a taxi, and used, in the absence of a larger appliance, to supply hoses with water. Every little helped.

Any fitment that goes on to the end of a hose is, even to this day, called a **Branch.** No, neither do I, and I suspect that the origin of the term has become lost in the labyrinth of time.

A **DP**, or **Dual-Purpose** Appliance is so called because it carries both an escape ladder and a pump, so that it can be used to save lives as well as for fighting fires. As such, it is well-represented by the modern service's motto: 'Save Lives, Protect Property.'

A **Sub-Station** was the smallest unit in the wartime fire service organisation. They were often based, for convenience, in school buildings, the children having been evacuated.

An **HU**, or **Heavy Unit** was an AFS appliance capable of delivering 1200 gallons of water per minute. It was usually a welcome sight.

The **Watch Room** was the room in which the telephones, the alarm panel and suchlike were located. It was often manned, if you'll allow the word, by personnel of both sexes, but the responsibility sometimes fell, as it does in this book, to the ladies.

The **WAFS** was the **Women's Auxiliary Fire Service**. Whilst not directly involved in fire-fighting, they performed a multitude of tasks and were indispensable.

Riders were simply the front-line firemen who rode on the appliance to an incident.

Red Riders crewed the red-painted appliances of the professional fire brigades, but AFS men who worked alongside them were still paid less than their professional counterparts.

The Bells Go Down was simply a reference to the alarm bells that called firemen to an incident.

'Knock off and Make Up' was the order to close the valves and stow equipment back on the appliance preparatory to returning to the station or sub-station. Needless to say, it was a popular order, especially at the end of an exhausting and harrowing incident.

An **Escape** was a wheeled ladder capable of being extended to 50 or 55 feet.

An **Extension Ladder** was carried on a motor pump, and could be extended to 40 feet. A smaller one, extending to 30 feet was also carried by auxiliary appliances for use where a wheeled escape could not be used.

A **Turntable Ladder** was operated hydraulically and powered by the appliance's engine. It extended to 100 feet and could be swivelled as well as extended and retracted.

Reichsmarschall Hermann **Göring** was head of the Luftwaffe, and therefore responsible for starting all those fires.

Shrapnel is the name given to fragments, large or small, of a shell or bomb casing. It could inflict terrible wounds and was the main reason for sheltering during a raid.

An **Incendiary** was a small, yet devastating bomb capable of starting a major fire.

An appliance is said to be **On the Run** when it is leaving the appliance room to attend an incident. It has nothing to do with evading capture. The term 'run' describes the sloping floor designed originally to help the horses overcome inertia.

An **HE**, or **High Explosive** bomb was the kind, other than the incendiary, most often dropped on British cities during the Blitz.

The **Stirrup Pump** was a manually-operated pump used in conjunction with a bucket of water to tackle incendiaries. It was so called because it resembled a stirrup, with a flat steel base on which the operator placed one foot to steady the pump in operation. The other part of the stirrup was placed in the water. It may sound puny, but it often provided the difference between safety and disaster.

The **Curtain** was the protective oilskin shroud that hung beneath a fireman's helmet. It was designed to enclose his head as protection against gas attack, but that never became necessary. Instead, it was worn over the back of the neck as a defence against water. It made little difference, because firemen still came off watch soaked to the skin, and auxiliary firemen were issued with only one tunic and one pair of trousers and waterproof leggings. Needless to say, drying facilities were scarce.

'**Valves Down**' was a warning that water was about to be passed to the pumps. The valves would be closed until the pumps were ready for use.

I hope that is of some help, and that, now you have been made privy to some of the language of Mr Churchill's 'heroes with grimy faces', you can relax and enjoy the story.

RH

PROLOGUE

LONDON, 1940

THE BLITZ

Lashed though it was to the top rung of the extension ladder, the hose bucked backward and upward as water surged at high pressure from the pump, and Ted was careful to keep the nozzle pointed at the base of the fire, where the water was most needed. As he did so, he felt the heat of the blaze on his hands and face. Perspiration had already saturated his underclothes and woollen uniform in spite of the severe winter chill.

It was impossible to see where the fire began and, perhaps more appropriately, where it ended. Certainly, it made a nonsense of the blackout, illuminating the skyline as it did; at times, it seemed that the whole of London's dockland were in flames, and that every fire appliance in Greater London and beyond had come to the incident to lend assistance. The hard-pressed London Fire Brigade and auxiliary firemen needed all the help they could summon.

On the other side of the conflict, the unrelenting Luftwaffe continued to drop its lethal cargo on the already stricken docks, buildings, and often the ships tied up alongside. Every now and again, a high explosive bomb would explode close enough for Ted to feel the shockwave at the top of his ladder. Most of the bombs were incendiaries, however, loaded into the bombers with the intention of consuming as much of London as possible by fire, or at the very least, paralysing the city's way of life.

Concerned though he was with his allotted task, Ted still found himself thinking about the curious chain of events that had brought him to the East End as an auxiliary fireman.

1

A West Riding Town

September 1938

Wilfred Dewhirst switched off the wireless set and sat in silence. After a few more seconds he looked across at his son, who had been similarly engrossed in the news from Heston Airport. The nation had been in suspense even before Neville Chamberlain's departure for Munich, and impromptu celebrations were already being reported throughout the country, although not everyone was so readily convinced by his claim to have secured 'peace for our time.'

'I don't know what to believe,' said Mr Dewhirst. 'I don't trust either of 'em, Hitler or Chamberlain.'

'Neither do I, Dad. I'd like to know who Chamberlain thinks he's kidding. If he's done any good at all, it seems to me he's given us a bit more time to prepare for the worst.'

'In that case, lad, all we can do is hope and pray.' Mr Dewhirst had served with the Army from 1915 until after the end of the war, and it was clearly an experience he was reluctant to revisit.

No one could have taken the two men for anything but father and son. They were equally tall and they shared the same powerful physique. Wilfred was a market gardener, whilst Ted, a master at Beckworth Boys' Grammar School, was an all-round sportsman. They even shared the same firm jawline and expressive, brown eyes, although Wilfred's face was naturally marked with the lines of a man of twice his son's age, and his dark hair was edged and flecked with grey.

Practical as ever, Mrs Dewhirst said, 'I'll put the kettle on and make us all a cup of tea.'

Her husband looked up at the walnut-cased clock on the mantlepiece and said, 'Eileen should be home by now. Where did you say she'd gone?'

'She went round to see one of her friends from school. Their cat's just had kittens, and she couldn't wait to see them.'

'Cats,' said Mr Dewhirst, making a face at the thought, 'the gardener's pest.'

'At least they keep the pigeons away,' Ted reminded him.

'There is that,' conceded his father. Then, waiting until Mrs Dewhirst was out of the room, he said, 'I suppose you'll be thinking of doing something daft if Chamberlain's efforts come to naught, like joining up.'

Ted had been wondering how to break the news, so he was glad his father had mentioned it first. 'I've been thinking about that new thing they've started, Dad, the RNVWR. They've opened a training centre in Bradford.'

'What's that when it's at home?'

'The Royal Naval Volunteer Wireless Reserve.'

'Oh, aye? What's made you suddenly interested in wireless?'

'I'm not, really, but it's the only training the Navy can offer so far inland.' Ted was spared his father's response for the moment, because his sister Eileen had arrived home and was chattering excitedly to her mother in the kitchen.

'Fifteen years old,' said her father, 'and she can prattle like a grown woman.'

As if to confirm that assessment, Eileen came into the room with unabated excitement. 'Have you heard the news? There isn't going to be a war after all. It's all settled, and they say that Britain and Germany will never go to war again. Isn't it wonderful?' She was a naturally cheerful girl, engaging, rather than conventionally pretty, with dark, shoulder-length hair and friendly eyes.

'You'll just have to keep your fingers crossed,' Ted told her, but I hope you're right, for once.'

'Why do you say, "for once"? You talk as if I'm never right.' She put her hands on his throat, pretending to strangle him. 'Shall I kill him now, Dad, or save it for later?'

'Whichever you like, love, but do it quietly.'

Kneeling beside Ted's chair, she said, 'I've got a favour to ask you.'

'You're going a funny way about it.'

'Don't be daft. Listen, will you help me with my Latin homework? It has to be in on Monday.'

'You should have done it when you came in from school, you scatterbrain.'

'I couldn't. I still can't. That's why I want you to help me.' She grasped his arm and shook it. 'Go on, say you'll help me.'

'Go on, Ted,' said his father, 'say you will, 'cause there'll be no peace in this house 'til you do.'

'All right,' said Ted. 'Bring it down and I'll have a look at it.' He would have a cup of tea first to celebrate the fact that he'd broken the unpopular news to his father about the Navy thing. The Great War had left a marked impression on his generation that left little enthusiasm for military service.

———◆◆———

When Ted telephoned the Wireless Training Centre, the instructor, a Petty Officer Telegraphist in the Royal Navy, invited him to attend the next 'drill night', as he called the training session, on Tuesday, which he did.

He was impressed by the number of recruits already under training, and he looked forward to joining them.

He was interviewed and given a selection test, and then he was told to make an appointment with the Admiralty Surgeon for his medical. The doctor in question was a GP with a surgery in a Victorian terrace house just below Bradford Royal Infirmary, where Ted waited, along with several patients, to be called in. Eventually, the doctor came to the waiting room and asked, 'Is Mr Charles Edwin Dewhirst here?'

Ted got up and followed him into his consulting room.

The doctor eyed him appraisingly and said, 'You look like a fit young man. Are you a keen sportsman?' His accent placed his origins in or around Edinburgh.

'Yes, I've played cricket and rugby, and I help with the coaching at the school where I teach. I've done lots of boxing, swimming and athletics as well.'

'I thought as much. Take off your clothes.'

Ted undressed, and the doctor went on to measure his height and test his sight and hearing before asking him to lie on the examination couch.

Ted asked, 'Are you likely to need a urine specimen from me?'

'Most certainly.'

'Good. Could I possibly do that now, before you start pressing on my bladder?' He'd been uncomfortably aware, since getting off the bus, that he needed to relieve himself.

'That's a good idea,' said the doctor, picking up a measuring flask and pointing to a screen in the corner. 'Go behind that screen and then bring me a specimen in this flask.'

Gratefully, Ted took the vessel and obliged, emerging with a full flask and a feeling of welcome relief.

'Very good,' said the doctor, dipping litmus paper into the specimen. 'Hm,' he said as the litmus reacted. 'No sugar, slight acid. Quite satisfactory.'

The doctor palpated his torso for a few minutes, declaring himself satisfied. 'Excellent. Now I need to ask you a few questions.'

'Ask away, Doc.'

'Is there any insanity in your family?'

'No, there's an acceptable level of eccentricity, but no one's barking mad.'

'None of your antecedents at all?'

'No, my ancestors all managed to stay out of the bin.'

'Good, good. Are you haemophilic?'

'Not that I've noticed.'

'You certainly would have noticed. Have you ever suffered from haemorrhoids?'

'Happily, no.'

'All right. Just bend over and let me examine your back passage.'

It seemed a lot to ask. 'Do you have to do that, Doc? I mean, I told you I'd never had haemorrhoids. Can't you take my word for it?'

'I'm afraid not. I must look. It won't take more than a second.'

'But I told you there was no insanity in my family, and you accepted that. Why can't you just believe me when I tell you I haven't got piles? I mean, if anyone would know, I should.'

'It's the nature of the examination.'

It was obvious that the doctor's heart was set on an inspection of the fundament, so Ted reluctantly bowed in submission and studied the pattern in the carpet as a distraction.

'Hm,' said the doctor, 'quite satisfactory.'

'You're the only one in this room who's surprised, Doc,' said Ted, resuming an upright stance.

'There are things that have to be checked, Mr Dewhirst. Now, have you, as far as you know, any allergies?'

'Only one.'

'Well, don't keep it to yourself. What is it?'

'I'm allergic to soya.' It had been an isolated reaction, but serious enough for him to remember the symptoms.

At the mention of soya, the doctor's eyebrows rose sharply. 'Oh, and when did you realise that?'

'When I was taken to hospital, covered in hives and struggling to breathe. It was when I was at university in Manchester. Largely in the spirit of enquiry, some of us had been to a restaurant in Chinatown. Never again.'

'I see.' The doctor put down his pen and eyed him gravely. 'In that case,' he said, 'I'm afraid I can't possibly pass you as fit for service in the Royal Naval Volunteer Reserve.'

'Why not? What has soya to do with operating a wireless set at sea?'

'It's what they might give you to eat at sea that would cause the problem, Mr Dewhirst. If this country were to go to war, foods that we currently take for granted would be in short supply, just as they were during the last war, and food substitutes such as soya would inevitably become part of our regular diet. That is why I cannot pass you. I'm sorry.'

———————

The medical for the Territorial Army also went well until the moment the doctor asked about allergies, and the verdict was, depressingly, the same.

'I'm sorry, Mr Dewhirst, I can't pass you as fit for military service.'

'But I'd surely run the same risk as a civilian,' he protested.

'As a civilian,' the doctor told him, 'you can exercise more care with the food you eat. The armed forces are not equipped to cater for individual needs.'

Ted wasn't going down without a fight. 'As I see it,' he said, 'the risk would be mine, and I'm happy to run that risk.'

'The Army would be responsible for your health, Mr Dewhirst, and they're not prepared to chance it. You must accept my decision.'

———————

The RAF was Ted's last resort. He'd never been particular keen on the idea, but his first and second choices had rejected him, so he went to the recruiting office in Leeds to make enquiries.

There, he found a warrant officer who resembled an amiable mastiff, in that he displayed the conflicting qualities of a commanding voice and an inviting manner.

''Ow can I 'elp you, young man?'

'I have a question about the RAF medical,' Ted told him.

'It's not really my line of country, if you know what I mean, but I'll do my best to answer your question.'

'That's kind of you. Would a food allergy cause me to fail the medical?'

The warrant officer put on a thinking face. 'What food would that be, to which you are allergic to, young man?'

In the interest of politeness, Ted tried not to wince at the man's muddled syntax. 'Basically,' he said, 'it's soya.'

'In that case, you would most certainly be rejected. The Air Ministry is quite….' He stopped and thought. 'What's the word I'm looking for?'

'Definite? Decided? Emphatic? Categorical? Insistent?' Any one of those words seemed depressingly likely.

The warrant officer smiled gratefully. 'The Air Ministry is, as you say, quite definite about that. There will possibly come a time when soya will be widely used—'

'I understand,' said Ted wearily, 'but thanks for your help.'

'It was no trouble, young fellow. Good day to you.'

'Good day.'

Ted left the recruiting office and made his way back to the bus stop in Aire Street, a man of sorrow, rejected and acquainted with grief. War was inevitable, and he was barred from playing his part in the defence of his country. It was too awful. He also realised that he'd just missed the bus, and the next one wouldn't be along for another half-hour.

While he was waiting, he heard an insistent bell in the distance. It was growing louder, so it was obviously approaching, possibly along Boar Lane. Like a small boy, he waited to find out if the bell belonged to a fire engine, a police car or an ambulance, and he was rewarded when a magnificent red fire engine sped past with its bell ringing and with firemen on the back still pulling on their boots and adjusting the chin straps of their helmets. The scene had a romance all of its own.

As he rode home, he gave some thought to his next step.

———▶◀———

The doctor greeted him as if he were an old friend. 'Come in, dear boy,' he said. 'I examined you recently, didn't I?'

'Yes, for the RNVR. I didn't realise they shared your services with other organisations.'

With the modesty of a philanthropist admitting to his good works, the doctor said, 'I help out various government bodies when I can.'

It sounded as if he had a few lucrative side-lines, but Ted kept that thought to himself. Instead, he said, 'before we go any further, can we address the question of allergies?'

'Oh, we'll deal with that in a moment. First of all, is there any insanity in your family?'

'No, they're as sane as they were the last time you asked me that question.'

'That was then, Mr Dewhirst. This is a completely different examination. Please remove your clothes.'

It felt remarkably similar to the first examination, another impression that Ted kept to himself as he disrobed.

'Now, are you haemophilic?'

Ted replied patiently, 'No, I'm not.'

'Have you ever suffered from haemorrhoids?'

'No.' It really was a case of *déjà vu*, and quite literally, as the doctor's next request confirmed.

'Very good. Please bend over.'

Ted knew better than to argue. Once again, he touched his toes and thought of pleasanter matters.

'Quite satisfactory.' The doctor handed him a flask, probably the same one as before, and said, 'Will you kindly oblige me with a specimen of your urine?'

'It'll be a pleasure, Doctor, but I think we should talk first about allergies.'

'All in good time, my dear fellow. See if you can manage a specimen.'

Ted went behind the screen and filled the flask.

'Very good.' The doctor applied the litmus test. 'No sugar, slight acid,' he reported yet again, quite probably for his own satisfaction.

The remainder of the examination went largely as before, and the doctor wrote busily on the form provided. Eventually, he screwed the cap back on his pen and addressed Ted. 'I think we can safely say,' he said, 'that you are sound in mind and body, Mr Dewhirst.'

It was almost too good to be true. He asked, 'Aren't you going to ask me about food allergies?'

'I don't think so. Why do you ask?'

'You refused to pass me as fit for the Navy because of my allergy to soya, the Territorials wouldn't have me for the same reason and, although I didn't submit myself for a medical, I learned that the RAF were similarly discriminating. Not surprisingly, I expected the sting to be in the tail, as usual.'

'Ah, that was the Navy, Mr Dewhirst. I can't speak for the Army and the Air Force, but I'm not in any way surprised that they take the same line. In the Auxiliary Fire Service, however, you will be part-time, and therefore presumably fed at home, unless you volunteer for full-time service, in which case, you will have to disclose your particular vulnerability to your station cook. It's all very straightforward.' He stood and offered his hand. 'Mr Dewhirst, I wish you every success as an auxiliary fireman.'

2

September 1939

T he school summer holiday had been more than a time for cricket, swimming, a week in Scarborough, and general self-indulgence. When he hadn't been helping his father at the market garden, Ted had also been busy at the Central Fire Station. After a year's training, he had satisfied his superiors with his knowledge of fire brigade organisation, watch room procedure, the fire engine, always referred to either as the 'appliance' or the 'pump', fire-fighting techniques, the motor pump, the trailer pump, escape drills, ladder drills, knots and slings, methods of rescue, fire prevention, and the other, numerous skills and areas of knowledge required of a fireman. He now had a uniform with a steel helmet of the kind issued to members of the armed forces, all of which he maintained with pride despite much teasing by Eileen and his friends. Boys at school were also amused to find that one of their masters was a part-time fireman, but he bore their playful remarks with good humour, confident that his training would one day prove invaluable.

He was at the fire station when the Prime Minister who, one year earlier, had assured the populace of peace for their time, broadcast the news that Britain and the Empire were at war once more with Germany.

It felt odd, the next day, to be returning to school for a new term, when infinitely more momentous events were about to occur. Even so, apart from conversations in the common room and the natural excitement among the boys, normal procedure took place as if the Prime Minister had never spoken. Assembly was followed by an hour of administration, during which timetables were given out, a more complex task than before for Ted, as he now had a fourth form for registration, and its members were embarking on their chosen curricula in preparation for the School Certificate exam. Some would pursue the Classics option, and within it, their individual choices of subject. Others had decided on Moderns with similar variations.

Eventually, timetable matters were dealt with, and ten minutes remained until the change bell, so that some relaxation was possible and pupils were allowed to ask non-curriculum-related questions.

'Sir,' asked one boy, 'will you be joining the forces, like Mr Enright?'

'How do you know about Mr Enright, Harrison?'

'My granny knows Mr Enright's mother, sir. She told her yesterday.'

'I should be inclined to keep that under your hat if I were you. He may not want everyone to know.' It was just possible that the school hierarchy were still in ignorance of his intentions.

'Everybody knows about it, sir.'

'You're a lot of washerwomen, aren't you, Four B? You can't resist a good old gossip. Anyway, for what it's worth, I've been turned down by all three services on medical grounds, so the answer to your original question is no, I'm not.'

Another boy, who had been following the conversation, asked, 'So, are you going to carry on being a part-time fireman, sir?'

'For the time being, Thompson. Of course, that's unless Four B drive me insane, in which case I'll be unfit for service in any organisation.'

His reply brought forth immediate laughter. He was thankful on that occasion that fourteen-year-old boys were easily entertained. It served as a gentle diversion at a time when he was thinking seriously about his immediate future.

———▶◀———

After more serious thought. he made his decision and caught the bus to the fire station immediately after school.

One of the senior firemen saw him arrive and said, 'You're keen, young Dewhirst, coming in at this time. Are you after promotion, or what? You won't get far, turning up in civvies.'

'No, but I'd like to see the Station Officer, if I can.'

'I'd go up now. I don't think he's got anybody with him.'

'Thanks.' Ted climbed the stairs and opened the passage door that led to the seat of power. As he did so, he came face to face with Station Officer Simpson. 'I beg your pardon, sir,' he said, 'I was wondering if you could spare a moment, but I'll come back later if it's not convenient.'

'No, that's all right, Dewhirst. Come into my office.' He ushered Ted into the office at the end of the passage and asked, 'Why aren't you in uniform?'

'I've come straight from school, sir, and I wouldn't normally be here on a Monday anyway, but I wanted to see you because I want to volunteer for full-time service.'

'Do you, by Jove? Well, you have an excellent record, and I'll be happy to have you at the station as a full-time auxiliary fireman, but what brought you to this decision?'

'I've had it in mind since the Prime Minister's announcement, sir, and then today, I learned that one of my colleagues is joining the Air Force. I just feel as if the war's somehow leaving me behind, and I want to catch up with it.'

'I've an awful feeling the war's going to overtake us all before long,' said the station officer with a rueful smile, 'but I see what you mean.' He stood up to pull out the top drawer of a filing cabinet and retrieve an official form. 'If you're absolutely sure, fill this in and leave it in my basket in the general office.'

———▸◄———

Ted's colleague wasn't the only one about to forsake Beckworth for the Air Force. David, the neighbours' eldest son, was due to report soon to the depot for new recruits at Warrington. He'd been a keen member of the Air Defence Cadet Corps for some time, so his early mobilisation was no surprise to anyone. His impending departure was already causing Eileen some distress, however, despite her natural pride at the object of her fancy joining the colours. When Ted arrived home, he found his mother trying to reason with her.

'Eileen, you've got to remember that he's eighteen now, two years older than you, and he's bound to be interested in girls more his own age.'

'Don't say that, Mum.' It was a plea from the heart. 'He says he'll write to me an' everything. He wouldn't say that if he wasn't keen, would he?'

'Oh dear,' said Ted, seeing his sister's tears, 'is this about David?'

'Yes, and where have you been until now? I'd nearly given you up for lost.'

'I've been to the station to see somebody.' There would be time enough to break his news after Eileen had calmed down.

'Well, now you're here, see if you can talk some sense into your sister while I get these vegetables on. Your dad's due home, an' I haven't finished peeling the carrots.' Glancing dismissively in her daughter's direction, she said, 'It doesn't look as if I'm going to get any help with them, either.'

Ted took his sister's hand and said, 'Come with me, Eileen.'

She frowned. 'You'll only tell me the same thing.'

'We've had this conversation before. What am I going to say to you?'

Like a pupil reciting an unpopular school rule, she said, 'You're going to tell me not to write your script for you.'

'That's right.' Looking theatrically from side to side, he said, 'Let's go where we won't be overheard.'

'All right, we can go into the garden.'

'Why not, when "One touch of nature makes the whole world kin"? And that, basically, is what we're trying to do, to heal a quarrel.'

'If you say so.' Eileen shrugged. 'Anyway, you heard what it was about when you came in. She says David's bound to find somebody older than me.'

'Who's "she"? The cat's mother?'

'No, *our* mother. She says he'll do that because he's eighteen, but he's not bound to.'

'No, he's not. It's always a possibility, but it's by no means a certainty.'

'He says he'll write to me.'

'Well, that's something to look forward to.'

'And he kissed me when he said it.'

'The libertine! The blackguard! It's going to be pistols at dawn before ever he gets a chance to catch the train to Warrington.'

'Not properly, not the way film stars do in the pictures.' She touched her cheek with her forefinger. 'Here.'

'Oh well, I suppose I can stretch a point and let him get away with that.' They reached the garden seat that Ted had made the previous summer. According to his father, it was over-designed, meaning that it was so robust that a family of playful hippos might romp all over it without causing it to creak or groan. Ted was proud of his workmanship. 'Come and sit down,' he said, 'and let me expound.'

She eyed him warily, but sat beside him. 'What does that mean?'

'It means I'm going to give you the benefit of my wisdom and experience.' He patted her hand in preparation. 'I'm not advising you to give up on David.'

'Good.'

'Don't give up, but don't *build* up, either. He's said he'll write to you, and he sealed his promise with a kiss. He's a nice lad, and I'd expect nothing less from him, but try not to imagine it burgeoning into a wild romance. For all we know, it might, but don't expect it, because that's the road that leads to heartbreak. Just take it as it comes.'

She looked down at her hands for a while, possibly digesting what he'd said, and then surprised him by asking, 'Are you still going with Lily Thornton?'

'No.'

'Why not?'

'Because she doesn't want to be a teacher's pet or even a part-time fireman's moll. A sailor, a soldier or an airman is more to her taste.'

'That's awful.' Judgement gave way to curiosity, and she asked, 'Are you right bothered?'

Ted sighed impatiently. 'Honestly, I've tried to teach you respectable English, and what do I hear? "Are you right bothered?" I despair, I really do.'

'Well, are you?'

'No, I'm not. It just shows how vacuous she is, and why I'm better without her.'

'I hope you mean that.'

'I do, and that's not the extent of it, Eileen. Believe it or not, she doesn't even know how to use the semicolon correctly. I ask you, how could I consort with such a girl?'

Eileen shook her head hopelessly. 'You're just daft, Ted.'

'I know, but you feel better now, don't you?'

———◆◆———

Ted's disclosure at the dinner table was as unpopular as he'd anticipated, but the deed was done, and it provided a distraction from Eileen's immediate problem, so he was in a reasonably sanguine state of mind when he went into school the next day.

He had a marking period after assembly and, having delivered the news of his likely departure to the Senior English Master, he took the opportunity to extend the same courtesy to F W Bower, BSc (Lond), Headmaster of Beckworth Boys' Grammar School. Bower had a mercurial temperament, and his reaction was predictable.

'Full-time? Are you out of your mind, Dewhirst?'

'No, Headmaster, I'm responding to the fact that we're at war. For medical reasons, I'm not allowed to serve in the armed forces, so I want to make my contribution as a fireman.'

'I've never heard anything so ridiculous in all my life. I remember you when you were a boy at this school, Dewhirst. You were capricious then and it seems that you have not improved. Tell me this,' he demanded, shaking his forefinger. 'How am I supposed to run a school efficiently, when half my staff are deserting me to pursue their *Boy's Own* dreams?'

'*Half* your staff, Headmaster?'

'First it was Enright, and now you.'

'I see. You're talking about Enright and me.'

'Yes, I am. Neither of you has given a thought to the school, to your pupils, or to the staff who will have to cover your lessons until replacements can be found.'

'As a matter of fact, Headmaster, I've given it a great deal of thought.'

'You amaze me.'

'And my decision stands. I'll naturally keep you informed of developments as they occur.'

'See that you do, Dewhirst. Just see that you do.'

3

It made sense to Ted that war was an urgent business, and that an application to undertake full-time service would naturally be treated accordingly. In the event, three weeks elapsed before the letter arrived, instructing him to report, not to Bradford Central Fire Station, but to Beckworth Fire Station, on Monday, the sixteenth of October, when he would assume full-time duties. The reason for his transfer was that all firemen were required to live within quick and easy reach of their station, in case they were called out.

His appointment served to renew his unpopularity at home and to re-open the wound he had allegedly inflicted on his headmaster.

'I'll be glad when the thirteenth comes and I can clear off,' he told Paul Enright. 'I'm sick of being Public Enemy Number One around here.'

'That's a superb number. Have you heard it?' Paul was a devotee of popular music, and particularly of musical theatre. 'It's from *Anything Goes*,' he prompted. 'Cole Porter, you know.'

'I know, and now I want to go, too.'

'You're not the only one,' said Paul. 'I'm still waiting for the RAF to send for me.'

'That's funny, now I think of it,' said Ted.

'What is? I can't see anything funny about being kept waiting.'

'No, not that. It's just that my neighbour was called up almost as soon as war was declared. Mind you, he was in the ADCC for two or three years.'

'That would help, I suppose.'

The lesson change bell came as a distraction from their joint frustration, and they went to join their classes.

———

' "It wavered an instant – then there was a heartrending crash – and the canary-coloured cart, their pride and their joy, lay on its side in the ditch, an irredeemable wreck." ' Ted put the book down for a moment to ask, 'Binns, what does "irredeemable" mean?'

'I don't know, sir.'

'Think about the context and the word "wreck". I'm sure you know what a wreck is, so have a wild guess at "irredeemable". Go on, take a run at it.'

'I don't know, sir,' insisted Binns.

'You're not trying, Binns. You give up too easily. Anyone, "irredeemable"?'

Several hands rose, and Ted chose the owner of one of them. 'Yes, Fenton?'

'My father says that no one is irredeemable, sir.'

Fenton's father was Vicar of St Jude's. His son was a bad choice. On second thoughts, though, maybe he wasn't. 'What happens to someone who is redeemed, Fenton?'

'He sees the light, sir.'

'Would you say that he is improved in some way?'

'Yes, sir.'

'Repaired, even?'

'Yes, sir.' Fenton agreed grudgingly, with the air of someone less than tolerant of silly questions.

'Right, Binns,' said Ted, 'if someone or something can be *redeemed*, or repaired, what does "*ir*redeemable" mean?'

'I don't know, sir.'

'Binns, you are exasperation in short trousers. Anyone?' He chose a hand at random. 'Yes, Parker?'

'Beyond repair, sir.'

'Hallelujah.' As the word left his lips, he winced at the gaffe. 'Sorry, Fenton.'

'That's all right, sir.'

'You're a sport, Fenton. Right, Grahame writes, "the canary-coloured cart, their pride and their joy, lay on its side in the ditch....". We know the colour of the cart – we were there when Toad, the Mole and the Water Rat embarked on the excursion – and we know they were quite enchanted with it, so why did Kenneth Grahame describe it again when it had been smashed to blazes?' He looked around the class. 'Binns, here's an opportunity to *redeem* yourself. Why do you think he described it again?'

Binns shifted uncomfortably. Finally, he ventured, 'In case we'd forgotten what it looked like, sir?'

'There is always that possibility, Binns, but I doubt it. Anyone else?'

A shy boy in a blazer at least one size too big for him raised his hand, which appeared to have taken refuge inside his sleeve.

'Yes, Sanderson?'

'He was making the accident look even worse than it was, sir.'

'Good lad! Yes, he was emphasising the tragedy by reminding us of the colourful and appealing caravan that was now in bits at the side of the road. An object of beauty and pride had been smashed to smithereens. The destruction of any old caravan would have been bad enough, but not Toad's exquisite pride and joy.' His eye fell on a boy at the back of the classroom, whose attention had been taken by something outside the building. 'I'd pay attention if I were you, Nicholls,' he said. 'I'm going to set the class a comprehension on this passage for homework.' Then, because he wasn't one to give up too easily, he asked, 'Do you see what I mean, Binns, about emphasising the tragedy?'

'Yes, sir.'

'Good lad.' Whether he understood it or he didn't, he would at least leave the lesson on a positive note. 'Be a good lad again and hand these out for homework, please. It's the comprehension exercise I mentioned earlier. It's to be in on Wednesday morning, One B, and no excuses.' That final warning was for the benefit of Harper, whose homework had so far 'fallen on the fire', 'had gravy spilt all over it' and been 'chewed by the dog,' and all within the first three weeks of term. His parents had so far been required to pay for three replacement exercise books.

The change bell sounded, and Ted asked, 'What's your next lesson?'

'Maths, sir,' said Fenton.

Binns suddenly looked cheerful. He was presumably good at maths, and the thought pleased Ted. It would be awful if the poor lad had to go through school struggling with everything.

At that moment, it also occurred to him that, come the thirteenth, and if the previous war was any guide, he might not see the boys of Form One B again for some years.

———•┤◄———

Ted was relieved. For the first time in weeks, a mealtime at the Dewhirst household had gone by without reference to his decision to serve full-time in the AFS. He felt as if a huge obstruction had been removed, and now Eileen was claiming his attention. It seemed that she was about to provide a distraction quite unexpectedly and for good measure.

'What is it, Eileen? Latin, French, History?'

'No, a lot nearer home. It's English Lit.'

'Right on my doorstep,' he agreed. 'What's the problem?'

As if the task were too much to ask, she said, 'I have to write a character analysis.'

'Don't keep me in suspense, little sister. Which character have you to analyse?'

'Peggotty.'

'Clara or Mr?'

'The maid.'

'Clara, then.' It was becoming clear to Ted that his sister was spending more time reading *Picturegoer* than *David Copperfield*.

'How do you see her?'

'I don't know.'

'Don't you?' It felt like the theme for the day. 'Think of two words to describe her.'

'*Two* words?'

'All right, one.'

After some thought, Eileen said, 'I suppose she's kind to David.'

'She certainly is. What does she do that David's mother can't after she marries Murdstone?'

'She sticks up for him.'

'Yes, she tries to shield him from Murdstone and his sister. Incidentally, you'd better start taking a note.'

'Right.' Eileen took a notebook and fountain pen from the top of the piano.

'So,' said Ted, 'she's kind to him and she tries to protect him from the Murdstones. Why does she do that?'

'I expect she feels sorry for him.'

'Oh, I think she feels more than that. You have to remember that she's known David since he was a baby.'

'She loves him.'

'That's right. His mother's not allowed to show him love, but Peggotty does. She gives him what he needs so desperately. If you want to use a grown-up word to describe her, she's the *antithesis*, the opposite, of what the Murdstones stand for.'

'How do you spell that?'

He spelt the word for her and watched her scribble a note. 'I hope you can read that, Eileen,' he said, 'because I'd challenge a codebreaker to make sense of it.'

'Good. That way nobody will copy what I've written.'

He let that go, and asked, 'How does Jane Murdstone treat Peggotty?'

'She behaves like a….' Eileen looked behind her and realised that both of her parents were listening to the conversation. 'She's a tyrant. She sacks her.'

'And what does Peggotty do then?'

'Oh heck, I can't remember.'

'Remember "Barkis is willin' "?'

'Oh yes, she marries Mr Barkis.'

'So she does, but it's very much a marriage of convenience, isn't it?'

'Is it?' She held her pen poised for the next gem of information.

'She marries Barkis so that she can be on hand to help David. Believe me, Eileen, Peggotty is not a minor character. She and Mr Peggotty are the all-round good eggs of the Dickens canon. Clara Peggotty, in particular—'

'Slow down, Ted. I can't write as fast as you talk.'

Ted waited.

'All right,' she told him, 'you can carry on.'

'That's big of you. I was going to say that Clara Peggotty is unfailingly loyal to both David and Aunt Betsey Trotwood, and she gives David love and moral guidance throughout her life.'

Eileen finished writing and asked, 'Is that it?'

'That just about covers it, yes.'

'Thanks, Ted.'

'Eileen,' said her mother, 'I think you should thank your brother properly for taking the trouble to do that.'

'Yes,' said Mr Dewhirst, 'he's got you out of trouble again.'

'All right.' She put her notebook back in her bag and replaced the cap on her pen. 'Thank you, lovely, kind, clever brother,' she said, planting a noisy kiss on his forehead. 'Mwa!'

'Be off with you and write your analysis,' he told her, 'and it would be a good idea to read the novel again before the exam.'

'All right.' She picked up her bag and left the room before anyone could challenge her further.

'And this,' said Mr Dewhirst, 'is the lad who went through three years of university and got himself a job at the Grammar School, and for what? So that he could dress up and ride on a flamin' fire engine.'

The peace couldn't last forever, and Ted always knew couldn't win.

————◆◄————

He was infinitely more popular with the personnel at Beckworth Fire Station, where he'd already shown himself to be keen and trustworthy. It was as well, because he was soon required, as a 'rider', one of the firemen on the appliance, to attend a fire at a woollen mill in Beckworth.

A head count had satisfied the mill manager that the building had been cleared, so hoses were brought into use. Ted had long-since learned that any fitment that went on to the end of a hose was called a 'branch', and he quickly attached a branch and an inch-and-three-eighths nozzle to his hose.

'Right, young Dewhirst,' said Fireman Watts, stationing himself behind Ted, 'brace yourself.' He signalled to the man on the pump that they were ready, and the two prepared themselves for the kick as water surged through the hose.

'Keep it low,' advised Watts. 'Aim at the base of the fire.'

The deluge swept through the open window, and Ted was grateful for the presence of Fireman Watts as the hose bucked.

He continued to direct the flow on to the base of the fire, gratified by his progress, and feeling that this must surely be his destiny, at least for as long as the war lasted.

The fire was a small one, and the crew quickly had it under control, but the occasion meant much more to Ted, because it was his first experience in the front line. Throughout his training, he had never been allowed on a hose or even to be so close to a fire.

As they coiled up the hose and stowed it on board the appliance, Watts turned to him to say, 'They won't all be as easy as that one.' He chuckled good-naturedly. 'Be thankful you got a little fire to practise on, young Dewhirst.'

'That's right, Watts.' Sub-Officer Wright was quick to agree. 'It was a gentle introduction, Dewhirst, but you did well. I will say that.'

'Thank you, Sub.'

'You're keen all right, and there's nothing wrong with that as long as you don't take unnecessary risks. There's many a fireman come to grief through taking shortcuts and leaving things to chance.'

'Thank you, Sub. I'll remember that.'

Ted would also remember his first fire. Small it may have been, but it was to be the precursor of many, larger, and more devastating fires that he would attend over the next five years.

His next big excitement, however, would occur the following August.

4

August 1940

On the night of the 31ˢᵗ of August, the duty watch at Beckworth Station became aware of aerial activity over neighbouring Bradford.

'Just when you think it's going to be a quiet night,' said Fireman Watts, 'the bells go down.'

Almost as he spoke, the alarm sounded, and every man in the room picked up his boots and leapt for the brass pole that took them down to the appliance shed. They scrambled aboard the dual-purpose appliance, the one with an escape ladder as well as a pump, and the message was passed to them that they were bound for the Odeon Cinema in Manchester Road, Bradford.

'I think we've missed second house,' said Watts, as the appliance picked up speed. It was 10:45 p.m.

'I don't know why the Jerries would want to bomb a picture house,' said Fireman Shaw. 'You'd expect them to go for the aircraft factory at Yeadon.'

'Maybe that was the idea,' said Watts, 'and maybe they're like you when you're throwing darts. Anywhere near the board will do.'

The banter continued during the short journey, until they arrived at the Odeon and found that Central Bradford was a townscape of fire appliances from everywhere within calling distance.

After a quick word with the senior officer at the scene, Sub-Officer Wright asked, 'Have you been up the ladder, Dewhirst?'

'Only in training, Sub.'

'Well, now you can go up in anger. Take this line, and when you get level with the top storey, give warning and then drop one end to us. We'll put a branch on a hose, and then you can haul it up and lash it securely to the ladder.'

'Right, Sub.' Ted took the light coir line and climbed to the top of the ladder, where he could feel the fierce heat from the fire. He yelled, 'Stand clear below!' Then, when he saw that everyone had retreated from the bottom of the ladder, he secured his end and heaved the rest downward. A reassuring shout from below told him that the hose was ready, and he hauled it up and lashed it to the top rung of the ladder. When he was satisfied that it was secure, he called down to the man on the pump, 'Ready!'

Water surged up the hose, and Ted felt it buck.

The sub-officer shouted, 'Down at the base of the fire!'

Ted directed the jet further downward, conscious all the time of the pandemonium going on around him. From his elevated position, he could see other fires in Thornton Road and stretching as far as Leeds Road. The worst fires, however, were those in the city centre, where the majority of appliances were in attendance.

He ducked instinctively when another wave of bombers came over, and he was surprised to find that, in the glare of the fires, he could see the bombs leaving the aircraft and falling to the ground. Their explosions sounded like giants' footsteps.

Inside his heavy woollen uniform, he was perspiring, and he had to pass a hand occasionally across his brow to prevent perspiration from impeding his vision.

A voice called, 'Are you all right, Dewhirst?'

He answered, 'Yes.' In the noise and excitement, politeness was a luxury.

He became conscious after a while that the inferno inside the cinema had receded thanks to the attentions of the crew at ground level and, he was pleased to note, due in some way to his own efforts, but he continued to direct his jet on to the diminishing blaze beneath him until he noticed that the water pressure was falling. Eventually, the flow became a trickle and then it stopped altogether, and he heard Sub-Officer Wright's voice.

'Come down, Dewhirst!'

He unfastened the lashing to release the hose, and made his descent, only realising, then, that his hands were aching from directing the hose nozzle during his stint on the ladder. He'd also lost all sense of time.

'Well done, Dewhirst. The lads are just damping down, but we'll stay here for now.' The sub-officer jerked his thumb towards the sky. 'Them buggers haven't finished with us yet.'

The Beckworth crew were directed later to Thornton Road, where they dealt successfully with another incident, this time at the Tatler Cinema. It seemed that it was their night for cinema fires.

At three-thirty the following morning, the All-Clear sounded, and Green Watch were able to stow their equipment and get a welcome mug of tea from the mobile canteen before returning to Beckworth.

Eventually, the night watch ended, and Ted made his way home, weary, but with a sense of great satisfaction. When he arrived, he found his mother cooking breakfast, and his father reading the paper. They both saw his soot-smeared face, and his father said, 'We heard a commotion over Bradford way last night. Is that where you've been?'

Ted nodded, too tired to talk.

His mother was by no means a demonstrative person, but she bent and kissed him. Her eyes were wet. 'I'll get you some breakfast,' she said.

'Thanks, Mum. Then, when Eileen's up and about, I'll have a bath and go to bed.'

'It's time she was up,' said his mother, looking at the clock.

'Don't chase her, Mum. It's not her fault I've been up a ladder all night.'

'Well, she won't get out of bed without persuasion.'

'Or a crowbar,' said Mr Dewhirst.

His wife went upstairs to shake Eileen.

His father asked, 'Bad, was it, lad?'

'Bad for some,' Ted told him, 'but we were all right.' Suddenly, he smiled as a thought occurred to him. 'If you're thinking of going to the pictures, I'd be inclined to give the Tatler and the Odeon a miss, because the Jerries didn't.'

Eileen came downstairs in her dressing gown and flung herself at Ted.

'I'm all right,' he told her. 'I've just been doing my job, that's all.'

'An' you've come back all mucky,' she sobbed. 'What have you been up to?'

'The top floor of the Odeon. You get a grand view from up there. I'm all right,' he told her again. 'Where's your hanky?'

'Upstairs.'

'I don't think I've got a clean one. Have you got one, Mum?'

'Here,' said his father, taking one from his pocket and handing it to Eileen.

'There,' said Ted. 'Wipe your eyes and blow your nose.'

When the necessary operation was complete, he gathered her up and hugged her. 'You're not to start worrying every time I go to an incident, you know. You'll grow grey hair and wrinkles, and then nobody will want to marry you.'

'Let Ted and your dad have their breakfast now,' said her mother. 'I'm afraid it's powdered egg, Ted.'

'That's all right, Mum. Is Miss van Winkle going to join us? She might as well.'

'All right, and then you'll have to hurry up and get ready for school, Eileen, and don't come down in your nightie and dressing gown again with menfolk in the house. You're seventeen now, remember.'

———◆►◄———

In the days and weeks that followed, everyone waited for another visit from the Luftwaffe, who must have decided that one raid was sufficient for the time being, because they proceeded to leave Bradford alone. Naturally, it was good news for everyone, except that Ted was now feeling restless again. Most of the British Expeditionary Force had been evacuated from France, and now, in the skies of southern England, the RAF were locked in combat with the Luftwaffe; the news was full of it every day, and all the time, the war was leaving him behind again. In fighting the fires in Bradford, he'd felt that he was making his contribution. He'd seen and heard the bombs come down, he'd witnessed the awful destruction, and he'd countered the Luftwaffe's efforts by helping to put the fires out. Now, however, he was reduced to attending an occasional animal rescue or chip pan fire, chimney fires being out of season for the time being. After much careful consideration, he asked to see Station Officer Taylor.

'I'd like to request a transfer, sir.'

Station Officer Taylor looked up in surprise. 'Oh? What's wrong with this station, Dewhirst?'

'Absolutely nothing, sir. I've been very happy here.'

'You haven't been here two minutes. What on earth's brought you to this decision?'

'Inactivity, sir.'

'Nonsense. Only this morning, I saw you washing the DP appliance. You were doing a thorough job as well.'

Ted explained patiently, 'I don't mean that kind of activity, sir. I'm saying that I want to go somewhere that's being bombed, where I'll be needed.'

Taylor closed his eyes, possibly counting silently to ten. 'Are you out of your mind, Dewhirst? Those places are bloody dangerous.'

'I know, sir. I want to help make it less dangerous for the people who live there.'

Taylor stared at him in wonder. 'Without realising it, Dewhirst, you've just answered my question. You *are* out of your mind. I don't need a psychiatrist to tell me that, because it's bloody obvious that you're round the bend.' He folded his hands on the desk and said, 'I've no doubt they'd welcome you with open arms in Hull, which – and don't you dare quote me – is being bombed to buggery almost as we speak, but what kind of station officer would allow one of his men to go somewhere like that? No, Dewhirst, the answer is "No".'

Not for the first time in his life, Ted was determined not to be refused out of hand. 'That's your privilege, sir.'

'I'm glad you recognise that, Dewhirst.'

'At the same time, sir, I have the right to make such a request and to go on making it.'

Taylor appeared to be mustering his patience. He asked, 'Have you got a family?'

'Yes, sir, my parents and my sister.'

'What do they think?'

'They think I'm round the bend, too, sir, and they've had longer to draw that conclusion than you have.'

Station Officer Taylor closed his eyes again wearily and said, 'Go away and... clean some equipment, Dewhirst.'

'Yes, sir. Thank you for your time, sir.'

———◆◆———

Ted continued to send in an application for transfer each day for the next week, until one day, he was surprised to be summoned by Station Officer Taylor.

'Dewhirst,' he said, 'you're a bloody nuisance, but you're not the only bloody nuisance in this brigade. I've just received a reminder that this station is over-establishment.'

'Sir?'

'It means that there are too many personnel here, and someone has to go.' Looking as harassed as ever, he went on to say, 'I've also received a notice calling for volunteers to be transferred to brigades that are *under* establishment, brigades that need extra personnel because of the pressures placed on them by our friends in Germany, so it looks as if you're going to get your transfer after all.'

———▸◂———

Ted carried on with his duties, waiting to hear from higher authority, but resigned to the knowledge that the inner workings of the AFS ran no quicker than the wheels of eternity. Patience had to be his watchword, although there were distractions, one of which occurred when he came home from the day watch and found his mother tight-lipped and displeased. It was one of those occasions when waiting for an explanation would be a wasteful use of his time. He had to ask, 'What's the matter, Mum?'

'It's Eileen. She's had a letter from David next door. He's going with a girl in the WAAFs.' She delivered the news angrily, as if it were all Ted's fault. 'I warned her. I told he was too old for her, but would she listen? Does she ever listen to me?'

'Where is she?'

'Upstairs, in her bedroom, behaving as if the world's come to its end.'

'If you like, I'll go up to her.'

'Tell her to pull herself together.'

Ted made no reply. Instead, he went upstairs and tapped on Eileen's door. 'It's me,' he said. 'Are you decent?'

'Yeah.' The word sounded muffled and it was sandwiched between sobs.

'Can I come in?'

'If you want.'

He pushed the door open and found her face down on her bed, so he perched on the five or six inches available and put his hand on her shoulder. 'I'm sorry to hear about David,' he said. He heard her mutter something unintelligible and decided to ignore it. 'It's an awful thing to happen,' he went on, 'and coping with it isn't easy.'

She turned her head gradually so that she was looking at him out of the corner of a red and swollen eye.

'Are you going to sit up and talk to me?' He stood up to facilitate the process.

'All right.' She swung her legs over the bed and shuffled up to make room for him.

'Thank you.' He sat down again. Taking a handkerchief from her bedside table, he invited her to blow. 'Go on,' he said, 'blow all your misery into that.'

She tried, and said, 'It id't ad eady ad dat.'

'Blow again. You've got too many d's in your alphabet. Mind you, I have to agree. It's not as easy as that, because it takes time.'

'I hope you're not… going to tell me… there are… plenty more fish in… the sea.' Her words were punctuated with involuntary shudders.

'No, I'm not, because you know that already. Just now, it feels like the end of the world, I know, but it does get easier.'

'Does it?' She sounded unconvinced.

'It must. Otherwise, we'd be a race of broken-hearted people, and there are more smiles than tears out there, believe me.'

After a moment's thought, she said, 'You're going… away just… at the wrong time.'

'I still don't know when or where.'

'It'll be… soon,' she prophesied. 'You'll… go away, and you're the… only one in this house… who understands me.'

He couldn't argue with that, because it was true.

'She doesn't… understand because she's never… felt anything in her… life.'

'Oh, there I have to disagree, Eileen. Everyone feels things, but we don't all show our feelings. Mum was brought up to keep everything inside. You know what Grandma Thomas is like.'

'Yes.'

'Well, she was her example, and it's very difficult to change that kind of behaviour. Besides….'

'What?'

'If she'd never felt anything in her life, how on earth do you think you and I happened?'

'Ergh!' She screwed up her face in horror. 'I don't want… to think about… that.'

He put a comforting arm round her and drew her closer. 'It's going to hurt for some time,' he told her, but it will get easier.'

'Have you felt like this?'

'Oh, yes. It felt like the end of everything, until one day it began to improve. Not all at once, you understand.'

'Of course not.'

'But then I had a distraction.'

'What was that?' She was looking up at him, eager to know.

'One of the boys in my form was going through a bad patch. He'd lost his mum, and I felt so sorry for him, I forgot I had a problem. It's worth remembering, you know. Care for other people, and you forget your own woes.'

———▶◀———

That evening, Mrs Dewhirst said, 'I thought you were going to wash your hair tonight, Eileen.'

Eileen gave a non-committal grunt.

'You'd better wash it now, and then you can get it dry before you go to bed.'

'Go on, Eileen,' said Ted, 'wash your hair.'

'Why should I?'

'Because there's a great big dollop of bird muck in it.' He pretended to inspect it more closely. 'Crow, I'd say, or magpie, at a pinch.'

'That's enough messy talk from you,' said his mother.

Eileen realised she was being teased. 'You horror,' she said.

'Go and wash it, and then come down, and I'll dry it for you the way I used to.' Ted had performed that service for her regularly when she was very young. She was much older now, but age was an artificial barrier. At least, he thought so.

His mother gave him her look that said she'd given up trying to understand either of them, and his father continued to hide behind the *Yorkshire Post* crossword.

At length, Eileen came downstairs with a dry towel, which she handed to Ted before sitting on the floor in front of him.

He began towelling her hair. 'Rub-a-dub-dub, three men in a tub, Who do you think they were?'

As he continued to dry her hair, his mother said, 'You spoil her, Ted.'

But Ted disagreed. Like Peggotty caring for David Copperfield, he was only giving his sister something vitally important that would otherwise be missing from her life. He would continue to do that through his letters long after his draft came through.

5

When his orders arrived, Ted was surprised to find that he wasn't being directed to Hull or anywhere else in the north of England. His destination was to be the East End of London, and he was ordered to report to Sub-Station 4C in Whitechapel.

After a long, stop-start journey by train to King's Cross Station in London, he had then to make his way to Whitechapel, a daunting experience for someone on his first solo visit to the capital, his previous one having been with a meticulously-organised school party. Happily, he found the natives friendlier than he'd been led to expect, and someone directed him to the bus that ran to Whitechapel.

Relieved, he stowed his kitbag in the luggage compartment beneath the stairs and took his seat. He was so distracted by the bomb damage he saw around him that the conductor had to nudge him to gain his attention. He paid his fare and returned his gaze to the damaged and wrecked buildings, which became more numerous as the bus approached the East End.

More passengers filled the bus, and Ted gave up his seat to an elderly woman.

'Much obliged,' she said.

'It's no trouble, love.'

'Where are you from, if you don't mind me askin'? You don't sound like you're from round 'ere.'

'I'm from Yorkshire,' he told her, trying not to look at the gaps between her brown teeth.

'I fort you was from a long way off. You come to lend a hand, then? We can use a bit of 'elp.'

'That's right.'

'What station are you joinin'?'

'Sub-station 4C.' He wasn't sure where it was, and he didn't imagine the woman would know it either.

She surprised him by saying, 'That's at my old school. Whitechapel

Road Board School it's called, even though it's not actually in Whitechapel Road. It's just off the main road,' she explained, 'where it turns into Mile End Road. Get off when I do, and I'll show you the way.'

'Thank you. That's very kind of you.'

'Nah, it's the least I can do. You give up your seat for me, didn't you? A lot of fellas wouldn't 'ave bovvered.'

'It's just the way I was brought up.'

Looking at him with new interest, she said, 'You're very polite for somebody what comes from the norf. What did you used to do before you was a fireman?'

'I was a schoolmaster.'

'Oh, that explains it.' As another thought occurred to her, she said, 'I expect you'll feel at home at the school.'

Ted hoped he would. According to the street sign he'd just read, he was almost there.

'The London Hospital,' announced the elderly conductor.

'That's our stop,' said the woman.

Ted helped her up and they shuffled to the back of the bus, where he took his kitbag from the luggage compartment.

When they'd alighted from the bus, the woman pointed along Whitechapel Road and said, 'The school's that way, about two hundred yards, on the uvver side o' the road.'

'Thank you. You've been very helpful.'

'That's all right, love. Best o' luck. You'll get plenty practice, anyway.' She looked up at the clear sky and said, 'It won't surprise me if the bleeders come over again tonight.'

'We'll do our best,' he promised her. 'Thanks again.'

He hoisted his kitbag on to his shoulder and followed her directions.

He found that her estimate of two hundred yards had been somewhat conservative, because he'd walked closer to five hundred before he spotted the playground railings and gate of the school. He was in the right place, though, because there were signs on either side of the gate telling him that he'd reached 4C Sub-Station. Further evidence in the form of a Heavy Unit stood in the playground, where several men were hard at work with soapy water, sponges and chamois leathers.

'Good afternoon,' he called. 'Which way is the Watch Room?'

'In through the main door, where it says "Boys", and it's the second on your right,' one of them told him. He had untidy, dark hair and a cheerful expression.

31

'Thanks.' He climbed the few steps up to the entrance just as a ruddy-faced man in his shirtsleeves appeared in the first doorway. He was possibly in his late thirties, so Ted imagined he might have some authority.

'Hello,' he said, 'my name's Dewhirst.'

'I'm Sub-Officer Prentice.' He offered his hand.

'Glad to meet you, Sub.'

'I'll take you to the Watch Room, and then I'll get somebody to show you round the place.' He opened the door next to his and beckoned Ted inside. 'This is our very own beauty chorus. Meet Mrs Chandler and Mrs Hearn. This is Dewhirst, who's joining us.'

The two firewomen each sat behind a desk. One was fair-haired and about forty, and the other was younger, maybe in her early twenties, with dark, loose curls held neatly in check by a blue ribbon. She was very attractive, although, with the ease born of practice, Ted had already spotted her wedding ring.

'I'm pleased to meet you, ladies,' said Ted.

Mrs Chandler said, 'You're the first man to call us "ladies", isn't he, Lorna? That makes you all the more welcome.'

The pretty one laughed and agreed with her.

'I'm glad to meet you both,' he said, shaking hands with them. 'I'm Ted, but I suppose I'll just be "Dewhirst" from now on.'

'That's right,' said the sub, winking at the two firewomen, you're in a man's world now.'

'And don't we know it,' said Mrs Chandler.

'I'll get somebody to show you where to stow your gear,' said the sub-officer, 'and then you can meet the rest of the watch.'

'Thanks, Sub.'

'That's a funny accent you've got. You're just down from Yorkshire, I believe.'

'That's right, Sub,'

'Can't say as I've ever been there.' He appeared to question his memory before confirming his original statement. 'No, I can't say I have. What did you do before you joined the AFS, Dewhirst?'

'I was a schoolmaster, Sub.'

'Oh well, you'll feel at home in this place.'

It was likely to follow him around like a tin can tied to a cat's tail. All he could say was, 'That's right, Sub.'

'Follow me.'

''Bye, Ted,' said Mrs Chandler.

The quieter one, who Mrs Chandler had just addressed as "Lorna" said, ''Bye, Ted.' The smile that accompanied it was a friendly one.

'You'll be in Green Watch with us,' said the sub as they went into his office. 'We're on days, in case you haven't noticed.' He walked over to the opened window and shouted, 'Jenkins, I've got a job for you!' Turning to Ted again, he said, 'The watches do month and month about. We used to do forty-eight hours on and twenty-four off, but they put an end to that nonsense. We've got another week on days and then it's our turn to warm our hands.' He looked up as the fireman who had pointed Ted towards the Watch Room appeared in the doorway.

'You want me, Sub?'

'Yes, Jenkins. This is Dewhirst, the new bloke.'

'Oh,' said Jenkins, offering his hand, 'pleased to meet you, Dewhirst.'

'He's not a rookie. Far from it, he's got some time in. Anyway, I want you to show him to the boudoir, Jenkins, and then take him to meet the rest of the watch.'

'Right-oh, Sub. Grab your kit, Dewhirst.'

Ted picked up his kitbag and followed Jenkins down the corridor. As they reached the end, he said, 'This is where we have our quarters. It used to be the gym in the old days, but the only action it sees now is the all-night snoring match.'

'Right,' said Ted, following him inside. 'Where do the other watch sleep?'

'In the old school hall, on the other side of the building. We're lucky to have both a hall and a gym. In some school buildings, the two watches have to share a hall.' He took Ted to a spare locker and said, 'Stow your kit in there, lock it, and take the key. It's yours for as long as you're here.' He eyed Ted warily and said, 'It's none of my business, but how did you come to be in this lot and not in the forces?'

'The forces wouldn't have me because of my allergy.'

'What are you allergic to?'

'Soya.'

'Is that right?'

'Guides' honour.'

'You'd better tell Olive about that.'

'Who's Olive?'

'Our cook. She'll need to know that before she kills you.'

Ted knew what he meant.

Jenkins performed an elaborate and delayed double-take, and said, 'Anyway, what was that you said about girl guides?'

'I couldn't say, "scouts' honour", because I've never been a boy scout and I don't know the first thing about them, but I do know about girl guides' honour.'

Suddenly, Jenkins was eager to hear more. 'What do you know, mate?'

'I know that they're pure in thought, word and deed, far too pure to be led astray by the likes of me.' He nodded to confirm it. 'At least, that's what I've found.'

'You 'ad me wonderin' for a minute.'

'I know.'

'Here,' said Jenkins, pointing along the corridor, 'are the grown-up heads. There's usually competition for them, because if you can't get in, you have to use the little boys' heads across the playground.'

The signs on the doors made translation unnecessary, but Ted still had to ask, 'Why are the toilets called "heads"?'

'Tradition.'

'How did it come about?'

'In the last century,' explained Jenkins, 'all the London Fire Brigade's firemen were ex-sailors. It was because they were good at climbing, tying knots and slings and doing what they were told, so it worked well, but because they were sailors, they brought their own language with 'em. That's why we say, "up top" and "below", we talk about "lines" instead of ropes, we "stow" equipment on the appliances, and we have "watches" instead of shifts. We also call the toilets the "heads", because in a ship, they're always at the sharp end, apparently. I don't know why.'

'Fascinating.'

'What did you do before you joined the AFS, Dewhirst?'

'I was a schoolmaster.' He waited, and when the expected quip failed to materialise, he asked, 'What did you do, Jenkins?'

Jenkins looked uncertain for a moment and said, 'I was a school caretaker.' It was his turn to wait. 'This is where you're supposed to say, "You'll be a handy bloke to have around in this place".'

'I wouldn't dream of it, Jenkins. You and I have the same problem.'

'We have, really. Let me introduce you to the lads in this watch.' He led the way to the front yard, where Ted had entered the building. The same men were still at work, some on the appliance, and others cleaning the equipment to be stowed in it.

'This is the new bloke, lads,' said Jenkins. 'His name's Dewhirst.'

There was a chorus of friendly greetings.

'That's "Spud" Murphy on the front of the appliance, Greg behind him – stand up and show yourself, Greg, don't be shy – and that's Turner and "Dusty" Miller cleaning hoses. You'll soon get to know the rest of 'em.'

There was a shout from the building, and Jenkins turned. 'Yes, Sub?'

'Ask Dewhirst if he can drive.'

'Right, Sub. Did you hear that, Dewhirst?'

'Yes, I can drive.'

'Just cars?'

'No, I've driven a fifteen hundredweight Bedford for my dad. He's a market gardener.'

Jenkins cupped his hands and shouted, 'Yes, Sub. He'll be able to drive Heavy Unit Two and give me a break sometimes.'

'Good. He can take it out tomorrow.'

'You haven't been here two minutes, Dewhirst,' said Jenkins, 'and you've already got star billing. Where is it all going to end?'

On the way back to the firemen's quarters, they passed the Watch Room. The door was open, and Mrs Chandler, who seemed to be alone, said, 'I hope you're not leading the new man astray, Albert.'

'Me lead him astray? It's the other way round, Mrs Chandler. He's a bad influence.' Leaning confidentially into the doorway, he said, 'You need to keep an eye on him.'

A voice behind them asked, 'Who are you talking about?'

'Pay no attention, Mrs Hearn,' said Ted. 'He's just giving me a bad name.'

'Typical.' She stopped in the doorway to say, 'Don't stand on ceremony, Ted. My name's Lorna.'

'Noted. Is your husband a fireman, Lorna?'

'No, he's in the army, in North Africa.'

'Bad luck.'

As they walked on, Jenkins said, 'It's a bloody waste an' all. Her being spoken for, I mean.'

Ted was inclined to agree.

———◆◄———

Jenkins introduced Ted later to Olive, an ample, good-natured woman of uncertain age, but with opinions that, according to Jenkins, she shared readily and universally.

'I have to tell you that I'm allergic to soya,' he told her. 'That's why I'm not in the forces.' He told her that in case she was wondering, but she seemed unperturbed.

'Don't you worry, love. You won't get none o' that foreign muck here. Good, plain, English cooking is what you'll get. Don't give it another thought.'

His new situation had so many facets to occupy his mind that he had no difficulty in following her advice.

———▸◂———

After dinner, which was as plain and wholesome as Olive had claimed and as over-cooked as Ted had feared, he and Jenkins went to the recreation room, where firemen were engaged in darts and snooker. On one side of the room, stood a bar with a carefully-painted sign that reminded its patrons that they were drinking at *The Hose and Hydrant*.

Jenkins said, 'We're limited to two. It's in case we get called out. Also, we let the night watch have first go at the bar and everything else.' He added, 'Don't worry, it'll be our turn next week.'

6

OCTOBER

Ted came to know the rest of the watch particularly well during that first week. Even if reticence had been possible within such a closely-knit community, it would never have become a feature while its members shared opinions and personal details so freely and without awkwardness. Some of the watch lived at home, being East Enders by birth and lineage, whilst others, like Ted, who had been drafted in from other parts of the country, lived at the sub-station, where privacy was an alien concept.

Ted learned, for example, that Auxiliary Fireman Gregory, a quiet and retiring member of the watch, was shy only when at work. At home, he had six children and another on the way.

If Ted had thought that Form 4B were like washerwomen, he found Green Watch just as bad. He was told that Mrs Chandler was a widow, and that she had admirers among some of the older men, not all of whom were married, but she'd given them no encouragement so far. Lorna was simply out of bounds to anyone, being newly married. It was all the same to Ted, who had made contact with a student nurse at the London Hospital when he and Jenkins were checking its hydrants. Her name was Iris, and she would be spending most of October on nights. She had agreed to meet him the following Friday, when she'd made the adjustment. She explained that it took about a week for her to become a night-owl.

Before that, though, was Ted's introduction to the East End Blitz. He'd lain awake in the sub-station as the bombs shook the building with each explosion, but now he was in the front line.

His cue came when Lorna interrupted the jollity in the recreation room by ringing the suspended bell vigorously and shouting, 'Heavy Unit Two to Pennington Street!'

The riders were out of the door in seconds. There was no brass pole, as there had been at Beckworth, only a sprint across the darkened playground, where HU2 was parked.

Ted went round to the driver's door, but Jenkins pushed him aside. 'I know the way to Pennington Street,' he said. 'Get in the back.'

With Sub-Officer Prentice in the front beside Jenkins, and everyone else in the back, the unit took to the main road, illuminating its way with the meagre light that passed through the letters 'FIRE' cut out of the headlamp masks.

Ted knew that Jenkins had been right to take over the driving; it was much easier for him to do that than it would have been to give directions, although it seemed he'd been reading Ted's thoughts, because he said over his shoulder, 'You can drive us back to the sub-station, Dewhirst.'

'Thanks,' said Ted, 'I'll look forward to that.'

They reached their destination, and a senior officer directed the unit to a colossal warehouse currently attended by more appliances than Ted could make out. Each man went to his allotted task, although, being new, Ted had to be directed.

'You're on the pump tonight,' Sub-Officer Prentice told him. 'I reckon we should have water in a minute.' It was urgently needed, as the fire was raging through the warehouse.

A district officer approached the unit and asked, 'Who's in charge here?'

'I am, sir. Sub-Officer Prentice.'

'Good. This warehouse is beyond help. We're going to isolate it and make sure nothing else goes up. Take your unit a hundred yards down the road and get your hoses on the next building.'

'Very good, sir.' Prentice summoned his team and explained what was happening. Recovering quickly from the false start, they stowed their equipment.

'Meet us down there,' said Prentice, climbing in beside Jenkins.

Ted and the others ran down to the end of the warehouse, where a smaller building was threatened. It was impossible to make out either the owner's name or the purpose of the building, because the heat from the warehouse had already blistered the sign over its double doors, but frantic equine noises were coming from within, and they were about to force the doors open, when a highly agitated civilian, an elderly man, arrived.

He said, 'The horses are in there! I've got to get them out.'

The unit drew up, and Sub-Officer Prentice asked, 'What's happening here?'

'I've got to get the horses out,' said the man, almost tearfully. 'Don't start squirting yet.'

'Get them out quick, then. Have you got the key?'

'Yes.' The man took out a bunch of keys and searched for the appropriate one while Prentice watched impatiently.

The man found the padlock key and opened the double doors. Immediately, the horses surged forward, carrying him between them in their terror. They trawled him into the road, where he established some kind of tenuous control, and the trio disappeared at speed in the direction of Wapping.

Gregory had found a hydrant, and the pump stood ready.

'Right,' said Prentice, wincing as an HE exploded less than half a mile away, 'let's start boundary cooling.'

———◆◆———

By the end of the night, the burning warehouse lay in smouldering ashes, but the buildings that bordered it were saved, and so, as far as Green Watch were aware, were the two draught horses.

'They've even got a nice, cool stable to come back to,' said Prentice. For Ted's benefit, he said, 'It is our first duty to save life, so we're not without feelings. It was the man that was annoying me, not the poor bloody horses.'

After the welcome order to 'knock off and make up', which was fireman's jargon for closing the valves and clearing everything away, Ted drove the unit back to the sub-station, where the men of Green Watch washed themselves at the handbasins that had been provided for the children of the school. They were a great deal less than adequate, and the situation gave Ted something to think about, not that thought came easily after such a night. That had to come later. For the time being, he and the other resident firemen took to their beds and lost consciousness for several hours.

———◆◆———

The watch was naturally called out every night to attend fires either in its own station area or to reinforce other areas, and it was starkly apparent to Ted why each watch spent only four weeks at a time on nights.

He left his bed readily, however, after only a morning's sleep that Friday, because he was meeting Iris.

He passed the Watch Room on his way out, and exchanged a cheerful word with the two firewomen of Red Watch. It felt strange, seeing them there, at the desks he associated with Lorna and Mrs Chandler.

One of them asked, 'Couldn't you sleep?'

'I have an assignation,' he told them as mysteriously as he could.

'There had to be a girl in it somewhere,' she said. 'Nothing else would get a man out of his bed at this time.'

Ted walked down Whitechapel Road and then right into Turner Street, which took him eventually to Newark Street and the nurses' home, where he told the matriarch on duty that he'd arranged to meet Student Nurse Wingate.

He hadn't long to wait, because Iris came downstairs and joined him after only a few minutes. To say that she, too, was on night duty, she looked remarkably fresh, with her fair hair down to her shoulders.

'Iris,' he said, 'you look like next week's wages.'

'If that's a compliment,' she said, 'thank you.' On a more practical note, she asked, 'Where are we going?'

'I wondered if you'd like to see *Night Train to Munich*. That's if you haven't already seen it, of course.'

'No, I haven't. Who's in it?'

'Margaret Lockwood and Rex Harrison.'

'Oh yes, I've heard about it, now I think of it. Let's go.'

He reached for her hand, and she transferred her gasmask case to the other shoulder to accommodate him.

As they walked, she asked, 'What have you been up to? Lots of exciting things, I imagine.'

'It becomes fairly routine after a while.' He delivered the information with a teasing smile.

'Beast. I bet it's one adventure after another.'

He wondered a little about her concept of firefighting, and then told her about the horses.

'Oh yes,' she said, 'we forget about the poor animals that are caught up in the bombing.'

'They were all right,' he reassured her. 'We last saw them dragging a dotty old man to Wapping.'

'A what?'

40

'A *dotty* old man.'

'I thought you said…. Anyway, I don't believe you.'

'That's up to you, and it's your turn to tell me about hi-jinks among the bedpans and whatever else you get up to.'

'You don't want to hear about my work,' she said a little awkwardly. 'I'm on obstetrics and gynaecology.'

'I'm impressed.'

'No, you're not. You don't know what it means.'

'No, I've never heard of it, but it sounds messy.'

'It is.' She accompanied her answer with a grown-up look.

'You're right,' he said, shuddering. 'I don't want to know about any of that.'

Happily, they reached the Picture Palace, and the topic was forgotten. Ted bought two balcony tickets.

'Oh,' said Iris, 'are we going upstairs?'

'Of course we are, I wouldn't take a lady into the one-and-tuppennies. Also,' he told her in a conspiratorial tone, 'it's darker up there.'

'Just behave yourself.'

He twitched his eyebrows theatrically as they climbed the stairs.

'Behave yourself, Ted.'

'Okay,' he sighed.

They took their seats to watch the remainder of a silly newsreel about how Britain's desert army was ready for anything, including an impromptu game of football, and Ted remembered similar items being shown in 1939. He wondered if anyone was taken in by it.

Eventually, the main picture began, and Ted was treated to a scene featuring Margaret Lockwood. Sensitively, however, he reached for Iris's hand to let her know he hadn't forgotten her in his excitement.

It was a glorious film, with some excellent scenes by Basil Radford and Naunton Wayne in their now-celebrated roles of Charters and Caldicott.

As they walked back to the nurses' home, Ted asked, 'What's your memorable moment from the film?'

'I don't know.' She thought about it and said eventually, 'I think it was right at the end, when we knew everyone was safe.' She asked, 'What was yours?'

'There's no contest, as far as I'm concerned. For me, it was the conjuring trick.'

'What conjuring trick?'

'The one Rex Harrison performed when he fired about twenty bullets out of a revolver that only held six.'

'Oh, that's typical of a man. You've no soul.'

'Actually, it was a superb film. I can forgive them for the *faux pas* with the revolver.'

When they reached the nurses' home, he asked, 'Do you like dancing?'

'I love it. Why do you ask?'

'I thought we might go dancing another time. That's if you're happy to meet me again, of course.'

'As you've been on your best behaviour,' she said, 'I'll meet you again.'

'Here?'

'Yes, here.'

'Oh, good. It's going to be our trysting place, Iris, a bit public, but rather special in spite of it.'

'You do talk nonsense.'

'How can you say that, when you trot out words like "gynaecology" and "obstetrics" that call for a Latin dictionary?' He put on a thoughtful face and said, 'Maybe I should bring one next time.'

Whether or not she thought that was a good idea remained a mystery, because she said, 'All right, we're going to meet here, but when?'

'Let me consult my mental calendar. When shall we two meet again?' He thought about it and said, 'How about next Saturday?'

'Saturday? That should be all right. Where shall we go?'

'You pose so many questions, Iris. I think we'll go to the Strand Palace Hotel. They do tea dances, I'm told, and that's perfect for two people on nights.' Mrs Chandler had told him that. 'We can certainly get the first hour or so in.' He gave her an enquiring look. 'Does that appeal to you? I take it you approve of, er, sandwiching the foxtrot between the sandwiches and cakes?'

'It sounds wonderful, but I have to go. Thank you for a really lovely afternoon.'

'You're more than welcome. I look forward to seeing you next Saturday.'

'Next Saturday, yes.'

He kissed her inclined cheek. 'Have a rewarding week on Obstetrics and Gynaecology,' he said, kissing her again.

'You remembered both words, and you said you'd never heard of them.' It sounded like an accusation.

'I hadn't, but I did Latin at school.'

'You big swot.' She smiled nevertheless. ''Bye for now.'

''Bye.'

7

Air raids had become so frequent and so devastating that it was no surprise that Green Watch was fully occupied every night the following week. Ted, whose sense of direction was fairly acute, was beginning to learn the layout of the station area and beyond. As well as driving back from various incidents, there were occasions when he was able to view a generous area of Tower Hamlets, including the parts that were on fire, from the top of an extension ladder.

Each morning, the watch returned, dirty and weary, to the sub-station, prompting Ted to ask Albert Jenkins one afternoon, 'Do you know where could I lay my hands on a sprinkler head and some steel tube and fittings?'

Albert gave him a strange look and asked, 'Are you thinking of setting up in business, then?'

'No, it's an idea I've had to turn the washroom into a shower bath for the whole watch.'

'I think you're out of your mind, but if you want a sprinkler head, the place to find one is in the caretaker's store. I do know that there's one the London Fire Brigade used for training before the war.'

'Let's go and look.'

Still shaking his head, Albert led the way to the caretaker's room and the store under the school. The key to the store hung conveniently from a hook inside the caretaker's room, a fact known, apparently, only to Albert. Ted naturally kept his curiosity to himself.

Once inside the store, they located, not one, but two sprinkler heads, a number of steel tubes, fittings, hemp, jointing compound, and the all-important hacksaw and pipe wrench.

'I don't suppose there are any threading dies,' said Ted, almost to himself.

'You expect a lot, Ted. If you want pipe threaded, you'll have to ask the plumbers up the street. I imagine they'll do it for you.'

'I suppose they might.'

'Mind you, before you can do anything, you'll have to get your idea past the sub.'

———————— ▸◂ ————————

'The washroom has its own floor drain, Sub. There's no problem there, and the pipe and fittings are just lying around unused. I can do the work,' he assured him. 'I installed the watering system for my dad's market garden, and that was harder because I had to drill the pipes at six-inch intervals.'

The sub-officer rubbed his chin. 'The pipes and fittings rightfully belong to the Council,' he said.

'But I wouldn't be taking them away, Sub. They'll still be here when this place is a school again.'

'I suppose so.' He gave it a little more thought and said, 'You're a bright lad, Dewhirst. I'm sure you can do it, but how much water is it going to use? Have you thought about that?'

'Yes, I've thought about it, and it'll use very little. The whole watch will use it together, and we only need to be under it for two minutes or so. It'll get us properly clean and it'll help keep up morale as well. I don't have to tell you how important that is after a long, hard watch.'

Sub-Officer Prentice gave him a lop-sided look and asked, 'Did you learn bullshit at university, Dewhirst? It sounds like it to me.'

'No, it just comes naturally, Sub.'

Sub-Officer Prentice scratched his head and said, 'Okay, you can start when we go back on days, but you'll still have your normal duties to do. There's to be no slacking.'

'Thanks, Sub. There won't be.'

Ted went to the recreation room, which was deserted for the moment. He wanted to reply to a letter he'd received from Eileen, and it was better done in peaceful surroundings.

Dear Eileen,

Thanks for your latest letter. I'm afraid I've been busy lately, on nights, so I'm a bit behind with my reply. I'm sure you'll understand.

To answer your question about Hamlet, and why he didn't kill Claudius earlier, I have to say that it seems Shakespeare left us with a mystery, although there are helpful references in the play. To begin with, Hamlet doesn't feel as angry as he believes he should, and this is an example of Shakespeare's acute understanding of human nature. Throughout the play, there are indications that Hamlet is losing his sanity, but nothing is ever black and white. He describes himself as 'unpregnant of my cause' (I can't give you references, because I haven't a copy here, so you'll have to find them for yourself). At all events, there he is, wondering why he doesn't feel more strongly about his uncle's crime than he does. Later in the play, he wonders if the ghost claiming to be his father is to be trusted. 'The spirit that I have seen may be a devil.' If the ghost is a devil, it may be trying to persuade him to commit a crime. In Act 3, he holds back from killing Claudius, because his victim is at prayer, and he is afraid that the murderer will go to Heaven if he is praying at the time of his death. Towards the end of the play, he can't decide whether killing Claudius is morally right, and he uses the excuse that he is a thinker, rather than a doer. In conclusion, I think Dickens had the right of it when he referred in the early pages of A Christmas Carol *to the ghost of Hamlet's father appearing 'to astonish his son's weak mind'. Had Hamlet not been a ditherer, the play might have been much shorter than it became! I hope you find that helpful. If not, there's a book in my room by A. J. Graham, called,* Hamlet's Casualties – a Post Mortem, *and you're welcome to use it.*

You've certainly been busy at home. By the sound of it, you've scarcely had time to incur the maternal wrath! She must be wondering what's happened.

I've met somebody new. Her name's Iris, and she's a nurse at the London Hospital, just down the road. I haven't had time yet to get to know her very well – we've only been to the pictures to see Night Train to Munich, *an excellent film – but she's good company, and we're going dancing tomorrow afternoon.*

Guess what as well? I'm going to install a shower here. It'll be much better than washing at the kiddies' hand basins after a dirty watch. I've got all the stuff I need, so I can make a start as soon as we're back on days. Do you remember helping me with the watering system at the garden?

Take care and keep reading the texts. You won't have me in the exam room when you sit Higher School Certificate, although I'll certainly be with you in spirit!

Lots of love,
Ted XXX.

———▶◀———

Ted viewed the cake stand critically. 'The sandwiches look all right,' he said, 'but the cakes are a shadow of their pre-war yumminess.'

'Well, there is a war on,' said Iris, pouring tea for them both.

'A feeble excuse.' The band began 'South of the Border', so he asked, 'Would you care to join me "down Mexico way"?' He took her hand and led her on to the floor.

'I've always liked this song,' said Iris.

'You and millions of others.'

'Don't you?' She sounded surprised.

'I'm happy as long as I'm dancing with you,' he told her sweetly. 'They could play Colonel Bogey for all I care.'

'You're full of it, Ted.' She smiled to show that she wasn't serious. 'But you make up for it by being a good dancer.'

'Thank you. You're not bad, either.'

They returned to their table at the end of the number. Iris cut into a sandwich and said, 'Somebody's been a bit miserly with the ham.'

'Well, there is a war on,' he reminded her mischievously.

'I suppose so.'

'You can bet Hitler's not tucking into a tea like this.'

'Now, there's a thought,' said Iris, putting her teacup down. 'Do you imagine the Germans go dancing like this?'

'Not like this,' he said confidently.

'I don't mean tea-dancing, particularly. I just wonder if they dance at all. They don't look as if they know how to enjoy themselves, do they?'

'I imagine they do, but they enjoy themselves seriously. As for dancing, why dance, when you can goose-step to "The Lambeth Walk"?' Memories of that film clip had them both laughing.

'I'm sure they've got music of their own,' said Iris.

'Oh, I'm not so sure. There is a war on, you know.'

'I wish I hadn't said that. You won't leave it alone now.' Just then, the band began to play 'Change Partners' from the film *Carefree*, prompting her to say, 'I love this one. Can we dance?'

Ted led her on to the floor again, and they joined the line of dance. Even if she'd not spoken a word, Iris's discernible involvement with the music would have told him how she felt about it. She was an excellent dancer and a rewarding partner.

When they sat down again, she said, 'That was truly wonderful.'

'It's just a shame,' said Ted, 'that Fred Astaire couldn't be here to sing it for you.' The vocalist, a stand-in for the afternoon event, was no doubt doing his best, but he lacked something.

'Well,' said Iris, 'there is a war on.' Immediately, she screwed up her face and said, 'I'm sorry. It just slipped out.'

Ted patted her hand understandingly. 'I doubt if it'll be the last time,' he said as an idea occurred to him. 'If we put sixpence into a "There is a war on" box every time we said it, we'd save a fortune.'

After a few more dances, it was time for them to leave, and they slipped discreetly out of the room. As they took their coats and hats from the attendant, Ted said, 'It's a shame you have to wear a coat.'

'It's cold out there, Ted.'

'I know. I'm just saying that you look so good in that dress, it's a shame to cover it up.'

She looked at him strangely. 'It's the same one I wore when I met you last week.'

'I know. I recognised you immediately.'

'Idiot.'

'Yes, I'd recognise your lovely features anywhere, not to mention your slender figure, your shapely—'

'Keep it clean, Ted.'

'I was going to say, "legs", nothing more *risqué* than that, but if you don't want compliments, just say the word and I'll stifle the poet within my soul.'

'You do talk nonsense.'

They walked into Embankment Station surrounded by people arriving early with their bedding to shelter from the expected Blitz. A station official was calling in a strident voice, '*Bona fide* passengers only this way!'

'Just imagine,' said Ted as they followed the woman's directions. 'If we didn't have to report for duty we could spend a cosy night wrapped up together on the station platform or in a darkened shelter, nice and intimate. Wouldn't that be grand?'

'You can forget all about intimacy.'

'Do you mean there's no point in bringing you down here during an air raid?'

'You know what I mean, Ted.'

'No,' he said, 'I don't think I do.'

She sighed impatiently. 'It's only fair to tell you for future reference that I don't want you to get ideas about... you-know-what.'

'I'm not likely to get ideas about it when I don't know what "you-know-what" is. How would I recognise it if I saw it? Does it have a label?'

'You're being difficult, Ted. What I'm saying is that there's line I won't cross, and you may as well know that now, before you build up on it and you're disappointed.'

'Oh, that.' He looked thoughtful for a moment and asked, 'What, in an air raid shelter?'

'Of course not. I mean anywhere. I'm just not prepared to take the risk.'

'Nor should you be,' he agreed, realising it was time to stop teasing her. 'Message understood, and don't worry, Iris. It's yours to preserve.'

'You've got the idea, but there's no need to sound so martyred about it.'

'I don't feel like a martyr. It's quite a relief to be spared yet another task.'

'Is it?' She sounded suspicious.

'Well, yes. I've got plenty to do without "you-know-what" on my list as well. There is a war on, you know.'

———— ▸◂ ————

He walked her to the nurses' home, where broad daylight demanded only the purest of pecks on her cheek.

'It'll be different when we're back on days,' she said, almost apologetically.

'There's always something to look forward to, isn't there?'

'There is to some degree,' she agreed.

'Don't worry, Iris. You shall remain "as chaste as is the bud ere it be blown." ' He looked around him to ensure they weren't overlooked, and kissed her again briefly, but full on the lips. 'When will I see you again?'

'Is next Friday all right?'

'It should be, and then we're both back on days.'

'' Bye.'

'' Bye.' On a sudden whim, he kissed her again.

He reflected as he walked back to the sub-station, that enforced celibacy made him no different from most young men. It was the accepted standard in respectable circles. Nice girls simply didn't do that kind of thing, and he would probably survive the experience anyway.

Later that night, as he stood on the extension ladder, directing his hose into yet another burning warehouse, he forgot about the lusts of the flesh and even Iris herself, as he concentrated on the immediate task of pitting his puny resource against the fire that threatened to pluck him from the ladder.

8

NOVEMBER

Ted's shower project suffered a hiatus when he realised that the sprinkler heads would give unsatisfactory performance at normal water pressure.

'It was like a lot of good ideas,' said Sub-Officer Prentice. 'It just didn't work in practice.'

'I haven't finished yet, Sub,' said Ted. 'I know where I can lay my hands on some shower roses.'

'Legally, I hope.'

'Legally, they belong to my dad, and he'll be glad to see the back of them.'

'How's that, then?' The sub took a packet of Woodbines from his pocket and offered it to Ted.

'No thanks, Sub, I don't.'

'No, course you don't. Go on, then. Why does he want rid of them?'

'When I planned the watering system, I was going to use roses, but then I realised I needed something that would reach every corner of each bed, so I drilled a series of lengths of tube with a fine drill, and they did the job. The roses have been sitting around ever since, an expensive reminder that we're all human and fallible. I'll write to my dad today.'

———◆◆———

However Ted's father felt about the roses, he acted quickly, and they arrived at the sub-station towards the end of the week, just as Ted was completing the pipework. The job called for eight of them, and he worked past his normal shift time on Thursday, fitting them and testing the system. It was important that he found the right setting for the valves to deliver a comfortable temperature and he was able to report to Sub-Officer Prentice by seven o' clock, that the installation was complete.

'Right,' said the sub, opening the door to the recreation room, ' Green Watch get your washing kit and yourselves into the washroom. We're going to christen the new showers. You blokes in Red Watch will have that to look forward to in the morning.'

A few minutes later, the washroom was filled with several naked firemen and one sub-officer, all laughing and singing, bearing out Ted's claim that the shower would be a great morale booster.

They were only under the shower for less than two minutes, so it was unfortunate that one of Red Watch's firewomen walked in during the course of an innocent errand. When she saw what was happening, she shrieked and retreated to the Watch Room.

Fully-dressed again, the watch returned to the recreation room. On the way, Sub-Officer Prentice stopped at the Watch Room to apologise to the unfortunate firewoman. 'I'm sorry, love,' he said. 'I should have warned you. It can't have been a pretty sight.'

'It certainly wasn't,' she confirmed, still embarrassed. Her colleague was still helpless with laughter.

'Now,' said the sub when they reached the recreation room, 'she can say she's seen more of this watch than she has of her own.'

———◦►◄◦———

When Ted met Iris on Saturday, she asked her usual question. 'What have you been up to since I saw you last?'

'Fifty feet on a ladder.'

'Funny man. You know what I mean. I know you don't like telling me about going out to fires, but there must be other things that happen to you.'

'One very important thing I did this week was to install a shower that'll take a whole watch at a time. Just imagine, Iris, all those firemen singing "Rub-a-dub-dub", and with only a cake of soap to preserve their modesty.'

'I'd rather not.'

'You'd love it. You and I could go in there together when no one's looking.'

She gave him a grown-up look. 'You only say these things to embarrass me,' she said.

'That's true.'

'What are we going to see tonight?' Films evidently interested her more than naked firemen.

'*The Stars Look Down.*'

'Who's in it?'

'Michael Redgrave, Margaret Lockwood and Emlyn Williams.'

'Lovely. What's it about?'

It had become apparent to Ted that reading had never been Iris's favourite pastime. 'It's based on a novel by A J Cronin,' he told her, 'about a mining community in the north-east.'

'Where's the north-east?'

'If you go up the London and North-Eastern Line and jump off the train just before it reaches Scotland, you'll be in the north-east.'

'I didn't mean that. I meant, what places are there in the north-east?'

Now he understood what she meant. 'There's the northern end of Yorkshire. That's Stockton, Middlesborough and Redcar. Then there's County Durham, and then a bit further up, there's Newcastle.'

Iris looked at him in amazement. 'How do you know all these things? When we did geography at school, we learned about sheep in Australia and rainfall in Brazil and all the bits we were never likely to visit, but I don't remember learning anything about England.'

'I read a lot.'

'Books?'

'And newspapers. I usually read them before they get used for fish and chips.'

'I should hope so.'

'Yes, the fat makes an awful mess. You can see the print on both sides of the page.'

'Are you always daft?'

'Not when I'm asleep, I'm told.'

They arrived at the Picture Palace, and Ted bought two tickets for First House. He asked, 'Can I put my arm round your waist as we go upstairs?'

'Why do you want to do that?'

'It adds to the excitement. Go on, be a sport, and I'll buy you an ice cream at the interval.'

'Don't be silly. Of course you can if you want to.'

They reached the balcony, where the usherette showed them to their seats. To Ted's relief, the newsreel was just ending. He always found them too artificial to be taken seriously.

They sat through trailers of forthcoming pictures, and he wished they'd get on with the main film before the inevitable bombing began.

Eventually, *The Stars Look Down* came on screen, and Iris and he were gripped from the start. Unusually, the film seemed to be remarkably true to the novel, and Ted, who'd read it a few years earlier when it was first published, was very impressed until the moment a notice came on the screen, saying, *An air raid is in progress. Please make your way to the nearest shelter.*

'Bugger!'

'Ted!'

'I'm sorry. I said it without thinking.'

As they made their way downstairs to the foyer, Iris said, 'I really need to get back to the hospital.'

'Okay, I'll cover you.'

'What do you mean?'

'I don't know. It's something they say in the westerns.'

'Come on, then.'

They joined the crowd that surged out of the cinema, the same crowd that had chosen to go to First House in case of an air raid. Unfortunately, it made little difference in winter.

They left the majority trying to get into a public shelter just along the road from the cinema, and took the most direct route to the nurses' home, arriving there about five minutes later.

'Thank you,' said Iris. 'It was a shame about the interruption. I don't know when we'll see the end of the film.'

'If you like, I'll lend you the book.'

'That wouldn't be the same, though. When you read a book, you can't see the people and the expressions on their faces.'

'I can.'

'You'd say anything.'

'I shan't speak for at least another minute.'

'I don't believe you.'

Looking around quite unnecessarily in the darkness, he bent and touched her lips with his, teasing, and then settling into a soft, lingering kiss.

After a few minutes, she asked breathlessly, 'Where did you learn to kiss like that?'

'Manchester,' he told her truthfully, 'when I was at university.'

'They don't teach that at universities.'

'Not all universities, granted—' He was about to say more, but then the air raid seemed to pick up in intensity. 'You'd better get inside,' he said. 'Is next Friday okay?'

'No, I'm on fire-watching duty.'

'Saturday, then?'

'Okay. Be careful, Ted.'

He kissed her quickly and then pushed her to the door, watching her until she was inside, before turning and running back to the sub-station.

———◆◆◆———

It was a noisier night than usual, with a heavy unit and two trailer pumps going out immediately. The rest followed shortly afterwards. A high explosive bomb that sounded close had Ted wondering if the hospital had been hit. He wouldn't know for some time whether or not Iris was safe.

Eventually, the All-Clear sounded, and sleep was made possible, but Ted was up early in the morning.

He learned that the hospital had been hit during the night, and that men from Red Watch had attended the fire. By that time, they were all under the shower, and they would all need their sleep. He would have to wait until he could speak with someone at the hospital.

———◆◆◆———

After breakfast, he walked out to the yard with the others to set about cleaning the vehicles and equipment that the night watch had brought back. As he passed the Watch Room, Sub-Officer Prentice called out to him. 'Dewhirst?'

'Yes, Sub?'

'Do you realise you're the most popular man in the station?'

'Am I, Sub? He'd been so preoccupied with the bomb that had fallen on the hospital that he'd been conscious of nothing else.

'Until this morning, the District Officer was top bloke, ever since he announced that they were doing away with the forty-eight hours on, twenty-four off routine, but now Red Watch are singing your praises. At least, that's what they were doing after their shower. They went to bed a happy bunch of boys.'

'I could envy them their shower,' said Mrs Chandler, 'but they need it and they deserve it after a night like last night.'

'It was a bad night,' said Ted. 'I believe a bomb fell on the hospital, but I don't know how to find out anything. If I ask about an individual nurse in a hospital that size, I'll just be a nuisance.'

'You will,' said the sub. 'Take it from me, son, that hospital's too big for Jerry to miss, and if you get into a state every time a bomb comes down on it, you'll be no use to anybody.'

'Drop her a line,' suggested Lorna, 'and if she's okay, she'll send a reply. You'll know something inside two days.'

It was the most helpful thing he'd heard that morning. 'Thanks, Lorna,' he said, 'I'll do that.'

———◆◆———

To speed up the process, Ted delivered his note by hand, leaving it at the hospital's reception desk.

His worries were heightened that night, when another high explosive bomb hit the hospital, and he tried to take the sub's advice, although it was far from easy. He'd only known Iris a short time; they'd been out together just three times, but she was already more to him than a casual friend. His fellow-firemen ribbed him about his new girlfriend and called him a Casanova and a fast worker, but that was all they knew. Men were slow to notice the important things, and he included himself in that assessment. Women, however, seemed to have an extra sense. He was reminded of it when he saw Lorna that lunchtime. Most of the watch had taken to the recreation room for a smoke before resuming work, but Ted stood by the entrance, watching the drizzle, but not really seeing anything.

A voice asked, 'Are you still waiting to hear from her?'

'Yes.' The voice was Lorna's, and with those few words, she sounded as if she genuinely cared.

'It's the same for both of us,' she said, 'except that Reg is about two thousand miles away. That's as the crow flies.' The thought made her smile. 'I used my old school atlas to work that out when he was posted.'

'When was that?'

'May, this year. His regiment left three days after we were married.'

'I'm sorry, Lorna. That was rotten luck.'

She shrugged. 'He's a regular soldier. It's only to be expected.'

'What's his regiment?' It seemed polite to ask.

'The Eleventh Hussars.' She smiled at his reaction. 'They don't ride horses now,' she explained, 'they're mechanised.'

Ted felt uncomfortable talking about a professional soldier serving abroad. 'I tried to join the Territorials back in nineteen thirty-eight,' he told her. 'That was after the Navy had turned me down. I only made enquiries at the RAF recruiting office, but they said they'd have rejected me for the same reason.'

'Is it very personal?'

'No, I'm fit enough. The problem is that I'm allergic to soya.'

She blinked in surprise. 'That sounds like a funny reason for turning down a big, strong chap like you.'

'I thought so too.' He told her about his feelings after he left the RAF recruiting office, and how he'd seen the fire engine go past. He laughed. 'It was like a sign from above,' he said, 'and it was all I was allowed to do, so I went full-time as soon as I could.'

'You're doing an important job,' she told him. 'You're serving your country just as surely as if you were in the armed forces.'

'That's what I keep telling myself.'

A familiar voice from inside the building said, 'Right, Green Watch, you've had long enough to rest and digest. Back to work, all of you.'

Ted turned up the collar of his overalls and said, 'It's been nice, chatting with you, Lorna.'

She smiled. 'Nice for me too. Let me know when you hear something.'

———◆◄———

The next morning, he received a note that was brief, but no less welcome. It read:

Dear Ted,
I'm fine. You mustn't worry. It's a big hospital, and I'm only a little target.
See you on Saturday.
Love,
Iris XXX

Just looking at the size of the hospital, it should have been obvious to him. He would bear her words in mind because they made him feel better.

9

The Athenaeum Ballroom in Bethnal Green was less grand than its name suggested, but it was conveniently situated for Ted and Iris, and it turned out to be a friendly place.

They took part in the usual silly activities: the Hokey-Cokey and the Lambeth Walk. The actual Siegfried Line, or 'Westwall', as the Germans called it, had long-since shown itself to be less than a joke, and the party game associated with it was no longer as popular with the public as it had been the previous year.

With those things out of the way, the proper dancing began, and the five-piece band started 'A Nightingale Sang in Berkeley Square', already one of the most popular songs with dancers and listeners alike.

'You look like next week's wages,' Ted told her.

'You always say that.'

'It's a different week each time, and it all mounts up, you know. I mean, not every girl gets told she looks like four weeks' earnings.'

'Idiot.' She smiled nevertheless.

'You won't say that this time next year. Fifty-six times a fireman's weekly wage will make it the most glorious compliment ever bestowed.' He whispered in her ear, 'And you'll deserve it.'

'When you say things like that, and I know you're not joking, I go weak and wobbly all over.'

'It's just as well the music's stopped.' He pulled out her chair for her. 'Come and sit down before you fall down.'

'They say Berkeley Square was bombed two months ago,' she said.

'Two delayed-action bombs.' He nodded. 'I know.'

'How do you know if they're delayed action bombs?'

'They don't go off straight away.'

She gave him a look of exasperation. 'I know that, but how do you know they're not just unexploded bombs?'

'They leave them alone, and then, if they don't go off, the army come and deal with them.' He reached for her hand and stroked it with his thumb. 'Let's not talk about bombs and air raids,' he said. 'We've come here to forget all that, at least, as far as we can.'

'All right,' she agreed. 'What are you doing for Christmas?'

'I don't know yet whether or not I'll have leave.'

'I'll get leave at some stage, and then I'll go home.'

'Where's home?' Strangely, it was a subject they'd never explored.

'My parents live in Cobham, Surrey.'

It meant nothing to Ted, who simply knew that Surrey was next door to London. 'Have you any brothers or sisters?'

'No, and it's your turn now. Where's your home?'

'A town near Bradford in the West Riding.'

She considered that, and said, 'You don't sound terribly northern. You do a little, but not like one of the cleaners at the hospital, a girl from Barnsley. I can barely understand her.'

'I went to a posh school. They don't let anyone in from Barnsley.'

'All right. Brothers and sisters?'

'One sister. Her name's Eileen, and she's seventeen.'

'What does she do?'

It seemed to Ted that women were born to ask questions. 'She's in the sixth form at school,' he told her.

'A clever girl, then. What did you teach at school?'

'English.'

'That'll be why you read books, I suppose.'

'It helps. Would you like a drink?' If nothing else, it would interrupt the barrage of questions.

'Mm, just lemonade, please.'

Ted went to the bar and returned with two glasses of lemonade, thereby surprising Iris.

'Aren't you drinking, Ted?'

'In London,' he explained, 'I usually drink Guinness, but I thought it might hang on my breath.'

'That's really thoughtful of you.'

'I suppose it is, but it's not so surprising.'

She gave him a corner-of-the-eye look and said, 'You're going to tell me that "Thoughtful" is your middle name, aren't you?' She was beginning to get his measure.

'Charles Thoughtful Dewhirst, that's me,' he confirmed.

'In that case, how do you come to be called "Ted"?'

'It was the vicar's idea. He said to my parents at my christening, "You can't have this poor child go through life with a name like 'Thoughtful'

", so they allowed me a pet name. I shall always be thankful to the Reverend Ernest Helpful-and-Obliging Whatmough for that. He knew what it was like to be given a daft name.'

Iris inclined her head towards the band, who had just begun 'Deep Purple'. 'Let's dance,' she suggested, 'and leave the silly stories for later.'

They danced without a word to 'Deep Purple', and Ted, who was as enchanted as Iris by the song, marked the final bar by lifting a lock of her light-brown hair and kissing her on the neck. As they took their seats again, he asked, 'Was that allowed?'

'Just about,' she told him with mock-severity.

The band were unusually silent, and Ted was wondering if they were about to take a break, when the bandleader spoke.

'Ladies and gentlemen,' he said, 'I'm afraid it's the Göring Excuse-Me again. The air raid siren has sounded. Will you please make your way to the nearest shelter, which is situated at the junction of Selby Street and Granary Road?'

Ted picked up his helmet and gasmask. 'This is becoming boring,' he said, offering Iris his arm.

They thanked the band on the way out. It wasn't their fault that the evening's entertainment had been cut short; in fact, they'd played particularly well up to the interruption.

'I must get back to the hospital,' said Iris. 'You don't need to come, Ted. I'll be all right.'

'Yes, I do.' He put an arm round her, guiding her through the crowd until they were outside, where most of them headed for the public shelter. Ted and Iris continued towards Whitechapel Road and the hospital. To the south, anti-aircraft guns were putting up a defiant barrage. In only a few minutes, the raiders would be overhead.

When they reached the nurses' home, Ted took her all the way to the outside door. The guns had stopped firing. Already, they could hear the monotonous beat of the engines. In what seemed no time at all, the aircraft were overhead and bombs were falling. The noise was coming, as ever, from the docks, but they were falling closer as well. There was a deafening explosion and shrapnel began to fall, some of it within yards of where they stood. Ted stood on the doorstep, shielding Iris with his body. He asked, 'Is next Friday okay?'

'Yes.'

He turned the doorknob and pushed the door open. 'I'll see you then.' He kissed her briefly. 'Be careful.'

'You be careful.' It was what people said. Even though they had no control over events, they felt they had to say it.

———◗◀———

Ted lay awake, listening to London in its agonies. Incredibly, men were sleeping through it, men who'd been there from the start. They must be inured to the explosions and tremors. Further along the room, though, the rasp of a cigarette lighter followed by a pool of flame told him he wasn't alone in his helpless vigil, and that knowledge held some strange comfort for him.

Eventually, the All Clear sounded, and sleep came like a long-awaited but welcome ally.

———◗◀———

After lunch, Ted stood, as before, in the boys' entrance. The mess room was filled with smoke, and he preferred to be out of it.

He was pleased when Lorna joined him. She was pleasant company, and that was always welcome.

'You'll be relieved to know they didn't bomb the hospital last night,' she told him.

'They showered it with shrapnel,' he said. 'I was there. You're right, though. I am relieved.'

'Are you going up to Yorkshire at Christmas?'

It was strange how everyone wanted to talk about Christmas, and he was surprised that Lorna of all people should raise the subject, parted as she was from her husband. 'If I get leave,' he said, 'I'll go and see my family.'

'What family have you?'

'My parents and my sister. She's seventeen, but she's still at school. She keeps asking me for help with her studies. When you have a brother who spoils you, you see, it's easier than finding out things the hard way.'

Lorna smiled, evidently finding the idea appealing. 'Yours must be a close family,' she said.

'Far from it. My sister and I are close, but my mother's a very buttoned-up person, and my father dodges anything even distantly related to closeness or affection.'

She looked puzzled. 'In that case,' she said, 'how did you become the sympathetic person you are?'

'What makes you think I am?'

'Things you've said.' She thought again. 'And the way you said them.'

'You're very astute.'

'I'm just nosey.'

He considered her original question. 'When I was four-and-a-half,' he said, 'my older brother Joseph died, and I was sent to stay with my father's sister and her husband, Auntie Jane and Uncle George. They are two of the best people imaginable, the kind of people whose mission seems to be to make others happier. Goodness knows, I needed it at the time. Auntie Jane is as openly affectionate as my father is inhibited, and Uncle George, who's only related to me by marriage, just accepted me as one of his own. They have no children of their own, and between them, they... well, they were a great influence on me. I stayed with them again when Eileen was born. They're still very kind to us both.'

'What an awful thing to happen, but thank goodness for your auntie and uncle.' She smiled and nodded, as if the knowledge gave her special pleasure. 'I'm lucky, you see. My family – my parents and my brother – are very close.'

The thought pleased him. With her husband away, her family would be supportive. He thought he should ask, 'How old is your brother?'

'Twenty-five. He's in the RAF. Nothing exciting, he's in intelligence.'

'But he's doing his bit.'

Lorna was about to respond, possibly with reassurance, but Sub-Officer Prentice's voice echoed down the corridor, sending the watch back to work.

'It's been nice talking to you again,' said Ted.

Lorna nodded. 'Now we know each other, we should do it again.'

———◄►———

Ted's conversation with Lorna had reminded him of an obligation, and that evening, he wrote an overdue letter.

Dear Auntie Jane and Uncle George,

I hope you're both well and not too frustrated by rationing and shortages.

As you can see from the address on this letter, I'm now in the East End of London. Being a fireman is all I'm allowed to do in this war, but people tell me I'm doing a worthwhile job. I hope that's true.

Uncle George, I hear you're in the Home Guard now, and Auntie Jane's in the WVS. Well done, both of you. I've always known you'd both pull your weight, and I'm delighted to hear that you're hard at it.

In case you haven't heard from Eileen recently, she's in the sixth form and, believe it or not, taking the same subjects I took at HSC. It's either hero-worship or else Eileen knowing I'll be on hand to help her when she gets stuck. She wants to do Modern History at university, and that's the only subject I haven't had to help her with – so far.

Unfortunately, Eileen's association with David next door came to a close when he wrote to her, telling her he'd taken up with a WAAF on his station. She was very upset at first, but she adjusted fairly quickly. She'll always be all right because she's quite uncomplicated – at least, as uncomplicated as a girl ever can be. I'm sure you know what I mean.

I met a girl last month. She's called Iris, and she's a nurse at the London Hospital. It's early days yet, but she's very nice indeed.

I was talking with someone on the station earlier today, and I told her about the times I spent with you, and especially when I was seven. I've never forgotten what a wonderful time I had, and I'm sure I never gave either of my parents a moment's thought during that time, and they – my mum especially – were having such a difficult time. Children can be horribly selfish and single-minded, can't they?'

Take care, both of you.

Lots of love,

Ted XXX

He folded and sealed the letter, wondering whether or not to write to Eileen while he had his writing things out, but he decided to leave it for another day. He'd just heard the Heavy Unit and its crew being called out, and it would be difficult to concentrate with raiders already overhead. When he'd told his Aunt and Uncle that he hoped he was doing a worthwhile job, he meant it, because there were times when the efforts of 4C Sub-Station seemed alarmingly puny against the colossal fires they had to face.

10

DECEMBER

The Luftwaffe returned on Sunday, the first of December, with previously unknown savagery, as wave after wave of bombers attacked the East End. Green Watch spent most of the night fighting a warehouse fire in Cable Street, and it was six o' clock the next morning before the fire was officially under control.

They were damping down when an excited District Officer shouted, 'That wall's not safe! Get everybody out!'

Sub-Officer Prentice looked up and saw the danger. 'Get up the road! Leave the pump,' he shouted, 'and run for it!'

Ted and the others were running to safety, when they heard the sub shout, 'Leave it and run!'

Turning to look behind him, Ted saw that Gregory was still at the trailer pump. He appeared to be closing a valve.

Prentice shouted again, 'Leave it, Greg! Run!'

Gregory finished turning the wheel and left the pump. He was running towards the rest of the watch when the wall began to collapse. Everyone in the watch was shouting to him now, urging him to run faster, and it seemed that he was clear of the falling brickwork. He glanced backward and ran across the road, instinctively trying to escape the threat, even though both sides of the road were equally dangerous.

As the brickwork folded, the heat from beyond the warehouse eclipsed everything for the moment. It was like an oven door being opened, except that the heat was greater than anything a kitchen had ever known.

Brickwork was still falling; the main part of the wall was down, but sections of it were hitting the road and bouncing. Ted watched in horror as a chunk of bricks still bonded by mortar fell on Gregory, causing him to fall.

'Come on, Greg!' Everyone was shouting to him, but he lay motionless with bricks still falling around him.

Looking back on the incident, Ted could never remember making the decision. He could only recall sprinting back to where Gregory lay, and turning him face down, as he'd been trained. He then grasped him under the armpits to lift him into a kneeling position, He was working with deadweight as his unfortunate colleague was clearly unconscious, but finally, he was able to take Gregory's right wrist in his left hand and haul him upwards and over his right shoulder. As he did so, a heavy weight caught the back of his helmet, and something also struck his head, stunning him momentarily and causing him to stagger. He gathered his wits, however, and ran as fast as his load would allow him, to where the rest of the watch were waiting. It was then that he became conscious of their frenzied shouts of encouragement.

He felt Gregory being lifted from his shoulder, and at that moment, his legs gave way and he fell to the ground.

'There's an ambulance on its way, and you're both going to hospital,' Sub-Officer Prentice told him.

'I'm all right, Sub,' he protested.

'You haven't seen the back of your head. It'll need more than a piece of sticking plaster, and you'll be needing more than a new helmet an' all.'

Ted felt around the back of his head beneath the brim of his helmet, and his hand came away covered in blood.

'Anyway,' said the sub, 'well done, Dewhirst. Good lad.'

'How's Greg?'

'He's conscious, but he needs to be checked over as well. For all we know, you might both have brain damage, although we've suspected it for a while, and you came close to confirming it tonight.'

An ambulance arrived while the watch were knocking off and making up, and Ted and Gregory were loaded on to stretchers and taken away.

Ted asked the attendant, 'Where are we going?'

'The London Hospital. I expect you know where that is.'

'I go there every week,' confirmed Ted.

The attendant said no more, probably suspecting she was in the company of a clever dick.

By the time they reached the hospital, Ted's head ached abominably, but he had to wait in a queue behind patients whose needs were obviously greater than his. He tried to ease the pain in his head by lying perfectly still and breathing regularly. It didn't work, but he persisted on the basis that it probably did no harm. Meanwhile, he kept his eyes closed. He needed a distraction, but not the horrible sights that the ambulances were bringing in.

The pain must have dulled to some extent, because he actually fell asleep, only waking when he felt his stretcher being moved.

'Now,' said a female voice, 'what have you been up to?'

He decided to spare her the one about the ladder. Instead, he said, 'Carrying a fireman.'

'Why on earth did you do that?'

'He has a wife, six kids and another one on the way. I thought his wife might like to see him again. It'll be a relief for the kids as well.' In the absence of any news, he said, 'I hope he's all right. He wasn't looking too good the last time I saw him.'

'The other fireman who was brought in is going to be all right.'

'Good old Greg. Thanks for telling me that, nurse.'

'Was he the man you carried?'

'Yes, but don't tell him that, or he'll expect me to do it every night.'

'Just be a brave fireman and roll over so that I can look at your injury.'

'All right.' He allowed her to turn him on to his side. 'Nurse?'

'Yes?'

'Do you know Nurse Iris Wingate? She's on Obstetrics and Gynaecology.'

'Not very well, but I know her to speak to.'

'Can you get a message to her, please?'

'What kind of message?'

'Just tell her, if you will, that I'm all right. If she hears that two firemen were brought in, she'll worry.'

'Okay, I'll leave a message at the nurses' home.'

'Thank you.'

It seemed that the nurse was no longer alone, because he heard her say, 'This patient has a nasty cut at the base of his skull, Doctor Woodley.'

'I can see that. Let's roll him on to his back so that I can examine him.'

Ted allowed himself to be rotated again, to come face-to-face with a tired-looking doctor, who said, 'Just lie still and let me examine you.' He shone a tiny light into each of Ted's eyes, asking, 'Do you feel at all dizzy?'

'No, but I've been on my back since they loaded me into the ambulance. If I sat up, it might be different.'

'It's not a good idea. Nauseous at all?'

'No.'

'Tired?'

'No more than usual at the end of a night watch.'

'Good. Vision okay?'

'I'm coping fine.'

'Headache?'

'Funnily enough, yes. Since you ask, it hurts like hell.'

'Hmm.' The doctor put his torch away. 'You have slight concussion. Any idea what might have caused it?'

'My money is on the chunk of masonry that caused the injury to which the nurse referred earlier, Doc. In fact, I'd say it was the prime suspect in this case.'

'He was carrying an injured colleague to safety,' explained the nurse, belatedly impressed.

'The chap I saw earlier?'

'Yes, Doctor Woodley.'

The doctor looked vaguely at his notes and asked, 'What's this patient's name, nurse?'

'Tell him it's Charles Edwin Dewhirst, nurse,' said Ted helpfully.

The doctor was unfazed, but chose to address Ted directly. 'Can you raise your left leg, old chap?'

'By all means.' Ted lifted his left leg.

'Right leg?'

Ted obliged. 'I can do the Hokey-Cokey as well,' he said, 'but I can't turn around.'

'Can you get his boots off, nurse?'

'Yes, Doctor Woodley.' She grasped each of Ted's fire boots in turn and removed them.

'Feel this?' The doctor tickled Ted's right sole with something small and firm, achieving the usual result.

'Now the left.' He repeated the process before writing something in Ted's notes. 'Hmm, we'll get your wound dressed and then we'll keep you in for a spell until we know you're not at risk. All right?'

'Right as rain, Doc, and thank you. You too, nurse. Please don't forget about Nurse Wingate.'

Later, swathed in bandages and feeling the benefit of the aspirin he was eventually allowed, Ted was taken on to the ward. As he was wheeled past a row of beds, a familiar but muffled voice asked, 'That you, Dewhirst?'

'Yes. Is that you, Greg?'

'Yeah, it's me. Thanks for what you did, Dewhirst.'

Ted saw that his colleague was lying face-down. It explained the muffled voice. 'Any time, mate.'

He hadn't long been in bed when a nurse came to take his details. It seemed that repetitive detail-taking was central to hospital admission routine.

When she had noted his name, address, religion and next of kin, she asked, 'Have you any allergies we should know about?'

'Apart from falling masonry? Only soya.'

'Good. Soya's not on the menu today. I'll see that it's entered in your notes for future reference.'

'Thank you. It follows me around like a bad reputation. It kept me out of the Navy, the Army and the RAF.' In fairness, he had to say, 'At least it didn't keep me out of hospital.'

'Good. Let's hope it doesn't get you *into* hospital some time. Try to get some rest.' She looked at her fob watch and told him, 'Lunch is in half-an-hour.'

Logic was a haphazard bugger, he decided, the way it left some people quite untouched.

Lunch was memorable in the worst sense, even worse than Olive's offerings on a bad day, but at last, he could have a nap, and he did so until two-thirty, when the first of the visitors arrived. He was still trying to shut out the noise of their greetings and disagreements when he found himself with his own visitor, a diminutive, dark-haired woman, who appeared to be in a state of distress. She was also more than a little pregnant.

She asked, 'Are you Mr Dewhirst?'

'That's right. What can I do for you?' He hadn't been aware that any civilians in the area knew of his existence.

'I'm Mrs Gregory. I want to fank you for saving my Arfur's life.'

'Oh, I wouldn't put it like that, Mrs Gregory. He'd have been all right on his own, you know. I just thought he'd like to be somewhere more peaceful than in the middle of the road, where it was all happening.'

'That's not what 'e said. 'E said the bricks was comin' down like rain, and now you've got yerself injured an' all.'

'I'm all right, really.'

'You don't look it.'

He reminded himself that she hadn't come to cheer him up. Had that been the case, her journey might have been less than successful. 'Honestly, Mrs Gregory, don't give it another thought. Just go and keep Greg... Arthur company. Thanks for coming to see me, though. It's been very nice making your acquaintance.'

'God bless you, Mr Dewhirst, and fanks again.'

'It was no trouble, Mrs Gregory.'

The noise had died down to some extent, and he was able to doze off for a while.

At four o' clock, the tea trolley came rumbling on to the ward. Members of the Women's Voluntary Service began handing tea to patients, to give the nurses a break, Ted imagined, and he admired them for their public spirit, but he was delighted to find his tea brought to him, not by one of the WVS helpers, but by someone even more welcome.

'Iris,' he said, 'what a perfect surprise.' It was too. Just the sight of her made him feel better.

The alarm in her eyes changed to relief at his apparent wholeness, but her first utterance sounded like a telling-off. 'What have you been up to? And don't say a hundred feet up a turntable ladder.'

'No, I was on the ground. Something hit me when I wasn't looking.'

'You'll have to be more careful.'

'I'll bear that in mind.'

'Whatever it was seems to have done the impossible,' she observed, examining his dressing. 'It must have hit you just beneath your helmet. You're lucky it didn't cause a spinal injury. They think it must have been the same thing that got the other man.'

'No, Greg got walloped on the head earlier. That's why I pulled him out.'

'I'm talking about the thing that caused the injury to his... bottom.'

'I didn't know about that.' It made sense, now, that Greg was lying on his front.

'Maybe your helmet and his bottom saved you from a worse injury.'

'It made me feel a bit weird,' he said, nevertheless feasting his eyes on the object of his affection.

She looked at him strangely. 'What's the matter? Why are you eyeing me up and down like that?'

'I'm just thinking that when I see you in uniform I could lose my heart all over again.'

'Don't be silly.'

'Don't mock sincere devotion, Iris.' An idea came to him, and he said, 'Iris?'

'What?'

'Could you put the screens round my bed?'

Startled, she asked, 'What on earth for?'

'Relax. I'm not suggesting you get into bed with me or anything like that—'

'I should think not.'

'Nothing like that, but I'd do anything for a kiss, and it would make me feel so much better.'

'Not in here. You'd get me shot.'

'Is that all?'

'Yes, you'd better think about something else.'

' "At length, I realise," ' he quoted, ' "the bitterness of life". In that case, I need to visit the heads.'

'The whats?'

'The toilet facilities. Will you support me?'

'I suppose so.' She drew back the bedclothes and waited for him to swing his legs over the side. 'Do you feel all right?'

'Never better.'

'Not dizzy or anything?'

'Only dazed with the immeasurable delight at seeing your lovely face again.' He hooked his arm round her shoulder and allowed her to lead him to the gents. When they'd turned the corner and were out of sight, he kissed her.

'Ted! Someone will see us!'

'Now, listen, Iris. It wasn't just a hoax, I genuinely need a jimmy riddle. Walking on a cold floor has that effect on me. It was most embarrassing when I was younger, and it always happened at dead of night. Linoleum was the worst, I seem to recall.'

'I'm sure it was, but that's a job you can do on your own.'

'And I shall. Back in two shakes.'

When he returned, he found her waiting to take him back to his bed. 'You're a ministering angel,' he told her.

'And you're a rogue. You'd get me into awful trouble if you could.' She saw the way he was looking at her, and said, 'I don't mean that kind of trouble, either, although you probably would, given half a chance.'

'And who could blame me? Let me tell you, Iris, in that uniform, you're not safe. It's as if it were designed with the intention of driving men wild with ungovernable desire.'

'Don't be silly. What's so special about a nurse's uniform?'

'I don't know. Let me examine it more closely.'

'Stop it, you horror, before someone sees you. Now, listen.'

'I'm listening.'

'Let me know when they discharge you, and we can make arrangements to meet again.'

'I can't wait.'

'Just behave yourself and you'll be out all the sooner.'

11

After two days, Ted was discharged from hospital on condition that he undertook light duties for the remainder of the week. Gregory, whose injuries were more serious, was to be kept in hospital a while longer.

'The District Officer's sent us two rookies,' Sub-Officer Prentice told Ted. 'They're better than nothing, but I'll be happier when you and Greg are back on the strength. Meanwhile, you'd better make yourself useful in the Watch Room. The girls will find you plenty to do.'

In the event, Lorna and Mrs Chandler allowed him to do very little, both fussing over him and insisting that he mustn't 'overdo it'.

'We know you're a big, strong fireman,' said Mrs Chandler in her motherly way, 'but you have to be sensible as well.' They were both in an excellent mood, having received an unexpected gift of soap and shampoo, both of which were in extremely short supply. Overjoyed that his warehouse had been saved from destruction, one proprietor had rewarded Green Watch with gifts from his stock, and Ted had naturally been given his share.

He insisted on brewing tea for the Watch Room staff and for the watch, as well, when they returned each morning. Delightful though the female company was, however, he really felt he should be with the rest of the watch. Unfortunately, the sub-officer was determined that he should follow medical advice.

After a week of frustration, he returned to normal duties, at least until Christmas. He was surprised and delighted to be granted leave from Tuesday, the 24th until Friday, the 27th. With any luck, that would give him two days and three nights at home.

———◄►———

He was even more surprised when, on stepping off the train at Bradford, he found Eileen waiting for him.

'Don't tell me,' he said, drawing her into a heartfelt hug. 'Everyone else has fallen out with me.'

'No, they haven't. I asked if I could meet you, and they said I could.'

'When's the next train to Beckworth?'

'You don't need one. You've got me.' She led him into the station yard, where the first object to meet his eye was his old friend the fifteen-hundredweight Bedford.

'Are you driving this now?' He knew his sister had been learning to drive, but the Bedford seemed a trifle ambitious.

'Girls are driving all kinds of things nowadays,' she told him airily.

'Have you passed the test already?'

'They've cancelled all driving tests for the time being,' she said, unlocking the passenger door for him. 'The examiners are too busy organising petrol rationing to be bothered with that sort of thing.' She climbed into the driving seat, checked her hair in the mirror, and started the engine.

'My little sister,' mused Ted, 'driving the old Bedford. Whatever next?'

'I'm driving it at weekends and in the school holidays,' she told him. 'At least, it gets me out of the house, and I'd rather deliver half-a-ton of King Edwards than be nagged at all the time.'

'Nothing much has changed, then.'

'Not much.' She gave the 'ahead' sign to the policeman on point duty and continued towards Manchester Road, saying, 'Isn't it funny? I mean, it's almost like the Hitler salute.'

Ted asked, 'How did you learn about that?'

'It was one of those rally-things I saw on a newsreel.' She thought about it and said, 'It was about two years ago. All the people who'd gone there were doing it and shouting like idiots. I don't know who was dafter, him or them. Why do you think they listened to him in the first place?'

'He was giving them what they wanted: full employment, self-respect, and the possibility of making Germany great again. It was the kind of thing Mosley was peddling before they locked him up.'

'It makes sense,' she said, stopping at the traffic lights at the bottom of Manchester Road.

'What does?'

'The extremes of politics always seem to want a return to greatness in one form or another.'

'Little sister, you've just impressed me again.'

'Again?'

'First of all, driving this thing,' he said, 'and now you're making erudite comments and presumably thinking for yourself as well.'

'I have to, now you're no longer around.'

'True.' He considered her earlier reasoning and decided to test it. 'You mentioned, "a return to greatness", but what about the original greatness?'

'That came about through acquisition.' The lights changed, and she turned left into Manchester Road. 'All the great empires in history came to prominence as a result of acquisition. That was the first time around, but it's the Fascists and those of their kind who, basically through misguided nostalgia, want a rebirth of greatness.'

'Well argued, Eileen. I'm impressed.'

'As I said earlier, when the fount of knowledge buggered off and became a London fireman, I had to start working things out for myself.'

'Do you still want to do modern history at university?'

'I certainly do, but not until the war's over. I want to do something useful, like joining the women's forces.'

'Which do you fancy?' He thought he knew already. Her choice would be dictated by the uniform.

'I'm not sure yet, but probably the Wrens. Even allowing for those awful hats, they've got the best uniform.' On a more grown-up note, she added, 'I really want to do something useful while the war's in progress.'

It was quite a thought. 'How do you see its progress?'

'Who can say? As I see it, we're still at the crease, and the umpire hasn't yet raised his finger.'

———◂▸◂———

Ted's welcome home was like a token gift, in that the intention was no doubt heartier than the reality. He had to remember that. In any case, Eileen's arrival at the station had compensated more than adequately for his parents' habitual reserve.

His father was still keen, however, to hear about life in London, a city he'd never visited, and which stirred his grudging curiosity.

'They say in the news that it's been bombed quite a bit,' he said.

'They come over regularly,' confirmed Ted, 'but nowadays only at night.'

'Oh well, that'll be an improvement, I daresay. They don't tell us a lot about air raids, you know, just that a northern town or a sea port has been bombed. Mainly, they tell us about London, but they say the emergency services are coping.'

'That's right, Dad, we're coping.' Ted thought about the Dock Road fire that had burned all night and taken appliances from all over London to bring it under control. It made sense to keep that sort of thing out of the news.

In a surprising change of topic, his father said, 'Our Eileen's been helping me at the garden when she's not been in school. She's doing all right. In fact, I'm thinking of taking her on full-time when she's finished her exams. Then, she'll be in a reserved occupation and there'll be no need to worry about National Service.'

'Oh, yes?' Ted thought about Eileen's plan to join the women's forces, and he resolved to speak to her about getting her application in before her father did. 'She's a good driver,' he said.

'I don't like her driving that lorry,' said his mother. 'She's too young to be driving something as big as that.'

'It's not exactly huge, Mum,' said Ted. 'In fact, it's not really a lorry, and you can't treat her like a child all her life.'

'I don't think I need advice from you about bringing up children, Ted. I've no doubt you'll spoil her while you're at home, but I'm the one who'll have to straighten her out when you've gone.'

'In that case, as it's Christmas Eve, you'd better have a timely word with Santa Claus,' he advised her. 'It would be too bad if he spoiled her, even once a year.'

'Don't tease your mother,' his father warned him. 'She's only got your sister's best interests at heart.'

His mother seemed to be bored with the subject, because, without looking up from her knitting, she said, 'I don't know about you, but we're only giving token presents this Christmas, what with rationing and shortages.'

'Don't worry,' he promised, 'I shan't rock the boat.' It occurred to him that "rationing and shortages" had been a cliché for so long, it sounded like a comedy double act; in fact, he was surprised no one had chosen to use it. It sounded almost as good as "Laurel and Hardy", and it was certainly better than "Murgatroyd and Winterbottom" or "Gert and Daisy".

He must have been occupied in thought longer than he realised, because his mother asked suddenly, 'What's the matter, Ted? Cat got your tongue?'

It really was a night for clichés. 'No, Mum.' He thought quickly.

'I was just thinking about one of the blokes at the sub-station, a chap called Gregory. He had an accident recently, and I hope he's all right.'

'Oh, what happened?'

'A wall fell on him.'

'That's just typical of you.' His mother put down her knitting to remonstrate with him. 'I ask you a civil question and you tell me something downright silly.'

'Silly or not, I'm going to telephone the sub-station tomorrow, to wish everyone the usual and to find out if Greg's out of hospital yet.'

———————

Christmas Day was, like Ted's homecoming, an occasion of muted affability, although there was a degree of excitement when the family opened their presents from him. Soap was not rationed, but it had become as difficult to find as any other cosmetic item, so his gifts of Palmolive toilet soap and Lux hair shampoo provoked expressions of delight on a scale previously unknown. Not surprisingly, Eileen's reaction outdid the rest.

'Now, don't waste that shampoo,' her mother told her. 'You can wash your hair too often, you know.'

'I'll see if I can get you some more,' Ted told her. He had two more bottles of shampoo, one of which he intended to give to Iris on his return, but Eileen could have the other.

'You're spoiling her again, I see.'

'And a happy Christmas to you, Mum.'

'I'm just saying. That's all.'

Ted was no physicist, but he knew about action and reaction, and that as long as Eileen with her positive outlook shared a home with her mother, they would always clash.

———————

Everyone enjoyed the Christmas meal, even though it was less sumptuous than in recent years, and disagreement was absent from the table, at least until cracker-pulling time, when Ted handed the larger half to Eileen.

75

She asked, 'What, all of it?'

'The hat and the mystery gift,' he confirmed, 'but I'd like to see the message, just to check that it's fit for your innocent eyes and ears.'

'It should be,' said his mother. 'I got them from the Co-op, and they don't have anything to do with... that sort of thing.'

'We shall see.' Ted unrolled the scrap of paper and read it to himself. 'I don't know,' he said, shaking his head. The Co-op's standards are not what they were.'

'Well, don't read it if it's questionable. Mind you, I'll have something to say to Mr Ormondroyd at the Co-op.'

Eileen asked, 'What does it say, Ted?'

'It says, "Why does the whistling thrush whistle?" '

His mother looked uncertain, as if half-relieved that the content was decent, after all, but no less mystified by the question.

Eileen said, 'Go on. Why does it whistle?'

' "Because it can't remember the words." '

'I don't believe you,' said his mother. 'Give us it here.' She took the message from him, and one glance was enough for her to say, 'You always have to do that, don't you? You've never grown up, that's your trouble.'

Ted held out his lower lip and made it tremble.

'What does it really say?' By this time, Eileen was impatient.

'Aye,' said her father, who had been ignoring the exchange, as usual. The mystery must have proved too much, even for him. 'Go on, what does it say?'

'It says,' said his wife in her poshest reading voice, "Good, better, best. Never let it rest, until the good is better, and the better best." '

'After all that,' said her husband with a sigh. 'Ted, you don't improve with keeping, lad.'

'I don't know why he has to do it,' said his mother.

Eileen squeezed Ted's hand beneath the table, no doubt trying not to laugh at her mother's humourless predicament.

———◗◖———

On the morning of Boxing Day, Eileen drove Ted to the station and bade him a tearful farewell.

'Don't forget what I said about the Wrens,' he warned her. 'You can apply on your eighteenth birthday without parental permission, and once it's in the system, they can't do a thing to stop you.'

'But it's ages yet.'

'Two months,' he agreed. 'I'm warning you in good time.'

'You really want me to join up, don't you?'

'Only if it's what you want,' he assured her. 'Anyway, if it gets you away from home, it'll be no bad thing. You'll just need to be on the lookout, then, for girl-hungry sailors.'

She gave him a cheeky look.

'It's time I was on that train,' he said, hugging her again. 'Take care.'

'You do, too.' As if it were necessary, she added, 'I mean it.'

'I will.' He picked up his kitbag and made for the waiting train, just a minute or so in time, before the doors were slammed shut and the whistle sounded.

Not surprisingly, he was unable to find a seat. Instead, he travelled the two-hundred-or-so miles standing in the corridor, hemmed in by impatient servicemen and women. There was usually an uneasy atmosphere when firemen and servicemen came together, and it wasn't long before a private in the Pay Corps looked at Ted's AFS badge and said, 'It beats servin' yer country, don' it? Free quid a week an' all.' He looked particularly young, although Ted saw that as no excuse. He asked, 'Where've you been?'

'Whaddayer mean?'

'Since you were called up, where have you been?'

'Aldershot.' With loutish defiance, he demanded, 'What's it to you?'

'All the time you've been sitting on your arse in your pay office, I've been up ladders, fighting fires that Nazi bombers have lit for us. I don't suppose Aldershot is high on Göring's list of targets, so you won't really know what I'm talking about, will you?'

'Don't see why I should. All I know is I'm doing me bit.'

'All right. When we get to King's Cross, I'll explain it to you properly. It'll give you something to think about when you're filling inkwells and scratching your arse in Aldershot.'

''Ang about,' said the soldier. 'Why can't you say what you 'ave to say now?'

'Because I'll need room to explain it to you in a language even you can understand. I can't do it in this corridor, because it involves giving you the hiding of your pathetic life.' He was gratified by the look of fear in the soldier's eyes. 'You know,' he said, 'I'm quite looking forward to it.'

'You wanna be careful, making freatenin'… freats like that.'

'It's no threat, soldier boy. It's a promise. As soon as we get on to the station platform, I'm going to carry it out.'

'Yeah, well,' said the soldier uncertainly, 'it might be 'arder than you fink. Anyway, I'm goin' to the latrines.'

'As scared as that, eh?'

Ted wasn't surprised when he stepped off the train, and the soldier was nowhere to be seen. The threat had been sufficient.

He enjoyed the luxury of a seat on the bus, at least part of the way to Whitechapel. Once again, he gave up his seat, this time to a pregnant woman who was suitably grateful.

Happily, he reached the sub-station while Red Watch were still on. It gave him ample time to prepare for the night watch, so he had a quick word with the firewomen on duty before making for the gym and his locker.

On his way, he met Sub-Officer Prentice, who seemed subdued.

'Hello, Dewhirst. Did you have a good leave?'

'Yes, thanks, Sub. What's it been like here?'

'Quiet. Jerry left us alone over Christmas.'

'That was unusually obliging of him.' Idle curiosity made him say, 'You're in early, Sub.'

'Yes, I wanted to catch you and the others before any of you goes to the Watch Room. The fact is, Lorna Hearn's husband's been killed. She got the telegram on the twenty-third, but she didn't say a word to anybody. She just took her two-days' leave. Nobody knew a thing 'til this morning.' He added, 'You're the first I've told.'

12

Incredibly, the Luftwaffe stayed at home again on the 26th, although Green Watch remained in constant readiness. With the news of Lorna's husband, however, the atmosphere was less lively than usual in the recreation room. They learned that Lorna had been offered compassionate leave, but that she'd elected to continue working her normal watches and taking off only the time to attend the funeral service.

During the night, Ted came across Mrs Chandler in the corridor outside the recreation room. Not surprisingly, she looked tired and worn.

He asked, 'Are you all right, Mrs Chandler?'

Smiling thinly, she said, 'I'm okay, Ted, but I'm not the one with the problem, am I?'

'No, but you're probably the best company for her, and it's quite a burden on you.' Because sympathy dictated, he put an arm round her shoulders and gave her a gentle squeeze.

She smiled and said, 'You'll have me in tears as well as her if you're not careful.'

'But you know you haven't been forgotten.'

'That's right, Ted.' With another weak smile, she said, 'I'd better get back to her.'

A watch of firemen all offering their condolences would be among the last of Lorna's immediate needs, so they simply gave her space. In the morning, however, when tea was late arriving, it occurred to Ted to call at the Watch Room, where he found Lorna alone and absorbed in grief. He walked over to her desk without her noticing, and put a hand on her shoulder. 'I'm sorry, Lorna,' he said. 'Stay where you are. I'll do the tea.'

She looked up with red, swollen eyes. 'Oh, the tea. I forgot.'

'Don't worry. I'll see to it.'

The kettle had evidently been used recently, because the water in it was still hot. Ted topped it up and lit the gas beneath it. He found mugs in the sink, but they were dirty, so he set to and washed them. No one could blame Mrs Chandler, who was working for two and had the additional responsibility of a grief-stricken colleague.

She returned to the Watch Room as Ted was pouring tea into the mugs. 'I'm sorry, Ted,' she said. 'I just remembered they hadn't been washed up.'

'They have now. Don't worry about it.' He gave her a mug of tea and did the same for Lorna. 'There you are, Lorna,' he said. 'Don't let it get cold.' He gave her shoulder another squeeze and took the tray of tea to the recreation room.

'Good lad, Dewhirst,' said Sub-Officer Prentice. 'None of us was in a hurry to go in there, things being the way they are.'

'It was no trouble, Sub. I've got a gentle touch with the ladies.' He'd had to exercise it on many occasions with Eileen during her troubled childhood.

——— ►I◄ ———

That afternoon, Ted met Iris at the nurses' home, where they exchanged presents and belated Christmas greetings. Iris gave him a copy of *The Mill on the Floss* by George Eliot because he'd read *Middlemarch,* but nothing else by her, and he gave her a more prosaic gift of a bar of Palmolive soap and a bottle of Lux shampoo, which delighted her as much as he'd expected.

They walked to the cinema, where they saw a matinee showing of *The Proud Valley*, starring Paul Robeson and Edward Chapman. The film earned their joint approval for a variety of reasons, including Mr Robeson's glorious bass voice. As Iris said on the way home, what Welsh choir wouldn't want a bass like him?

When they were within sight of the nurses' home, Iris said, 'I suppose it's too much to expect the German air force to stay at home again tonight.'

'I'd be very surprised if they did,' said Ted.

On a practical level, she asked, 'What did you do last night?'

'We sat around, ready to move if we had to.' Then, because it had never been far from his thoughts, he said, 'One of the girls at the station heard that her husband had been killed. He was with the Army in the desert.'

'Oh, no.'

'They'd only been married a few days when he left for North Africa.'

'That's even worse. Has she anyone to turn to for support?'

'She has her parents, and she spent Christmas with them, but she insisted on coming back and doing her watch. I suppose she wants to keep herself occupied.' The image returned to him, of her hunched over her desk, and he wondered if she'd made the right decision. It was hardly a time for rational thought.

'It's impossible to put yourself in her position, isn't it? Working with her, it must be difficult for you to know whether you're doing right or wrong.'

'That's basically what the sub-officer said last night. I just let her know I was sympathetic, and I tried not to intrude on her feelings.'

'I suppose that's all you can do.'

'Yes.' Ted looked at his watch and said, 'I have to leave you.'

'Oh heck.' Seeing the time, she said, 'Me too. I'm off next Friday. Are you back on days?'

'I will be. I'll see you on the third.' He kissed her until she broke away.

''Bye. Be careful.'

''Bye.'

———◆I◆———

The Luftwaffe returned, refreshed by its Christmas break, to resume its onslaught on the East End, and Green Watch worked at full stretch for twelve hours, after which a shower and bed felt like the greatest luxuries on earth.

Two nights later, on the twenty-ninth, it was as if the whole of London were on fire. At least, that was how it seemed to Ted from his place on an extension ladder, seeing the flames stretch from Tower Hill as far as he could make out. He could only concentrate on his immediate task and hope everyone else was doing the same. There was a sense of climactic fury about the raid, because was easily the worst yet, but there was no guarantee that the bombers would not return to inflict even greater savagery.

He'd never seen so many fire appliances; it would be impossible to count them from where he stood. It would also be an unnecessary distraction when he had to concentrate his hose on the base of the fire, regardless of the heat that seared his lungs with each breath, and that created a thirst such as he'd never known.

The torment continued until well into daylight, when he heard the welcome words, 'Dewhirst, come down off that ladder!' The water was reduced to a trickle, the valve on the pump having been closed, and Ted unlashed the branch, using the free line to lower it to the waiting hands below.

'Well done, Dewhirst,' said Sub-Officer Prentice when he reached the ground. 'Get yourself a mug of tea before you knock off and make up.'

'Right-oh, Sub.' Ted joined the queue at the mobile canteen.

Albert stepped aside and said, 'You go first, Ted. You need it more than I do.'

'Thanks, mate.' Exhausted, Ted waited until his turn When it came, he asked, 'Can you let me have some water as well as a mug of tea?'

'Of course I can, love.' The woman who was serving poured cold water into a mug and handed it to him.

'Thanks.' He drained it in one gulp.

'Let me fill it again.' She repeated the process, and Ted relieved his thirst. 'Will you have that mug of tea now?'

'Yes, please.' Behind him, someone voiced his impatience, and he heard Albert say, 'He's earned it up that bloody ladder, so wait your turn.'

Ted took his tea and stood aside, content to lean against the canteen in silence.

Albert joined him. 'Sub says there were more than two hundred pumps here earlier. They came in from Middlesex, Surrey and everywhere else.'

'You wouldn't think there was enough water in the river for all of them.'

'There nearly wasn't. The bastards always come over at low tide, just to make the job harder for us.'

Still thirsty, Ted tested his tea and found that it had cooled sufficiently for him to drink it. 'That's all you can expect from a nation that doesn't play cricket,' he said.

'And one that drinks lemonade, apparently.'

'I think it's a kind of beer. At least, that's what they call it. It just looks like lemonade.'

'Whatever it is, I hope it chokes 'em.'

Sub-Officer Prentice called, 'Knock off and make up!' Ted and Albert returned their mugs to the hatch and set about the task of clearing the site.

———— ►◄ ————

The journey home was a quiet one, with most of the watch either asleep or about to droop. When they reached the sub-station, however, they recovered sufficiently to stumble into the washroom, where they undressed hurriedly and stood beneath the shower, feeling that deliverance was finally nigh.

Ted was dressing when Prentice came to him. With an apologetic look, he said, 'Will you do me a favour, Dewhirst?'

'Okay, Sub. What is it?'

'It's not for me, exactly. It's Mrs Hearn. Her water's been turned off at home for two days now, and with everything else the poor girl has to cope with, she has to use a standpipe.'

'Poor lass.'

'Yes. She's asked me if she can have a shower after the lads have turned in, and I said she could.'

'Quite right, Sub.' He wondered what on earth the sub wanted him to do.

'The thing is, I know you're as desperate as the rest of us for sleep, but will you turn the shower on for her and make sure no bugger goes near the window or the door while she's in the buff? I know I can trust you.'

'All right, Sub.'

'As soon as she's dressed and gone, you can get your head down, son.'

'Right-oh, Sub.' Ted sat on one of the wooden chairs outside the washroom and waited for the watch to disperse. After a while, he heard Prentice say, 'Don't worry about anything, love. Dewhirst will look after you.'

A moment later, Lorna appeared with her towel and sponge bag. She was still red-eyed and her attention seemed far away, which it no doubt was.

'Hello, Lorna. I'll make sure you're left alone. Just knock on that door when you want me to turn the water on, and knock again when you're finished, so that I know to turn it off.'

'Thanks, Ted.' She went into the washroom, leaving Ted to concentrate on staying awake.

After a short time, he heard a knock on the door, and he opened the valves, making sure the temperature was rather lower than the watch usually had it. To be scalded on top of everything else would be too much for her.

Two minutes or so later, she knocked again, and Ted turned off the water.

He was almost asleep when she came out fully clothed, but he roused himself to say, 'Sit here and dry your hair before you go, Lorna. Will you be all right?'

'Yes,' she said vaguely. 'Thank you for....'

'You're welcome. I'll see you tonight.'

''Bye.'

''Bye.' He left her and made his way to the gym, looking forward as never before to sinking into bed. As he reached the door of the gym, however, the image came to him of Lorna, hopeless and somehow separated from reality, and his concern for her made him stop. A second later, he turned and made the return journey to the washroom.

She was sitting just as he'd left her, with her sponge bag and hand towel beside her and a bath towel across her lap. Her head was bowed, and her hair was still wet and glistening.

'You're going to catch a chill, going outside with wet hair,' he told her. She made no perceptible response, so he picked up the hand towel that lay on top of her sponge bag and began drying her hair as he'd done so often for Eileen. To save his back, he knelt in front of her, rubbing her dark curls between handfuls of towel.

She made no demur; in fact, it was as if she were completely unaware of his attentions, so he continued until the towel was soaked and useless. Then he found a dry section of the bath towel and used that, painstakingly finishing the job. 'There,' he said gently, 'you'll have to brush it yourself. That's one skill I never learned.'

She looked at him as if seeing him for the first time. 'Thank you,' she said vacantly. 'I'm an awful nuisance.'

'No, you're not.'

'You should be in bed.'

'So should you. Are you ready to go home now?'

'Yes.' She stood up, and Ted handed her the towels and sponge bag.

'Let the sub know if you want to use the shower again.'

'Thank you, Ted.' A solitary tear trickled down her cheek, and she mopped it absently with one of her towels.

'It was no trouble. Take care.' He watched her disappear towards the exit, waiting until she was gone before returning to the gym. He was aware of an ache deep in his abdomen that he'd known once before, when one of the boys in his form had lost his mother, and he recognised the sensation as helpless pity. He felt desperately sorry for Lorna, but there was nothing he could do to help her. Wearily, he undressed and sank into bed.

13

JANUARY 1941

Although raids continued to be heavy, they lacked the ferocity of the twenty-ninth to the thirtieth, which remained in everyone's memory as the awful climax of the Blitz.

Once more on days, Ted and the others began to recover from the exhaustion of recent nights, and a brighter mood naturally began to emerge. On the first Friday of the month, he met Iris and took her once more to the Athenaeum Ballroom in Bethnal Green.

'If there's a raid,' he told her, 'and there most likely will be, there's nothing we can do about it.'

'All the same,' she said, 'it's very frustrating.'

'But the days are getting longer, and that'll give us more time before they come.'

'What an optimist you are, Ted.'

In the event, they had a drink and one dance before the sirens sounded. It was a shame, because the band was really quite good. It seemed that the musicians were also disappointed. Ted heard the leader ask no one in particular, 'What has Göring got against dancing?' It was a question no one could have answered, so he was right to keep it rhetorical.

They reached the nurses' home before the aircraft were overhead, and took their usual position between a high wall and a laurel, both of which afforded excellent cover.

'This place might have been designed to encourage mild naughtiness,' said Ted.

'No, it wasn't, and neither was I.'

'That's very true. You inspire it, but you don't encourage it.'

'How do I inspire it?' She asked the question out of sheer curiosity.

'By being good enough to eat.'

'To eat?'

'Mm.' He slipped his arms round her and kissed her neck repeatedly. 'Yum, yum, yum.' He put his last kiss, a long one, just below her ear.

'Don't do that, Ted.'

'What? Don't you want me to eat you?'

'No, I mean, please don't kiss me there.'

'All right, but it's quite safe. Whatever anyone's told you, it won't make you pregnant.'

'I know, silly, but it makes me…. Please don't do it.'

'Okay. For what it's worth, it makes me… too, and as that's not going to happen, there's no point in getting over-excited.'

'It's not that I don't feel that way, Ted. I just daren't.'

'Don't apologise. There's no need.'

'But….'

'No apologies.'

'I really….'

'It's your choice and yours alone.'

'It is, really,' she agreed.

It was an exhausted topic, so he pre-empted further discussion by kissing her lengthily and acceptably in the approved place.

'I don't want to be a spoilsport,' she said as soon as she could speak. 'That's what I was trying to say.'

'There's no need, and there's another excellent reason why we shouldn't get carried away.'

'What's that?'

'We'd both catch our deaths, baring our all out here in January. It must be at least five degrees below freezing.'

'You'd get me sacked as well.'

They both heard the throb of aircraft engines at the same time, and Ted said, 'You'd better go inside.'

'Okay. I'm fire-watching next Friday.'

'Saturday, then?'

'Perfect.' He kissed her again on the lips. 'You see? I'm a reformed character.'

'You're a lovely man, even when you tease. 'Bye.'

''Bye.'

He had a conversation of a different kind the following lunchtime, when freezing conditions led him to choose the Watch Room rather than the front doorway to escape from the canteen. Mrs Chandler had gone to lunch, leaving Lorna to guard the telephone.

She saw him enter the room and said, 'I'm glad you're here, Ted. I haven't thanked you properly for Monday morning.'

'Haven't you? I've been too tired to notice, but there was no need. Have they got your water on again at home?'

'Yes, thanks. I'm not talking about the shower, although that was very welcome. I was thinking about…. You know.'

He tried to recall the episode. The events of Monday morning were partially obscured by a veil of exhaustion. 'Whatever I did for you, Lorna, was little enough. I only wish I could do more.'

'I was in a hopeless state. My senses had deserted me…. I just couldn't function.'

'I know.' He wondered how to phrase the question he wanted to ask. In the end, he settled for, 'Are you finding life any easier?'

'It's easier to cope, yes.' Sensing his wariness, she said, 'I know you meant everyday life.'

'Yes. Anything else will take a long time, and I'm sure you don't want to think about that now.'

'No.' She smiled gratefully. 'But it's good that you don't try to avoid the subject. The others in the watch don't want to speak to me. It's as if it's too embarrassing for them.'

'They're all sharing your hurt, Lorna, just as I am, but they don't know what to say to you, or how to show their sympathy.'

'You do.'

'I suppose I find the words more easily than they do.' Feeling that it was possibly time to introduce a lighter topic, he asked a question that had occurred to him when they first met. 'I've been wondering, although you've probably been asked the same question a thousand times. Did your parents name you after Lorna Doone?'

She smiled self-consciously. 'Yes, my mother's a glutton for nineteenth century novels. My brother's name is Fred. Not Frederick,' she added, just Fred.'

'Let me guess. Fred Vincy in *Middlemarch*?'

'That's right.' She seemed pleased that he'd identified the character so readily.

'I'm reading *The Mill on the Floss* for the first time,' he admitted. 'I'm enjoying it so far, but not as much as I enjoyed *Middlemarch*.'

'What do you like particularly about *Middlemarch*?'

'Oh, let me think. The characters are complex, but very real, and George Eliot was quite fearless in the way she challenged the injustice of the time.'

Down the corridor, Sub-Officer Prentice boomed, 'Look lively, Green Watch. Playtime's over.'

'That's a shame,' said Lorna. 'I was just enjoying my first proper conversation since... Christmas.'

'I'm sure we'll have more.'

———◂▸———

Lunchtime the following day offered no opportunity for conversation. The sausages looked and tasted different from any they'd ever known, but Ted gave it no thought. He was hungry, having helped clean the pumps after a particularly hectic night, and lunch was welcome. It wasn't until he'd cut into the second sausage that he sensed something was wrong. There was a tingling feeling in the back of his throat, and his chest and arms were beginning to itch. That was warning enough. 'Sub,' he said, 'I've got to get to hospital. It must be these sausages. I'm having an allergic reaction.'

'Jenkins,' said the sub, 'you've nearly finished, you greedy sod. Get Dewhirst into a vehicle and take him to the hospital.'

'Right, Sub. Come on, Ted. Can you manage, or do you want me to carry you?'

'I can manage.'

'That's a relief.'

Ted followed him out to the yard, where Albert opened the passenger door of one of the Hillman saloons they used to pull trailer pumps.

'In case you're unconscious when we get there, what did you say you were allergic to?'

'Soya, you cheerful bugger.' It was actually a timely precaution on Jenkins' part, because Ted was already finding speech difficult. Breathing was also becoming a problem, and the itching, which had now reached his scalp was contributing to an already intolerable situation.

Albert covered the distance to the hospital in a matter of seconds and drew up beside the sign that read *Casualty Only. No Parking*. Running round to the passenger side, he opened Ted's door and bundled him out, propping him against the car. 'Come on, mate.' Then, seeing that Ted was almost helpless, hoisted him on to his shoulder and carried him in to Casualty Reception.

A nurse asked, 'What's the problem?'

'He's allergic to soya and he can hardly breathe,' explained Albert.

'Right. Bring him through here. We'll need you to give us his details.'

A doctor took Ted's pulse and said, 'Oxygen, nurse. Also adrenalin and antihistamine.' Addressing Ted, he asked, 'Apart from soya, old chap, are you allergic to anything else?'

Unable to speak, Ted shook his head.

As the nurse fastened the oxygen mask and opened the valve, the doctor asked, 'Are you haemophilic?'

Ted shook his head again.

'I'm going to give you two injections that will ease the symptoms. Okay?'

Ted nodded. He would have welcomed any number of injections to stop the mad itching, but he knew from experience that the treatment would take time to work.

After the injections, he lay helpless as a baby while the nurse removed his clothes. When he was down to his underpants, she began dabbing the hives with a mysterious substance that felt cold, soothing, and therefore, more welcome than he could say, or could have said, had the power of speech not been temporarily denied him.

As he lay there, he recalled his attempts to join the armed forces, and his frustration at being rejected for the very condition that had brought him, itching and fighting for breath, to his current state of helplessness. The regulations weren't so idiotic, after all.

'I'll leave you to do your bits and pieces,' the nurse told him, handing him the swab and delicately turning her back while he performed the intimate application.

Gradually, the itching began to recede, and as his breathing became easier, he was able to relax again to the extent that he was asleep when the doctor returned.

'Sorry, Doc,' he said. 'I must have dozed off.'

'That's the antihistamine working. Otherwise, how do you feel?'

'Very much better, thanks.'

'This obviously wasn't your first reaction, or you wouldn't have known about your allergy.'

'No, I had one several years ago, when I was at university. The treatment seems to have improved since then.'

'New drugs are appearing all the time.'

'I'm glad to hear it. I must say, though, that this episode has taught me a lesson.'

'Oh?' The doctor waited to be enlightened.

'I tried joining the Navy, and I couldn't understand why an allergy should bar me from entry, but I can now.'

'Yes, if you'd been serving in a small ship with no medical facilities, you'd have had a problem. Instead of going home, as you shall quite soon, you might have been buried at sea.' The doctor looked at his notes and said, 'We'll keep you here for another hour, and then we'll think about discharging you.' He looked around the room and added soberly, 'We'll need the space tonight, as usual.'

———►◄———

Ted walked back to the sub-station, enjoying the fresh, cold air and resolved to give Olive a curt reminder about his allergy.

When he arrived, he learned that Sub-Officer Prentice had already spoken to her.

'She's feeling very humble,' he said. 'I've told her that if anything arrives that's even on nodding terms with soya, she's to make you something different.'

'Thanks, Sub. I'd better have a word with her. I don't want her to feel too bad about it. For my money, it was ignorance rather than carelessness that caused it.'

The sub laughed. 'You're just a softie, you are. Go on, then, undermine my bollocking if you feel you must.'

It was as well that Ted took the trouble, because it seemed that Olive was being even harder on herself than Prentice had been, and she was still in tears when he arrived.

'Oh, Mr Dewhirst,' she said, 'I can't tell you how sorry I am that it was me what got you taken to hospital.'

'Forget it, Olive. I'm all right now.'

'Oh, but it was a terrible thing.'

'You're telling me.'

'I mean, it was a terrible thing for me to do.'

'But it's all right. Listen, Olive, and I'll tell you what to do.' He waited for her to finish blowing her nose, and said, 'If something comes in with "Soya" or just "Soy" in the ingredients, just make me a sandwich or anything, really, and make sure that what you give me hasn't been in contact with soya. That way, we'll both live a bit longer.'

He left her chastened but relieved. His next call was at the Watch Room. He wanted to see Mrs Chandler and Lorna before Red Watch were due to arrive in about ten minutes' time.

Mrs Chandler was the first to look up when he opened the door. 'Just look who's here, Lorna,' she said.

'Oh, Ted! Are you all right?'

'We were so worried about you when we heard about you going to hospital,' said Mrs Chandler.

'Yes, we were.'

'You know,' said Ted, 'at this rate, I'm going to be too big for my fire boots, with two lovely ladies worrying about me like this.'

'Well, it sounded serious,' said Mrs Chandler.

'It was, but Albert Jenkins got me to hospital in time. I'll find him in a minute and thank him properly. I was nearly out for the count, but he carried me into Casualty.'

'Oh, Ted.' Lorna's utterance seemed to be prompted not so much by Albert's act of mercy, as the knowledge that Ted had been so infirm as to require his assistance.

'I'm all right now, but I appreciate your sympathy.' He blew them both a kiss before leaving.

His subsequent words of thanks to Albert were somewhat more manly, but no less sincere.

14

January continued as it had begun, and shortage of fuel meant that the extremely cold weather was experienced everywhere, inside and out. The ubiquitous ice even menaced fire-fighting operations, and stories returned from Red Watch, of men driven backwards, as if on skates, as water rushed through their hoses. Their opposite numbers in Green Watch could only sympathise, knowing that similar conditions might soon exist during their spell of night duty. Meanwhile, they strove to keep the water flowing so that pumps and equipment could be cleaned and kept serviceable.

A break in the normal routine occurred when Sub-Officer Prentice called Ted and Albert into his office. Even the meagre warmth of the sub's office was an improvement on outdoors, and Ted was beginning to glow, when Prentice said, 'You lads are going to be red riders for a week, at least. You're wanted at C Station to cover for two blokes who've been injured.'

'Red riders' were the firemen who crewed the red-painted appliances of the professional London Fire Brigade, and Ted had to admit, albeit to himself, that the prospect carried with it a sense of prestige.

Albert asked, 'Why us, Sub?'

'Because they've asked for two reliable and experienced men, and you two are the most reliable and experienced blokes I've got. Try to create a good impression, won't you?'

Ted thought it was worth asking, 'Will we be paid LFB wages?'

'No you won't, and something else you need to know is that you'll be on nights, so you'd better get your heads down while you can.'

Ted and Albert duly arrived at C Station's Watch Room half-an-hour before the change-over and reported for duty. A grim-faced sub-officer arrived and took them to the fire house, where they met the rest of the watch as they arrived.

'I make no concessions for AFS men,' the sub-officer told them. You'll be required to do everything the LFB does. Right, get yourselves settled in, but don't get too comfortable, because you won't be there for long.'

Happily, the rest of the watch turned out to be friendlier than their officer. A senior fireman asked them, 'Have you used a pole yet?'

'No,' said Albert, 'we haven't got one at our place.'

'I have,' said Ted, 'but advice is always welcome.'

'Oh well, it's not difficult. When the bells go down, grasp it with your hands, wrap your legs round it, relax your grip and use your legs to control the speed of your descent, rather like going down a line.'

'Thanks for that,' said Albert. 'We'll soon get the hang of it.'

'Oh, you will,' promised the senior fireman, looking at his watch, 'starting any time now.' The air raid sirens were beginning their nightly wailing chorus.

Before long, aircraft were overhead. In what seemed like no time at all, the bells sounded and the occupants of the fire house launched themselves on to the pole. Strangeness, rather than misplaced good manners, caused Ted and Albert to follow them, taking their turn, but they all boarded the appliance before it went 'on the run'.

'We're going to Mansell Street,' the senior fireman told them, looking at the already illuminated sky, 'although it seems to me that one fire's as good as another.'

When they reached the fire at a huge office building, Ted located a double hydrant, reporting the fact to the senior fireman, who seemed surprised that an auxiliary was able to recognise one. Together, they connected two hoses, and the crew began fighting the fire. The rest was routine; the fire was eventually brought under control, and although the building was reduced to a blackened shell, the fire had been prevented from spreading to nearby buildings. The crew were finally ordered to knock off and make up. It had been a relatively easy night, a state of affairs that was bound to change. They had no doubt about that.

———◆◆◆———

Two nights later, they were called to a fire at a tenement block in Stepney. A warden at the scene told the sub-officer that a family was thought to be trapped on the sixth floor. 'It looks as if the fire's already reached the third floor,' he said.

'Right,' said the sub, 'two men on the turntable ladder.' He pointed to Ted and Albert. 'You two.' Turning to the warden, he asked, 'How many of them are there?'

'They say two, a woman and a child.'

'Right, you two, you're looking for a woman and a kid. Get moving!'

Ted and Albert began scaling the turntable ladder, which was now up to the sixth floor. Ominously, smoke was already issuing from a broken window.

It was beyond Ted's powers of reasoning why there were still children in the East End, but if there was one up there, he or she along with the mother had to be brought down.

They reached the platform, which was about five feet away from the wall. Albert picked up the telephone. 'Below!'

'Up top!'

'Take us a bit further in.'

The ladder moved slowly forward until Albert said, 'Stop! That's fine.'

Ted reached through a broken pane to release the sash window and pull it upward. It was sticking, and he had to use his axe to prise it away from the frame before he could gain any purchase with his fingers. With a great deal of effort, he managed to get it high enough for them to climb in, and they entered the room.

Albert looked around him, and his torch picked out a mattress on the floor and a broken cot where a baby had slept, probably until very recently. 'Bloody hell, Ted,' he said, 'no one should have to live like this.'

Ted had opened the bedroom door and was searching in the smoke and darkness for another that would lead to a passageway. He found one, opened it and called out, 'Hello!' He tried again, 'Hello! Is there anybody there?'

The roar of the fire beneath them made it almost impossible to hear anything else, but he thought he detected a high-pitched voice. He called again. 'Hello! Is there anybody there?'

'Here!' said the voice. It seemed to come from his left, so he walked along the passage, alarmed now by the smoke that was billowing freely from below. He'd no way of knowing how far the fire had progressed. 'Keep shouting,' he called. 'Where are you?'

'Here!' A door opened, and someone, a woman, judging by the voice, leaned into the passageway.

'Come this way,' he said, 'and we'll take you down.'

'My daughter! My daughter is in here. She cannot move!'

'Why not?'

'She cannot walk. She is paralysed!' Her accent sounded foreign.

He called, 'Albert!'

'I'm here, mate.' He was only feet away.

'Can you take this woman, Albert? I'm going to find the daughter.'

'Right, mate.' Albert took the woman by the arm, but she held back.

'My daughter!'

'You've no need to worry. We'll get her out as well.' He pulled her towards the room where they'd entered the building.

'Dorota!'

'I'll bring Dorota,' Ted told her, hoping he'd heard the name correctly. 'Dorota, are you there?'

'She cannot speak,' said her mother helpfully.

Ted saw her. She was lying on a mattress by the window. 'Hello, Dorota,' he said. 'I've come to take you to safety. I'm just going to pick you up.'

Outside the room, in the passage, the girl's mother was shouting, 'Dorota! I'm not going without Dorota!'

He heard Albert say, 'Come on, love. My mate's bringing Dorota.'

'Dorota!'

Dorota was completely helpless, only able to make incoherent, panicky, squawking noises completely unrelated to speech.

'Come on,' said Ted, lifting her and noticing as he did so that she was wet underneath. Given the circumstances and her disability, he wasn't at all surprised, and it was no time to be squeamish. He reckoned she must be adult, or at least in her late teens. It was impossible to tell in the darkness and rapidly increasing smoke. From the passage, he could hear Albert struggling with the woman, who was desperate not to be parted from her daughter.

He lifted Dorota as close to standing as he could and hoisted her across his shoulder, the way he'd carried Greg. Then, with only Albert's torch to guide him, he made for the passage. The woman was still shouting Dorota's name, so he called back, 'I've got her! We're coming!'

He saw Albert drag the woman into the room where they'd entered the building, and was horrified to see flames at the end of the passage. He shouted, 'Get her on the platform and take her down, Albert!' There was scarcely room for two.

'Okay, mate.' Albert half-coaxed and half-pulled the woman through the opened window amid cries of terror and fear for her daughter.

'You'll be all right, Dorota,' Ted told the girl, who was understandably terrified. He had no way of knowing how much she could understand. Maybe her brain functioned normally, but all he knew was that she was helpless and out of her wits with fear. 'Just hang on, Dorota. You'll soon be safe.' He hoped so. With two people on the platform, the ladder was descending quite slowly in contrast with the fire behind Ted and Dorota, which was making rapid progress.

He carried her to the window so that she could get the benefit of what fresh air there was, all the time painfully conscious of the terror he'd seen in the girl's eyes. 'Everything will be okay,' he kept telling her and himself.

He could hear the flames in the passage now. They had little time left, but then he saw the turntable ladder returning, quicker than it had gone down. Releasing Dorota's wrist to free one hand, he thrust the window as far open as it could go, and shifted Dorota more securely on his shoulders. 'Hang on, Dorota!' He knew she was incapable of that or anything else. It was just something encouraging to say.

The platform drew level, and whoever was controlling it was bringing it closer to the window inch by inch. It touched the wall beneath the window sill and stopped. Ted could only admire the skill of the man at the controls.

'Here we go, Dorota!' The fire was now behind them in the room. Ted strode over the window sill, careful not to let Dorota's head hit the frame, and felt a rush of relief as his foot touched the platform. Unable to steady himself with his hands, he stumbled when he caught his other foot on the sill, but righted himself. Gently as he could in the urgency of the situation and with flames now engulfing the room, he lowered Dorota to the platform floor and spoke into the telephone. 'Below!'

'Up top!'

'Take us down!' He knelt beside Dorota, holding her hand and telling her everything was all right. There was a roar from the room, which was burning furiously, but mercifully, the ladder began to descend.

The ladder completed its descent. The sub-officer and an air-raid warden were waiting beside the appliance.

'This is Mrs Shilhavy, and you've just rescued her daughter Dorota,' said the sub. 'They're from Czechoslovakia.'

'Czechoslovakia, yes,' said Mrs Shilhavy between sobs.

'Dorota is completely paralysed,' Ted told him. 'She has no movement in her arms and legs and she can't speak. That's why it took so long.' By way of further explanation, he added, 'That, and Mrs

Shilhavy was naturally concerned about Dorota, so it wasn't easy for Jenkins to get her out either.'

'They have different names from ours, being foreigners,' the warden told him with the erudite confidence of a man in authority.

One of the firemen on the pump said to a colleague, 'They went to all that trouble for a bloody foreigner, and the kid's an idiot an' all.' With a superior officer standing close by, Ted had to pretend he hadn't heard him.

———◆�►◄———

After breakfast at the station, Ted and Albert stood to one side while the others went their various ways.

'I think,' said Albert, 'you and I did a bloody good job last night. It was teamwork of the highest order.'

'Yes, but I wonder what kind of report we'll get. That sub's a cold fish. He'd hardly anything to say to us after we got down.'

Only a moment had gone by, before the door opened, and the sub-officer walked in with a station officer. 'These are the men, sir,' said the sub. 'Jenkins and Dewhirst.'

'Which is which?'

'I'm Jenkins, sir,' said Albert.

'I'm Dewhirst, sir.'

'Well, I'm glad to meet you both. You did an excellent job last night, and I'm going to make sure it goes on your official records.'

'Thank you, sir.'

'Thank you, sir.'

'I imagine you'll be pleased to know that the survivors are now comfortable and being cared for in a place for bombed-out families.'

'Thank you for telling us that, sir.' Ted could only hope that the place they were in was more comfortable than some he'd heard about.

'Another thing you'll be pleased to know is that the injured men you're replacing are making a satisfactory recovery, and you'll soon be free to return to your sub-station.'

———◆►◄———

Their return came two days later, sooner than expected, and it seemed that an account of their deeds had gone before them, because Sub-Officer Prentice welcomed them by congratulating them warmly. 'You've done the reputation of this sub-station and the AFS a power of good, lads,' he said. 'Well done, both of you. I expect you'll want to turn in.'

'Not me, Sub,' said Ted. 'I have a date.'

———— ▸◂ ————

Frustrated as they had been by air raids, Ted and Iris took a bus to Soho and found a café for afternoon tea. It provided a hint of luxury with the possibility of completing their outing before having to seek shelter.

'I don't normally have tea,' said Iris. 'I know we did when we went dancing, but hospital routine means we don't always get the time off.'

'Hard luck.'

'The food at the hospital is generally good. They say it's better than at most hospitals.' After a moment, she asked, 'What's the food like at the fire station?'

'Pretty awful, even when she's not putting me in hospital.'

'Oh, don't. That was too frightening for words.'

'The worst thing is that vegetables have always been an important part of my diet, and that's fine as long as they're cooked properly, which is what I'm used to, but Olive doesn't think they're done if they've had less than half-an-hour.'

'Never mind,' she said, looking over his shoulder. 'Relief is on its way.'

Ted looked round and saw the elderly waitress painstakingly bearing sandwiches and cakes. 'Oh, good.'

They thanked the waitress, and Ted made a mental note to leave her a decent tip for her hard work.

When she'd left them, Iris asked, 'Did anything exciting happen while you were at the big fire station?'

'Only the usual things. We managed to get a woman and her daughter out of a burning tenement in Stepney.' It had been on his mind almost since the incident. 'They were Czech immigrants, and the daughter was completely paralysed.'

'Before the fire?'

'Yes, she'd no use in her limbs and she couldn't speak a word. I had to carry her to the window and on to the ladder.'

Iris squeezed his hand. 'Is it still troubling you, I mean, that she was like that?'

'No, I felt sorry for both of them, but the thing that affected me was something one of the LFB blokes said when we brought them down.'

'LFB?'

'Sorry, the London Fire Brigade, the professionals. He said, in effect, that we'd wasted time and trouble rescuing a foreigner and an idiot.' He shook his head, as if to rid himself of the memory. 'If the sub-officer hadn't been there, I'd have knocked his block off, I was so disgusted.' A memory that had seldom been far from his thoughts sprang immediately to mind. 'I spent a holiday in Germany with a school party when I was fifteen,' he said, 'and I saw Hitler's Brownshirts, the Sturmabteilung, at work. They were the worst kind of mindless bullies, and no one was safe from them, especially Jewish people. I only mention it because a remark such as that fireman made was the kind of thing I associate with those thugs, not a British fireman whose first duty is to save life, whatever its nationality.'

'Oh, Ted,' she said, smiling indulgently. 'You've led a sheltered life so far.'

'Why do you say that?'

'Grammar school, then university and back to grammar school. People in the world you know would never say what that fireman said, but many's the time I've heard patients argue that foreigners have no right to take up hospital beds.' She let go of his hand and said seriously, 'If only everyone could be as kind and high-minded as you are.'

'Oh well,' he said, more than a shade embarrassed, 'we mustn't let these sandwiches go to waste.' It was time to talk about happier things.

15

Dear Ted,

Thank you, thank you, thank you for the shampoo! I'm using it in tiny drops to make it last as long as possible. I need to keep my hair nice because of a recent development. Read on!

Guess what? David's WAAF has chucked him for a navigator! He came home on weekend leave with a tale of woe. He says aircrew have all the luck, and I think he was surprised when I wasn't very sympathetic. Anyway, he wasn't all that pleased when I went to the pictures with his brother Geoffrey last night. Do you remember him? He was always quiet when David was around, but he's a lot nicer.

I think you mentioned that you'd seen Night Train to Munich. We saw it last night at the Picture Palace. Caldicott and Charters are priceless, aren't they? I must say, I'm quite keen on Rex Harrison and, naturally enough, Geoffrey only had eyes for Margaret Lockwood.

I got an A-minus for an essay on the Evacuation of Corunna. Don't you think it must be awful to be like Sir John Moore, remembered for only one thing? Still, I suppose it's better than being completely forgotten, and anyone who was around at the same time as Sir Arthur Wellesley was always going to be in the shade, even before he became the Duke of Wellington.

We've got a new girl in the first year. Her family escaped from Poland before the Germans arrived, and I've been given the job of looking after her. She's a nice kid, and she speaks better English than some of the kids who are trying to bully her. I gave one of them a thick ear for it last week, and I was told off by Miss Stevens, the Senior Mistress, but it was worth it. I'll do it again if I have to.

Anyway, write soon and tell me what's happening. Take care as well.

Lots of love,
Eileen XXX.

Ted folded the letter and put it into his locker. He was proud of his little sister, not so much because she'd smacked that horrible girl, but because of her sense of fairness. As he'd told Auntie Jane and Uncle George, she was as uncomplicated as a girl could ever be.

To be fair, he had to confer the same accolade on Iris. He knew exactly where he stood with her; there was no need to read between the lines, as there had been with other girls he'd known, and he saw no reason why that should change. It was important, because he'd been giving the future a great deal of thought. In the relatively short time he'd known Iris, his feelings for her had developed to the extent that he found it difficult to visualise a life without her, and he was fairly sure she felt much the same. He meant to introduce the subject when he saw her again.

For their next meeting, they chose the tea dance at the Strand Palace Hotel, and they arrived during the first dance. The band were playing 'When You Wish Upon a Star' from the Walt Disney film *Pinocchio*.

'Let's dance,' suggested Iris, 'and find our table later.'

They took to the fairly empty dance floor, still swerving to avoid a Free French soldier and an ATS girl, neither of whom appeared to have a sense of direction.

'I can't wait to see this film,' said Iris.

'I'll take you to see it, but you'll have to promise not to cry during the sad bits. I'm told there are quite a lot.'

'What about the nice bits?'

'There'll be no need to cry then.'

'Don't you believe it. You can't beat a good cry at a happy ending.'

'I'll take your word for it.'

They danced to the end of the number and claimed their table.

'Do you remember a song from nine or ten years ago, called "Love is the Sweetest Thing"? Al Bowlly recorded it with Ray Noble,' he prompted.

'No. At least, I know the song, but I was very young nine or ten years ago, so I can't remember it from then.'

'But you know the song. That's the important thing.'

'Why is it important?'

He took her hand between his and held it. 'Because the lyrics are all wrong.'

'Who says?'

'I do. They're wrong because love isn't the sweetest thing.'

'And I suppose you know what is.' Her eyes teased him.

'Of course I do.'

'All right, Clever Clogs. What is the sweetest thing?'

'You are.'

She hesitated, surprised. 'Are you serious?'

'Deadly serious.' He corrected himself quickly by saying, 'Well, not deadly, but as serious as it's possible to get without taking deadly's name in vain.'

She stared at him. 'Do you really think that?'

'Yes, you're the sweetest thing in my life, and that's what matters where you and I are concerned.'

'It's just that no one's ever said that to me before now.'

He shrugged. 'I don't suppose any of your previous admirers was in love with you, or they might have mentioned it, albeit in passing.'

'Ted, be serious. Are you really telling me... you love me?'

'Yes, I am. Choirboy's honour.'

'Oh, Ted....'

'What? You're not going to spurn my suit, are you?'

'No, I'm not. I want to hold you close and tell you things, but it's just too public in here.'

'We're in agreement, then?'

'Of course we are.' She beamed at him and said, 'I can't really imagine you in one of those white smocks that choirboys wear,' she said.

'Surplices, they're called, and I was a lot smaller and I had a squeaky voice in those days.'

The bandleader announced the song 'Only Forever'. Even without Bing Crosby, it was irresistible, so they got up and joined the line of dance.

Ted pressed his cheek against hers, relishing the moment and wishing he could preserve it for all time.

'Ted?'

'Mm?'

'When you breathe in my ear, it makes me go....'

'Wobbly?'

'How did you know?'

'I can feel you wobbling. Get into practice. You've a lot of wobbling to do.'

At the end of the song, they returned to their table, and Iris asked, 'What happens next?'

'I've managed to save some money, so I suggest we find a jeweller's that hasn't been bombed out and then we can make it official.'

'That'll be lovely, but we really need to speak to my parents,' she said.

'It would be good manners,' he agreed.

'That, and I shan't be twenty-one until June.'

'Won't you?' Oddly, he hadn't thought about that.

———◆◄———

Outside the nurses' home, they made plans to apply for two days' leave in March, when they would both be back on days. It would make it much easier. In any case, they shouldn't have much difficulty in getting to Cobham and back.

As the air-raid sirens began their nightly wail, Ted asked, 'Which is better, Friday or Saturday?'

'Friday. I'm fire watching on Saturday.'

'Let's make it Friday, then.' He hated to think of her exposed on the hospital roof. Fire watching involved simply spotting the fall of incendiaries and smothering them with sand or water before they could burst into devastating conflagration, but any exposure to enemy action was dangerous enough, and he was increasingly sensitive to danger where Iris was concerned.

'Saturday,' she agreed. They kissed, and he watched her until she reached the sanctuary of the nurses' home.

He ran back to the sub-station, elated but reluctant to tell anyone his news until it became official. He'd already endured a wealth of ribbing about Iris, and he felt that he needed time to enjoy the feeling in private.

———◆◄———

Because of a change in manning, Friday the twenty-fourth saw Ted on fire-watching duty. His new rooftop partner was Lorna, who seemed to be coping much better than of late.

The Blitz was so much a part of everyday life that there seemed nothing surreal about sharing a flask of tea on the rooftop during a raid. As Lorna poured it out, she asked him, 'What do you make of Jeremy Durrance, the new chap?'

'I haven't had much to do with him yet, although the sub's mentioned putting him with Albert and me when we go on nights.'

'That's a compliment, Ted. It means he trusts you both to keep him out of harm's way.' She winced when a high explosive bomb fell some distance away. They were safe, but HE's were not to be ignored. 'I'm not being awful,' she went on, 'when I say that he sounds like someone in a story by P. G. Wodehouse—' She broke off abruptly. 'Incendiary,' she reported. 'I'll deal with it.'

He had to admire her for her coolness, and so soon after being pitched into widowhood, but he still kept an eye on her even though, technically, she knew what she was doing, priming the stirrup pump and directing the jet of water on to the incendiary. When it was under control, she turned the nozzle to 'spray' and drenched the bomb and its surroundings.

'Well done, Lorna,' he said.

She shrugged. 'I'm a firewoman, after all, even though I don't climb turntable ladders and rescue helpless victims.'

'You heard about that, then?'

'The sub was so pleased, he told everyone about it. You did a grand job, Ted.'

'It wasn't just me. Albert rescued the girl's mother.'

'I know. You're quite a pair.' There was another explosion from the south, although the aircraft seemed to be operating north of the river. Simultaneously, they said, 'Delayed action.' As they took their seats again, she asked, 'How are things between you and Iris?'

'Very good.' He left it at that, his thoughts divided between his wish to preserve the secret, and surprise that, in the light of recent events, Lorna wanted to raise the subject.

With a mischievous look, she said, 'You're smitten, aren't you?'

He nodded, neither willing nor able to deceive her.

'I shan't tell anyone, Ted.'

'Thanks. I prefer to keep quiet about it for the time being.'

'Quite right.' She sat in silence. After a while, she said, 'Reg and I didn't know each other all that well when we got married.'

It seemed an odd thing for her to say. 'Well enough to get married,' he argued.

'I don't know. A professional soldier spends very little time at home.

Most of the communication goes on through letters, and Reg wasn't a ready correspondent.' She added, 'Or a very inspiring one.'

'I'm sorry to hear that.' It was difficult to know what else to say.

'They sent me his personal effects,' she said, 'including a half-written letter to me.'

Ted said nothing, but waited for her to continue.

' "Dear Lorna, I hope you have a nice Christmas with your folks, It should be all right here. The Eyeties are all left footers" – I think he meant Roman Catholics – "so they won't be in a rush to do any work over Christmas. After the pasting we've just given them, I'm surprised they haven't caught the next boat home." There was some personal stuff,' she said, 'and the rest was about a football match against another regiment.'

Ted wondered how many times she'd read the letter, to be able to recite it as she had. 'If he included some personal stuff, it wasn't such a bad letter,' he said.

She smiled. 'That bit was written in the most basic terms. The officer who censored the letter must have raised an eyebrow or two, although Reg wouldn't care about that. He never cared what people thought.' After a moment's thought, she said, 'That didn't mean I wasn't embarrassed at the thought of his officer reading it.'

Ted saw that she was still smiling, but her cheeks were wet.

'Just one of his engaging characteristics, eh?'

'Yes.' She sniffed. 'I'm sorry, I didn't mean to get maudlin.'

'You're allowed to be as emotional as you need to be,' he said, offering her a clean handkerchief. He gave her a quick squeeze of sympathy before his attention was diverted. 'Incendiary,' he said. 'No, that's two. Come on, Lorna.' They hurried over to where the incendiaries lay fizzing their malevolent warning.'You take the stirrup pump. I'll use the sand.' He picked up a bucket of sand and smothered his bomb until he was sure it was extinguished. When he looked, Lorna had snuffed hers out. 'You're a dab hand with that stirrup pump,' he said. 'They should give you a special badge for it.'

'Like the Brownies?'

'I wouldn't know about that.'

She looking at her dowsed incendiary and asked, 'Why don't they let us use fire extinguishers on these things?'

'They have to be recharged. Even the water and foam extinguishers take time, and the carbon tetrachloride ones are quite unsuitable for this kind of thing, anyway.'

'Why?'

'When carbon tet. comes into contact with hot metal, such as these things are made of, it gives off phosgene, which is very toxic.'

'I'm glad you're here, Ted. You're a mine of information.'

'You asked me, so I told you.'

'That's right. You're not a show-off, like some of them.' She opened the paper bag they'd been given along with the flask, and asked, 'Would you like a sandwich? I'm afraid they're Spam.'

'You know, I don't mind if I do. I'll eat anything but soya.'

'Help yourself. I'll be back shortly.' She disappeared into the building.

While she was at the heads, Ted took stock of his good fortune, which included having excellent colleagues, both male and female, and now his unofficial engagement to Iris. He peered across Whitechapel Road and imagined Iris on the hospital roof, doing the same thing. He couldn't see her at that distance, but he knew she was there.

16

FEBRUARY

The new man was tall and slim, with delicate-looking hands. He wore wire-rimmed spectacles, and his expression seemed to convey either friendly tolerance or benign indifference. It was difficult to decide which. Either way, though, Lorna's description was quite appropriate.

'I'm putting Durrance with you two,' the sub told them. 'I get the impression he's been used to gentler company than ours, and I know you'll make sure the others treat him right.'

'Okay, Sub,' said Ted.

'Right, Sub,' said Albert.

They found their charge in the recreation room, looking lost.

'Durrance,' said Ted, 'I'm Dewhirst and this is Jenkins.'

'How d' you do?' Durrance offered his hand.

'Right, that's the official introduction out of the way. I'm Ted, and this is Albert. I believe you're Jeremy. Is that right?'

'Spot on.'

They shook hands.

Albert asked, 'What made you join this outfit?'

'The AFS? Blackballed by the armed forces, basically. The eyesight's a trifle dodgy, you know.'

'Well,' said Ted, 'you should be able to see a building on fire. You'll see enough of them to recognise one, anyway.'

'I'll certainly do my best.'

'That's all we can ask.'

Albert asked, 'What did you do before this?'

'I worked for a ladies' fashion magazine. I was pictures editor.'

'That sounds like a nice job to have.'

Ted nodded his agreement. 'Time to get ready,' he said. 'Get your boot socks and leggings on, Jeremy. Have you got everything else? Pouch, axe, respirator, hemp line, hose spanner, webbing belt, knife and helmet?'

'Mm, I'll go and get them, shall I?'

'That's the general idea.'

When he was gone, Albert asked, 'What are we supposed to do with him?'

'All we can do is protect him from himself as well as from some of the baser elements in the watch.'

'We can only try.'

Jeremy returned with the requisite equipment, and Ted said, 'Let me buy you a drink. The bitter's off, so it'll have to be mild.'

'Oh, rath-er.'

Ted disguised his amusement by ordering three pints of mild. When they arrived, he handed one to Jeremy.

'My dear old soul, how very kind.'

'Cheers, Jeremy.'

Albert peered through the doorway, the windows being blacked out, and said, 'It's dropping dark. I'd go for a jimmy riddle if I were you, Jeremy. You might not have time to do it later.'

'A jimmy riddle?'

'A piddle, strain the potaters, syphon the python, shake hands with an old friend, point Ernie at the earthenware, dangle your handle....'

'Oh, I see.' Jeremy disappeared down the passage to heed Albert's advice.

Albert looked at Ted and shook his head. 'And what's more,' he said, 'there's something wrong with a feller who *sips* a pint.'

'Maybe he doesn't like it much,' suggested Ted. 'I'm not keen, either.'

'One of these days,' said Albert, 'I'm going to travel to Yorkshire and try some of that famous ale, just to find out if it's as good as you say it is.'

They had just reached the end of their pint when Lorna rang the bell vigorously and called, 'Trailer Pumps One and Two to Bishopsgate and Liverpool Street!'

Jeremy moved, but Ted restrained him. 'Wait your turn, Jeremy,' he advised him.

He hadn't long to wait before Lorna repeated the process, calling, 'Heavy Unit Two to Bishopsgate and Liverpool Street!'

'Come on, Jeremy.' Ted propelled him to the door. 'You can put your fire boots on in the unit,' he told him as they climbed aboard.

'Liverpool Street,' complained Greg. 'Why can't it be the Palmolive warehouse again? I've never been as popular with my Brenda.'

'Yes, you have,' said Spud, 'at least seven times. Didn't you say you had six, and one on the way?'

'It'll soon be seven,' confirmed Greg.

'I think it's time you chained your dog up, Greg,' said Albert, 'or at least found yourself a new hobby.'

''Ere, that's a personal fing you're talkin' about.'

'Leave Greg alone,' said the sub, 'or he might not give you a piece of the christening cake.'

'Liverpool Street,' reported Albert, much to Greg's relief. 'It was good of them to light it up for us.'

'Pull in behind this DP pump,' said the sub, 'and I'll find out what's what.'

Albert parked the unit behind the dual-purpose appliance, as ordered.

The District Officer stopped by Prentice's window and asked, 'Are you in charge, Sub?'

'Yes, sir.'

'This place has had it, so we're boundary cooling again. Go down past that HU and get your hoses on the next building.'

'Very good, sir.'

Albert pulled out and drove the length of the warehouse, pulling in behind a heavy unit from 6C sub-station.

The sub-officer from 6C shouted, 'The water's dried up!'

'Right,' said Prentice, 'we'll find some more.'

'There's the swimming baths, Sub,' said Spud.

'Where?'

'The next block. It's staring at you.'

'All right, let's get in there and start pumping.' Seeing a trailer pump arrive, he shouted, 'Come here and get ready to pump! Relay it to the HU!'

In a remarkably short time, they were into the public baths and pumping water from the swimming pool into the heavy unit via the trailer pump. They could now turn their hoses on the next door warehouse.

'Jenkins and Dewhirst,' said the sub-officer, 'stay on the pump with Durrance. You can have a quiet night for a change.'

'Thanks, Sub.'

Ted added his thanks, watching the pressure gauge carefully.

The sub left them so that he could supervise the boundary cooling, but before long, they had another visitor, an excited civilian.

'Just what do you people think you're doing?'

'We think we're fighting a fire,' said Albert. 'Haven't you noticed the street's on fire?'

'I'm the manager of the public baths and swimming pool,' the man told them.

'And your pool is now making its contribution to the war effort,' said Ted.

'What gave you the right to enter those premises without permission?'

Ted pointed upwards. 'What gave those buggers the right to bomb this city?'

'Who's in charge here?'

'Our senior officer.'

'Right, I want to speak to him.'

'You'll find him over there,' said Ted, pointing to where the sub-officer was overseeing the operation. 'He's busy, though, trying to ensure that the fire doesn't reach your swimming baths. I shouldn't distract him if I were you. I don't think the council would be very pleased.'

'About what?'

'About their public bath house being burnt to the ground.'

The manager shuffled angrily. 'You haven't heard the last of this,' he said.

'We'll tell the sub-officer you were here,' said Albert.

'You people think you're a law unto yourselves.' He favoured them with a final glare before leaving them.

Jeremy asked, 'Does this kind of thing happen often?'

'Hello, Jeremy,' said Albert. 'We thought you'd gone to sleep.'

'What kind of thing? The fire or the unwelcome visitor?' Ted needed to know.

'That man. He's an absolute disgrace.'

'That's a fair assessment.' Ted saw the sub approaching. 'We could have done with him five minutes ago,' he said.

The sub asked, 'Who was that man who was talking to you?'

'He's the manager of the public bath house, Sub,' said Albert. 'He was a bit upset that we'd gone in there without his permission.'

'He's not an easy man to reason with,' said Ted.

'If he comes here again, he'll get a flea in his ear.' He tapped Jeremy on the shoulder and asked, 'Have you been on a hose yet, Durrance?'

'Only in training, Sub.'

'All right, come with me and widen your experience.'

'As the actress said to the bishop,' said Albert.

'You know,' said Ted, 'it's the innocent ones, such as Jeremy, that are the biggest worry, because they're daft enough to do anything.'

'They certainly are,' agreed Albert, 'and it's up to us to make sure that doesn't happen.'

———◆◆———

'There's been a complaint,' said Prentice the next evening. 'The public baths manager spoke to District and complained about nearly everything.' He counted on his fingers. 'There was the fact that we entered the baths without his permission, that we took the water without his permission, that no one in authority took the trouble to speak to him when he arrived, and that the firemen at the scene treated him like a bloody nuisance.'

'All of that's true,' said Ted, 'so what happens next?'

'Nothing. The District Officer telephoned the Amenities Department at the Town Hall and answered his list of complaints, adding that we'd saved his precious bath house from the fire. I'd say he's in for a bollocking. That's if civil servants do bollockings. I really don't know.'

'As long as we're in the clear,' said Ted, 'I don't care either way.'

The sub looked around him to see who was in earshot and, having satisfied himself, asked, 'How's Durrance coming on? He did okay on the hose last night.'

'He'll be fine,' said Ted. 'He just needs time to settle in. He's only half-trained, and you must agree, this is a bit different from choosing pictures for a fashion magazine.'

The sub asked incredulously, 'Is that what he was doing before he joined this outfit?'

'He was a pictures editor, yes.'

'I bet he's seen a few sights.'

'He probably has, but he's been well brought-up.'

'They're often the worst kind.'

Spud Murphy came into the room and made, as usual, for the piano.

'I'm glad we've had our talk,' said the sub, ''cause when he gets started on that joanna, you can't hear yourself think.' Spud compensated with enthusiasm for his lack of musical ability, but his efforts were generally appreciated in the recreation room, where a rowdy sing-song was often the prelude to a call-out. It puzzled Ted that, with all the popular songs recorded by the dance bands, watch-members still preferred the old music-hall standards, and 'The Old Bull and Bush' and 'One of the Ruins that Cromwell Knocked Abaht a Bit' were staple favourites. He concluded that if they entertained the majority they were doing a good job.

The sub asked, 'Where's Durrance? I haven't seen him for a while.'

'He'll be along,' said Ted. 'I told him to be back here with his fire equipment by five.'

The sub nodded.

Five minutes later, Albert and Jeremy came into the room fully equipped.

Prentice could only say, 'Well done, Dewhirst. I can see you've got the job in hand.'

The rowdier members of the watch were giving a boisterous performance of 'On Mother Kelly's Doorstep' when Lorna rang the bell and called, 'Heavy Unit Two to Eastcheap!'

'Eastcheap,' commented Albert. 'Trouble down at the docks, just for a change.'

'Come on, Jeremy,' said Ted. 'You're going to be a hero with a grimy face. Mr Churchill says so.'

They climbed aboard the heavy unit, and Albert drove off, picking his way through the darkened streets until the whole area began to grow lighter, illuminated as it was by the burning dockland buildings.

They came to the end of Eastcheap where a District Officer stopped them.

'The next hydrant is two hundred yards that way,' he said, pointing along Eastcheap, 'and that's where you're needed, Sub.'

'Very good, sir.' Turning unnecessarily to Albert, he said, 'Two hundred yards that way, Jenkins.'

'I just knew you were going to say that, Sub.' Albert pulled out again and made the extra journey.

'I can see the hydrant from here,' said Albert, switching off the engine.

The sub was looking at the building. 'Get the extension ladder up against that wall,' he said. 'We can fight the fire on two levels. Dewhirst, take Durrance up the ladder with you. He's got to learn some time.'

'Right, Sub.'

When the ladder was in place, Ted took Jeremy aside and said, 'You go up first. I'll be behind you. Have you got your hemp line?'

'Yes.'

'Good, you'll need it.' He followed Jeremy up the ladder. When they'd reached the top, he said, 'Secure one end of the line to the ladder.' He watched him carefully before shouting, 'Stand clear below!' As the men at the bottom of the ladder moved to safety, he said to Jeremy, 'Right, chuck the rest of it down to them.'

When a hose and branch had been attached to the line, the sub shouted, 'Ready!'

'Haul it up, Jeremy, and then lash it to the top rung.' He watched him again, making sure the branch was tied securely to the ladder. When he was satisfied, he said, 'Tell them you're ready, Jeremy.'

'Ready.'

'You'll have to shout louder than that.'

'Ready!'

'That's better. Now, hold on tight. The branch is secured to the ladder, but it'll still buck when the water comes through.' From his position behind Jeremy, he felt the backward pressure. 'Now, aim the jet at the base of the fire.'

'Okay. I say, this is fun, isn't it?'

Ted closed his eyes momentarily before concentrating on the task of supervising his new colleague. Given a fair chance and Ted's patient tutelage, Jeremy would probably be all right. Whether or not the job would continue to be 'fun' was a different matter.

17

The watch were all dressed and ready for duty when the sub came to the recreation room. Beside him stood a dark, unsmiling man with a full moustache that emphasised his grim appearance. He wore the shoulder badges of a senior fireman.

'This is Senior Fireman Binford,' said the sub. 'He's an experienced fireman in the LFB, so he should be an asset to the watch. To Binford he said, 'I'll introduce them but I don't expect you to remember all their names immediately.'

'I expect I'll learn them soon enough, Sub.'

'Good. This is Murphy, Gregory and Durrance. Durrance is new, still learning the ropes, but he's got two good men to help him. These two, in fact – Dewhirst and Jenkins.' He went along the row, introducing the others whilst Binford gave no more than a nod to each man. 'I'll leave you to get to know them, Binford,' said the sub.

When he'd gone, Binford stood in front of them like an inspecting officer. 'I don't know what jobs any of you did before joining the AFS,' he said, 'and I'm not interested. My job is to make you lot into something like proper firemen, so you'd better be ready for that.'

Spud said, 'We've been putting fires out for some time now, Binford. We're not as green as you might think.'

'We'll see.' Binford gave him a dismissive look before leaving the room.

Albert asked, 'What have we done to deserve him?'

'What has anyone done to deserve him?' Ted was gazing in dismay at the space Binford had vacated.

'Talking to us as if we were all rookies,' said Greg, 'and after all we've done.'

'He certainly looks the part,' said Ted. 'Whether or not—' He put a finger to his lips in warning as the sub reappeared.

'Where's Senior Fireman Binford?'

'We don't know, Sub,' said Spud. 'He left us a few minutes ago.'

'I think he got bored with our company,' said Albert. 'We're all rookies, you see.'

Prentice gave him a sharp look. 'He was promoted only a few weeks ago,' he said, 'so he's keen to make his mark.'

'He's done that all right,' said Albert. 'He's made quite an impression.'

'He's keen,' said the sub.

'You've told us that twice, Sub. He must be very keen.'

'Learn what you can from him, Dewhirst. He comes recommended.' He left, presumably to look for Binford.

'Chances are,' said Albert, 'some bugger recommended him to get rid of him.'

Ted's mind was on gentler matters. Having seen Mrs Chandler go to eat, he went down to the Watch Room for a word with Lorna. Happily, he found her alone.

'Hello,' she said, evidently pleased to see him.

'Hello, Lorna. How are you getting on?'

'I'm coping, Ted.' She smiled. 'I appreciate your concern, but you mustn't worry about me.'

'It's difficult not to feel concerned,' he said, recalling the image of her outside the washroom, helpless with grief, with her towel in her lap. 'Will you see your family soon?'

She shook her head. 'Not for a while. It's better if I carry on working.'

'I expect you know best.' He was about to leave her when the door suddenly opened, and Binford said, 'What's happening in here, then?'

'A private conversation,' Ted told him. 'In other words, none of your business.'

'Anything that happens on this station is my business, and while we're on the subject, I'll trouble you both to keep your love life off the premises.' He looked Ted up and down, as if seeing him for the first time, and asked, 'What's your name?'

'Dewhirst.'

'Well, just watch it, Dewhirst.'

'And you'd better watch out, Binford. I find your remarks insulting, and not just on my behalf.'

Lorna said, 'Don't get into trouble on my account, Ted.'

'Don't worry,' he told her. 'It'll take more than this little Hitler to make trouble I can't handle.'

Binford was clearly rattled. 'Just watch it, Dewhirst,' he said. 'That's all.'

'It doesn't pay to make enemies, Binford.' Unfortunately, his advice went unheard, because Binford was already down the corridor.

'Don't get yourself into trouble, Ted,' insisted Lorna. 'It's not worth it.'

'There's no need to worry about me, Lorna. You heard him say, "Just watch it. That's all." That was an empty threat, a sure sign that he doesn't know what to do next. He can't have me disciplined, because all I've done is argue with him, and if he tells the sub I've been less than respectful, I'll just put my side of the argument forward.'

'Well, don't do anything silly.'

'Who, me? "Sensible" is my middle name.'

Lorna was about to say something, when feminine footsteps in the corridor hinted at Mrs Chandler's return, an event that became evident when she opened the door and sighed.

'Olive doesn't get any better,' she said. 'The vegetables were done to death.'

'As they always are,' agreed Ted, 'but we have to eat. Come on, Lorna.'

<hr>

'Binford keeps looking at you, Ted,' said Albert.

Ted smiled and nodded. 'The trouble is, it's difficult to put a name to that kind of look, because his normal one is just as unfriendly.'

'What's happened between you?'

'Ted had just called into the Watch Room for a quick word,' said Lorna, 'and *he* arrived and accused us of romantic goings-on on sub-station premises.'

'I told him to mind his manners,' said Ted with a shrug, 'so now he's trying to think of a charge he can lay on me, and that means that, being a stranger to thought, he's struggling. That's why he looks as if he's trying to digest one of Olive's offerings, little realising that he's got that ordeal to come.' He pushed the overcooked cabbage to one side of his plate and said, 'I wonder if I dare attempt the pudding.'

'The last sitting seem to have survived it,' said Lorna. 'Mrs Chandler was still alive when we left her.'

'I suppose it's too much to hope that this meal will do Binford a mischief,' said Ted.

'Far too much,' agreed Albert. 'It would also be too much like justice.'

'We ate worse fare than this every day at school,' said Jeremy, belatedly joining the conversation. 'It only proves that anyone can survive bad cooking.'

'You know, Jeremy,' said Ted, 'there's a curious irony about privilege, isn't there? I mean, your education presumably cost your parents a great deal of money.'

'It wasn't cheap, old man.'

'But you still had to eat rubbish, and I don't mind betting that your masters ill-treated you in other ways, too.'

'It would be a safe bet,' confirmed Jeremy. 'They applied floggings liberally and often for the pettiest misdemeanours.'

'I'm sorry, mate,' said Albert.

'It wasn't your fault, old man.'

'No, I'm sorry for everything I've ever said about the rich and powerful, now I know how they're treated at school.'

'My dear old soul,' said Jeremy gently, 'I'm not rich and not the least bit powerful.'

'You're okay, Jeremy, and we're going to turn you into a first-class fireman not unlike our goodselves,' said Ted.

'Trust them, Jeremy,' advised Lorna. 'They will.'

'Mind you,' said Ted, 'according to Binford, we're no better than raw recruits.'

'Don't antagonise Binford,' warned Lorna, getting up reluctantly to leave them.

'We don't need to,' said Ted.

Albert waited until Lorna was out of earshot before saying, 'Someone needs to warn Binford about accusing Lorna. I mean to say, your back's broad enough, but it stands to reason that she's going to be fragile for a long time to come.'

'I'll speak to the sub about him,' said Ted.

In fact, he waited until Sub-Officer Prentice was in the recreation room with Binford standing importantly beside him, before raising the subject.

'Good evening, Sub,' he said.

''Evening, Dewhirst.'

'Binford, about that remark you made in the Watch Room, I really don't care what you say to me, because it's so much water off a duck's back, but there's something you need to know before you make your next offensive remark. Lorna lost her husband just before Christmas. That was only six or seven weeks ago, so you'd better start taking lessons from someone who knows what "tact" means, and learn quickly. Right?'

Shocked rather than surprised, Prentice opened his mouth, but Binford was the first to speak.

'How was I supposed to know that? I just know I found you two together in the Watch Room.'

'We were talking. It's what intelligent people do when they want to communicate. You just barged in and jumped to the daftest possible conclusion.'

'Leave it, Dewhirst,' said Prentice. 'I should have warned Binford about Lorna.'

'And he should have thought before opening his mouth.'

'Leave it,' repeated Prentice meaningfully.

'Okay, Sub.'

———◆◆◆———

The watch was called out again to a dockside fire that occupied them for almost the whole of the night, during which Binford was quiet, at least by his own lights, confining his activities to the issuing of unnecessary orders. The men of Green Watch simply got on with what they had to do. Sub-Officer Prentice was happy, and that was what mattered.

Ted's thoughts, when he wasn't concentrating on his duties, were naturally and frequently of Iris, and he looked forward with boyish impatience to the weekend, when they could spend a few hours together.

———◆◆◆———

She had news for him when they met at the nurses' home, and they'd exchanged discreetly rapturous greetings.

'I've spoken to my parents,' she said. 'Have you?'

'I'm afraid I don't know your parents.'

'I mean yours, silly.'

'No, I thought I'd surprise them,' he said, giving her his arm. 'What was their reaction?'

'Basically, they're pleased and excited. Naturally, they want to meet you, but it was welcome news.' She asked, 'What are we going to do?'

'We're going for tea and stickies. It's about all we have time for.' As they walked along, he said, 'So your folks don't mind you taking up with an impecunious schoolmaster?'

'No, they don't. Why should they?'

'Why indeed, when I'll have endless access to free fruit and vegetables.'

She waited until they were on the bus before asking, 'How will you manage that?'

'My folks have a market garden. Didn't I tell you?'

'I think so, but you didn't say much. I know very little about your family.'

He filled her in with thumbnail sketches of his parents and Eileen, after which he learned that Iris's father was a civil servant, although not a very senior one, and that her mother was kept busy by the Women's Voluntary Service. By that time, they'd reached their stop.

As they reached the teashop, Iris asked, 'What's been happening at the fire station?'

'Nothing good. We have a new senior fireman who thinks we're all beginners.' He told her about Binford's introductory speech.

'That's disgraceful, and after all you've done.'

They gave their order to the elderly waitress who'd served them on their previous visit.

'That's not all. He accused me of having a romantic liaison with Lorna, whose husband was killed at Christmas.'

'The beast. How could he even imagine it?'

Ted told her the story. 'I imagine the sub-officer's spoken to him about it,' he said, 'because he's been fairly quiet. As far as I know, though, he hasn't apologised to Lorna.'

After brief reflection, Iris said, 'It's a nice name, isn't it?'

'What, "Binford"?'

'No, "Lorna", you nitwit.'

'So is "Iris", and, contrary to what Binford might think, I only have eyes for you.'

She took his hand. 'That's a song, isn't it?'

'I believe so. Paul Enright, one of my colleagues at school could have told you which show it's from. He was a whale on musical comedy.'

'I know the answer to that,' she said. 'It's from *Dames*. I saw the film the day after my fourteenth birthday.' She added dreamily, 'That visit to the cinema was a birthday afterthought by my dad, but it eclipsed everything else. Dick Powell was wonderful.'

'Now I know what to do when I need to put you in a good mood,' he said. 'I'll just take you to see a musical with Dick Powell in it. I hope he hasn't retired yet.'

The waitress brought the set tea. When she'd gone, Iris said, 'You don't have to do anything special to put me in a good mood. You do that with no effort at all.'

'But when we're old and irritable and getting on each other's nerves—'

'Don't be silly, Ted,' she told him with the certainty only young love can offer. 'That'll never happen.'

18

One of the relative luxuries anticipated with eagerness was the mug of tea back at the sub-station before the shower, and Lorna's appearance with the familiar tray was always greeted with a weary but sincere cheer. On this occasion, however, Mrs Chandler performed the task, prompting Ted to ask, 'Is Lorna all right, Mrs Chandler? Not that you're any less welcome, but I wondered.'

She motioned him away from the others and said, 'No, she's struggling, Ted. It comes and goes, you know. She seems to be coping well for a while, and then it hits her again. The sub could see she was upset, so he sent her home early.'

'Good.'

'She should have taken compassionate leave when she was offered it, you know. She'd have been better staying with her family than she was coming back here.'

As always, Ted could only feel helplessly sorry for Lorna. 'You know,' he said, 'it's almost twenty years since I had to deal with bereavement, and I had the kindest aunt and uncle to help me. I had to go home eventually, though, and although I was only five, I remember the way it affected my mother.'

'Who had she lost, Ted?'

'My elder brother. He died of rheumatic fever.'

'I'm sorry.'

'It was awful,' he said, 'and my mother, who's a very private person, didn't cope with it at all well. Grief came and went without warning, just as it does with Lorna. I'd go to my mother for something, and then find that it wasn't the right time to bother her. After a while, I came to recognise the signs, rather like watching traffic lights.'

'That's an awful thing for a little boy to have to learn.'

She seemed so affected by what he'd told her, that he put his arm round her and gave her a squeeze. Then, remembering his manners, he said, 'I'm sorry, Mrs Chandler. I'm a northerner, and we do tend to hug.'

'Don't apologise, Ted.'

He put his empty mug back on the tray and said, 'The shower beckons.' Men were already collecting their washing tackle from the sleeping quarters.

'I don't know how men can do that,' she said. 'I mean going in the shower together.'

'We don't look at one another all that closely,' he assured her, 'and it's only like being at school. If it comes to that, at the rugby club, we all used to climb into a communal bath.'

'The things you boys get up to.' With an indulgent smile, she began gathering up the empty mugs. Ted went for his washing gear.

———

He slept for seven hours, only waking when Spud accidentally kicked one of the legs of his bed.

'Sorry, mate.'

'That's all right, Spud. It's time I was up, anyway.' That was how it was between members of the watch, at least when Binford, or 'Bumfluff', as the watch had dubbed him, wasn't around. He was the only source of friction and, as he lived locally, they were spared that during off-watch hours.

He went down to the Watch Room and chatted for a while with the girls of Red Watch before taking his tea to the Boys' Entrance. It had become a habit, even in cold weather, because it was both quiet and private.

He was thinking idle thoughts when a voice he recognised said, 'Hello, Ted.'

'Lorna, you're early, aren't you?' The words were out before he could stop them, and he wasn't surprised by her answer.

'I didn't sleep very well,' she said, 'so I got up early and I decided to come in because I may as well be here as anywhere else.'

'I'm sorry, Lorna. That was clumsy of me.'

'Not really.' She smiled weakly and said, 'Don't treat me as a special case, Ted.'

'I'll try not to.' To change the subject, he said, 'If you go to the Watch Room now, you'll find there's some tea made.'

'Thanks, I will.' She turned to leave, but hesitated and asked, 'When are you seeing Iris again?'

'Friday.'

'The last night of the month? If you'd left it one more day, you'd have been on days again.'

'I know, but she's fire-watching on Saturday.'

'That's tough luck when she's just come off nights.' She thought for a second and said, 'I believe you and I are on the roster for Thursday next week.'

'I'll look forward to it, Lorna,' he said glibly.

'I'll believe you.' Her look suggested otherwise. Fire-watching was universally unpopular.

———▶◀———

Almost as the bombing began, Green Watch were called out to Shadwell Dock, where Binford put Jeremy on the HU pump.

'He's had hardly any experience of that,' protested Ted. 'He needs to do it under supervision before you let him loose on it.'

'I don't need you to tell me my job, Dewhirst.'

'Well, some bugger needs to.'

'That's enough from you. Come on, Durrance, get on that pump, and try not to make a meal of it the way you do everything else. Let's see what you can do when you haven't got Dewhirst to change your nappies.'

Ted knew he would have to sort Binford out, but more important matters were pressing, so he climbed the extension ladder and joined Albert on the warehouse roof. 'I'll swing for that bugger Bumfluff,' he said.

'If no one else swings for him first. What's he done?'

'He's put Jeremy on the HU pump.'

'The stupid bastard.' Albert lashed the branch to the ladder and called down, 'Ready!' The hose remained dry, so he shouted again, 'Ready!'

There was unintelligible shouting below, and Ted saw Binford push Jeremy out of the way and open one of the valves. The hose heaved, and water gushed forth.

Binford shouted, 'Aim for the base of the fire!'

Ted shouted, 'Where you think we're aiming it, you daft bugger?'

They continued to fight the fire from above until the water pressure fell dramatically.

Albert called down, 'What's happened to the water?'

Binford shouted, 'We'll have to pump some out of the dock!' He seemed to be shouting at Jeremy about organising a relay, and then the sub arrived, and things proceeded more quietly. Meanwhile, the fire was threatening the top storey.

Prentice shouted, 'Come down, you two!'

Albert unfastened the hose and took it down as he descended the ladder. Ted followed him. They looked around for the sub, but Greg told them he was organising the relay of water from the dock to the HU.

'Your mate made a complete mess of the job,' Binford told Ted with visible satisfaction. 'I told him he wasn't at one of his posh bloody cocktail parties, but it made no difference.'

'Of course he made a mess of it, Binford. I told you he'd never done it before. What have you got between your ears? A bloody turnip?'

'That's enough from you, Dewhirst. As for Durrance, I'm going to make his life a misery until he gets his act together.'

Ted grabbed him by the tunic and dragged him to the other side of the HU so that they were unobserved. 'Listen, Bumfluff,' he said, slamming him against the body of the unit. 'I'll tell you what you're going to do. You're going to stop victimising the poor bugger, or I'm going to knock you into the middle of next week!'

'I'll have you disciplined, Dewhirst!' There was fear in Binford's eyes. 'You won't get away with threatening me.'

'I'm not just threatening you. I mean it. I'll knock the living daylights out of you, and then you can have me disciplined. Then, when I've been disciplined, I'll do it again. You'll tire of it before I do!'

Albert shouted, 'The sub's back. Valves down again!'

Ted operated the valve while Albert, Spud and the others held the hoses.

'You're in deep trouble, Dewhirst,' said Binford with undisguised loathing in his voice.

'Just concentrate on fighting this fire, Bumfluff.'

Ted wasn't surprised when Prentice took him aside after their shower.

'Senior Fireman Binford tells me you've threatened him with violence, Dewhirst.'

'That's right, Sub, but I'll only carry it out if he continues to pick on Durrance.'

The sub gave a tired sigh. 'If Durrance has a complaint about Binford, he should come to me.'

'I thought you were busy enough, Sub. I was only saving you a job, and it was no trouble. As I see it, Binford knows what he'll get if he goes on victimising Durrance, so he's probably seen the error of his ways by this time. That's if he has any sense at all, which is a matter for speculation.'

'Dewhirst,' said Prentice wearily, 'if Durrance has a complaint, he must bring it directly to me. When I told you to look after him, I didn't mean you had to take matters into your own hands.'

'All right, Sub, I'll speak to Durrance. Meanwhile, and purely from my own point of view, Binford is a disaster, the blokes have no respect for him, and all he does with his scathing remarks is create ill-feeling.'

'All right. Leave it with me. I'll speak to you tonight.'

Weary as usual after a night watch, Ted thought no more about the matter, but enjoyed six hours' uninterrupted sleep. He would normally have had more than that, but it was Friday, and he was meeting Iris at two-thirty.

———⋗⋖———

They went to the teashop that had become their regular haunt when they were on nights. They took their usual table, and Ted sat down in silence, content to feast his eyes on Iris. Her wardrobe was as limited as her income, but her taste was excellent, and she wore her clothes well. On that day, she wore a navy-blue dress with a white collar and short sleeves also trimmed with white, but from Ted's point of view, it might have been a priceless creation by Chanel.

She asked, 'Is something the matter?'

'Nothing at all. I was trying to imagine you in a white bridal gown.'

'Carry on dreaming, Ted. Those things cost a lot of money, not to mention clothing points.'

'It's a shame we don't know someone in the Navy, who could get us some parachute silk from one of those unexploded mines.'

She frowned. 'Why does the Navy get the job of doing whatever they do with those things? You'd think the Army would do that.'

'It's because they're mines, rather than bombs. They're supposed to fall into the river or the docks, but I suppose they're at the mercy of the wind.'

'It's more like we're at its mercy. We got an unexploded bomb in the tennis courts that held things up for ages until the Army dealt with it.'

He nodded. Bombs or mines, they were all the same to those they threatened, so he wasn't prepared to argue the difference with her. Besides, the elderly waitress, whom they'd come to regard almost as a friend, was coming to take their order. They exchanged familiar pleasantries and ordered the set tea.

Iris asked, 'How are you getting on with the new senior fireman?'

'Bumfluff? Oh, he's a dead loss.'

'That's not a very nice name to give him.'

Ted considered the matter briefly and said, ' "Bin lid" might be better, except that dustbin lids are useful.'

'What's he been up to, anyway?'

'Bullying Jeremy Durrance, the new chap. He has it in for him because he's from a higher plane, public school, gently brought up and all that.'

'What's Jeremy like?'

'He's a decent enough bloke, but he's a natural victim for the likes of Bumfluff, who's just a bully. Anyway, the sub-officer told me to take Jeremy under my wing, and now it seems I've exceeded my duty.'

'Oh.' Iris eyed him doubtfully. 'What have you done?'

'I've only threatened Bumfluff, I haven't touched him yet.' Realising that wasn't entirely true, he added, 'Not much, anyway.'

'Don't go getting yourself into trouble, Ted.'

He nodded submissively. 'Respectable married men don't go around laying into bullies, and neither do auxiliary firemen, according to the sub.'

'Nor recently-engaged men,' added Iris, putting a finger to her lips as the set tea arrived.

Feeling that a gentler topic was called-for, Ted waited until they were alone again before mouthing silently, 'I love you.'

Iris mouthed, 'I love you too.'

Thereafter, and without further disagreement, they set about the sandwiches.

When, all too quickly, the time came for them to leave, Ted paid the bill, and they took the bus to the nurses' home, sitting close together and holding hands tightly, as if each were afraid the other might be whisked away by some unforeseen event. That was how involved they were.

Back at the nurses' home, in the relative privacy of their favourite laurel, they kissed with deep commitment, parting reluctantly and only when they could delay it no longer.

'Next Saturday, then?'

'Next Saturday,' she confirmed.

'Love you.'

'Love you too.'

Ted walked briskly to the sub-station, where Binford greeted him.

'What have you been up to, Dewhirst? You've cut it a bit fine.'

Ted looked at his watch. 'I'm here on time,' he said, 'and what I've been doing is my business.'

'You'd better watch it, Dewhirst.'

'So you keep telling me.'

'Anyway,' said Binford with a leer, 'the sub wants to see you.'

'I'm not surprised. I expect he'd rather see my face than your ugly mug any day, although, now I think of it, my arse would win that contest easily.'

'Watch it, Dewhirst.'

Ted pushed Binford against the wall, saying, 'Stand aside, Bumfluff.' He walked past the Watch Room, exchanging greetings with Mrs Chandler and Lorna, and knocked on the sub's door.

'Come in.'

Ted opened the door and walked in.

'Ah, Dewhirst.' The sub was looking particularly serious. 'I've had a word with Binford about his attitude and I've told him he's got to treat Durrance fairly.'

'Right, Sub.'

'And I'm telling you now, to leave matters to me in future. Above all, don't go around threatening people with violence.'

'I don't make a habit of it, Sub.'

'Don't do it at all.'

'Okay, Sub.'

'You're a good man, Dewhirst, and I'm glad I've got you in the watch.'

'Thank you, Sub.'

'Just remember who's in charge.'

It was enough for Ted, who'd only ever wanted fair play. Now satisfied, he called into the Watch Room for a quick word with the ladies. Lorna had already gone to eat, so he stayed and chatted with Mrs Chandler.

'I see you've got a spring in your step,' she told him.

'Who's been talking?'

'Nobody's said a word. They don't need to.'

'Evidently.' Leaning forward confidentially, he asked, 'Is this the magical feminine intuition I've heard about?'

'I think it must be.' She smiled at the thought.

'Lorna keeps asking me about it,' he said.

'She hasn't mentioned it to me,' she assured him.

'No, I never thought she would.' He decided to confide in her. 'Look, Mrs Chandler, I haven't told anyone yet, because I want to save it for when it's official, but yes, your instinct tells you right.'

'Oh, Ted.' She stood up, checked that the door was firmly closed, and kissed him on the cheek. 'Congratulations! I'll keep it under my hat, honestly.'

'I know you will.'

As he went in to eat, it occurred to him that, at some stage, he would have to tell his family, and that would be interesting. He would leave it for a day, until he'd slept off his last night on watch, and then he intended to write to them. There would be two separate and distinct letters, because one would be to his parents, and the other would be to Eileen who, he knew, would be delighted.

———— ►◄ ————

They were called again to Shadwell Dock, where they succeeded in containing a fire at a tea warehouse, although the tea within it was unlikely to be of any value after the thorough soaking they'd been obliged to give it.

On this occasion, Ted had been obliged to supervise Jeremy on the heavy unit, and had been able to train him sufficiently that, should he be called upon in future to man the pump alone, he would do so confidently and effectively.

As they approached Whitechapel Road on their way home, Ted was obliged to slow down and pick his way between bricks and rubble.

'While we've been at the docks,' said the sub, 'it looks as if there's been trouble at home.'

They had to stop while a team of wardens lifted masonry out of their way. One of them said, 'This whole area took a clobbering last night.'

Ted asked, 'What about the hospital?'

'That too. Round the back, the laundry and the nurses' home. They got a right bloody packet.'

It was like a recurring nightmare. Ted drove on with a knot in his stomach, desperate to find out if Iris was safe.

'Concentrate on your driving,' the sub warned him. 'You'll find out soon enough.' But it wasn't true. Soon wasn't enough, because Ted couldn't wait that long.

He parked the HU in the yard. Then, without a word to the sub, he ran down Whitechapel Road to the hospital, desperate for news.

The front of the building was untouched; the damage must all be behind it. The warden had mentioned the laundry and the nurses' home. There were several nurses' homes, but the one Ted knew was close to the laundry. He remembered Iris mentioning it when she first gave him directions. But surely, she would be on the ward when the bombs fell. She would be safe there.

He hurried into the main entrance and made for the reception desk, where a nurse was on the telephone. He waited impatiently for her to end her conversation, and when she did so, she looked and sounded weary.

'Hello, fireman,' she said. 'What's the trouble?'

'Were there any nurses among the casualties last night?'

She closed her eyes, as if the question had been asked many times, and asked, 'Who are you interested in?'

'Student Nurse Iris Wingate. She'd be on Obstetrics and Gynaecology.'

The nurse closed her eyes again. 'Just a minute,' she said, searching her desk for a document. 'Nurse Iris Wingate, you said?'

'That's right.'

The nurse scanned her list.

He asked, 'Is she on your list?'

She regarded him, presumably, with what compassion she could muster in her current state of exhaustion. 'What was your relationship to her?'

Her use of the past tense came like a savage blow that seemed to leave him breathless. He said, 'We were engaged... to be married.'

She put the document down and touched his arm, 'I'm sorry, fireman,' she said. 'I really am sorry.'

19

MARCH

The high-explosive bomb that killed Iris fell nowhere near the nurses' home or the laundry; she'd been making a necessary journey between buildings when it fell, and the likelihood was that she knew nothing about it. Certainly, no trace of her was found, such was the devastating power of the bomb. He was told that the hospital authorities were going to organise a memorial service for the victims of the raid.

That was as much as Ted was able to learn, but it was enough for him to know that the girl he loved and had been going to marry was now dead, and because the hospital would not divulge her parents' address to a non-relative, he couldn't even attend her funeral. He'd considered searching the telephone directory for Wingate in Cobham, but the thought died within seconds. It would be cruel of him to intrude on her parents' grief. Life as he had come to know it had reached a full stop. From time to time, he wondered if it were some dreadful mistake, and Iris had been nowhere near the explosion, but he realised, even in his shocked state, that his mind was simply coming to terms with her death the only way it knew.

Weariness eventually took pity on him, and he fell asleep until five.

Waking at first, he was conscious of his usual buoyancy after a sound sleep, but only for a second before the horrors of the morning returned like a battering ram.

One by one, his discomfited colleagues expressed their sympathy as word went around, and a muted 'Sorry, mate' served as shorthand for the message they couldn't properly express. Mrs Chandler and Lorna were more articulate, each underlining her words with a sympathetic kiss on his cheek, but their tear-filled eyes made him feel unaccountably guilty.

Prentice greeted him in his office with the words, 'I'm truly sorry, Dewhirst. I'll speak to the District Officer and arrange compassionate leave. I can probably catch him now, before he leaves the station.' He reached for the telephone, but Ted held up his hand.

'No, thanks, Sub. I'm better carrying on here with the blokes I know.'

'It's up to you, Dewhirst, but I think you're wrong.'

'I may be, Sub, but let me find out for myself.'

'All right.' The sub took his hand from the telephone. 'This is going to sound harsh, but if I find that your effectiveness as a fireman is reduced, you *will* go on leave, because the DO will order you to take it. Do you understand that?'

'Of course I do, Sub. Thanks for your concern.' Ted didn't fully understand or care. He was operating in a state of abstraction in which nothing mattered except the loss of the person who had mattered most.

———————

He went about his duties in the same bemused state of mind, doing what he had to do whilst vaguely conscious of his colleagues' awkward sympathy.

There had been another incident involving Binford and Jeremy, but Ted followed the sub's orders and left it to Jeremy to make his complaint. In his current state, he would have struggled to keep his temper, anyway.

When he arrived on the rooftop the following Thursday night for his stint of fire-watching, he was surprised to find that his partner was now Mrs Chandler.

'I persuaded Lorna to swap duties with me,' she explained. 'She hasn't been at her best these last few days and, you two being in the same predicament, it wouldn't have been a good idea.'

'We wouldn't have done each other any good,' he agreed absently, adding 'Lorna's suffered more than enough already.'

'So have you.'

'I'll be all right.' It was empty assurance, a clichéd response learned in earliest childhood, when his mother insisted that he must never 'make a fuss'.

'You will,' she said, 'but it'll take time.'

'You're surrounded by casualties, Mrs Chandler. I don't know how you cope with it.'

'Two of you,' she pointed out. 'I'm hardly surrounded, and my name's Sarah, by the way. You're very polite, but I can't be more than about fifteen years older than you.'

'As much as that? I had you down as no more than thirty.'

She smiled, amused by his gentle flattery. 'You just can't help it, can you?'

'I was genuinely surprised, Sarah,' he insisted. 'In any case, a woman should be paid regular compliments. It goes a little way towards compensating for life's unfairness.'

She made no response, but took the nearer of his hands between hers. Ted had no idea what that simple action did for her, but for him the feel of her small hands at that time was the greatest comfort.

Unfortunately, the Luftwaffe were less sympathetic, and the ominous beat of their engines was already audible. Ted and Sarah concentrated now on keeping watch.

At the deafening blast of a high-explosive bomb close-by in Whitechapel Road, Ted said, 'That was probably the hospital again.'

'According to Lord Haw-Haw, only the RAF bomb hospitals. Have you heard him lately?'

'I try not to.'

'Living out, as I do, I hear him sometimes. Do you think anyone takes him seriously?'

Ted realised she was trying to distract him from thinking about the hospital, and he was grateful for her gesture. 'I don't know,' he said. 'Some people will believe anything. Parachutists disguised as nuns, and cigarette ends visible from five thousand feet both spring ridiculously to mind.'

There was a *thud* as something solid landed on the rooftop, and Ted said, 'Incendiary. I'll do it.' He picked up a bucket of sand and ran over to the place where the incendiary's fuse was already burning. 'There,' he said, smothering it with sand, 'that is as much as I can do.' His tone was wistful.

'That's all it needs,' said Sarah, 'or were you referring to your part in the war?'

'I suppose I was.'

'I'll deal with this one,' she said, as another incendiary landed about twenty feet away from them. She picked up the bucket Ted had used and emptied the remainder of the sand over the bomb.

'You've helped put out countless fires,' she reminded him as she put the bucket down, 'and saved three lives, counting Greg's.'

'Two lives. Albert rescued the girl's mother, and she was hard work.'

'Don't belittle your achievements, Ted. If you do that, you make fools of those who admire you.'

'I'm sorry, Sarah. I didn't realise you felt like that.'

'Of course we do. Mr Churchill's "heroes with grimy faces" are our heroes too.' An instant later, she said, 'Mine.' Taking a bucket of water because it was nearest the fizzing incendiary, she worked the stirrup pump until the fuse was drenched and harmless.

'Well done, Sarah. That's two to the firewomen and one to the men.'

'Let's just call it co-operation.'

By the end of their watch, they dealt with a further three bombs, and Ted also realised that for much of that time he'd been distracted from the awful pain of his loss. It was a passing luxury, but it was no less welcome for that.

Sarah looked at her watch and said, 'Our reliefs should be here soon.'

Affected by Sarah's kindly presence, he took her in his arms and hugged her. 'Thank you, Sarah,' he said. 'You've been the best possible company.'

'Any time,' she assured him, kissing him lightly on the cheek. 'Don't suffer alone.'

That weekend, there was a gas explosion, unrelated in any way to the Blitz, in a tenement block in Stepney.

When Green Watch arrived at the incident, the warden reported that the gas main had been isolated and that almost all the residents were accounted for.

'Almost?' The sub turned to see a procession of ambulances arriving. 'Who's still missing?'

'A woman and three kids. They're on the first floor.'

Prentice looked around for his senior fireman. 'Binford,' he said, 'organise a search for the missing tenants while I have a look at this fire.' He hurried along the road to gauge the extent of the blaze.

'They're just coming out now,' said the warden. A woman and what looked like two children had just emerged, coughing helplessly and with streaming eyes, from the doorway.

'Durrance,' said Binford, 'get in there and find the other kiddie.'

'I'll do it,' said Ted.

'No, Durrance can do it. He got me a bollocking from the sub, so it's his turn to suffer.'

'You're just bloody evil, Binford.'

Binford made no response but pushed Jeremy into the building.

He could only have been inside for a minute when Ted caught sight of the toddler being picked up by one of the auxiliary ambulance crew. Between bouts of coughing and choking, the mother was fussing over the child, who was now being given oxygen.

Ted asked, 'Is that your little boy?'

The woman nodded, still coughing.

Ted reckoned that the child must have come out with the others and, being so tiny, he'd gone unnoticed. 'So all your children are out of the building?'

She nodded again.

Snatching breathing apparatus from the appliance, Ted ran to the door, where Binford was peering through the smoke. 'You incompetent bastard, Binford. All the kids were safe.' He fastened the mask and opened the oxygen valve. 'Get out of my way!' He pushed Binford aside and stepped into the house, barely able to see a yard in front of him. Crouching as low as he could, where the smoke was least dense, he stumbled around for a minute before deciding to try the staircase. The family had come down from the first floor, so it made sense. As he moved towards the door, his foot encountered a soft object, and he tripped and fell over it. Then, picking himself up, he touched the obstacle and felt a woollen tunic with metal buttons. Through the thickening smoke, he felt for Jeremy's head, and his hand encountered the helmet. Having ascertained by touch which end was which, he turned his colleague over and hauled him up so that he could lift him. The bulky breathing apparatus was making the task very difficult, but he finally managed to hoist Jeremy over his shoulder and head for the diffused daylight that marked the doorway.

An agonising minute later, he staggered outside, where a pair of helping hands took Jeremy from his shoulder. He had no idea whose hands they were, until he tore off his mask, intending to give Jeremy oxygen, and that was when he realised that his helper was Prentice. An ambulance crew were putting Jeremy on to a stretcher.

'Okay, Sub,' said Ted, 'I'll take over the pump now.'

Assured, at least, that Jeremy would soon be receiving hospital treatment, Ted attended to the valves and pressure gauges on the pump. He would tell his story later.

Eventually, word came that the fire was under control, and it was possible for the crew to relax. It was also an opportunity for Sub-Officer Prentice to find out what had been happening. He started with Ted, because he was the most closely involved, and because he was available.

'Why did Durrance go into the building, Dewhirst?'

'Binford sent him in to look for a child he thought was missing.'

'But why Durrance?'

'He made him do it in revenge for the bollocking he got from you.'

'I see, and where's the child?'

'He was already out, Sub. Binford hadn't seen him.'

Prentice shouted, 'Binford, come here!'

A voice Ted didn't recognise said, 'The fireman's regained consciousness.'

'Hear that, Dewhirst? Durrance is conscious.'

'That's a relief. His lungs must be like a fireback.'

'Binford,' said Prentice, 'I understand you ordered Durrance into the house.'

'He was the only man available, Sub.'

'I offered to go in instead of him,' said Ted, determined not to let Binford get away with it.

'Why did you send him in without breathing apparatus?'

'He was in there before I could stop him, Sub.'

'That's a bloody lie,' said Ted.

'Not only that,' said the sub, 'you sent him in because he'd complained about you.'

'That's a lie, Sub. Dewhirst doesn't know what he's saying. His mind's still affected by that little number of his that got herself killed.'

'You bastard, Binford.' Ted heard the sub's warning, but it was too late. The callous and insulting reference to Iris's death and the inhuman way Binford had treated Jeremy left Ted without a vestige of self-restraint, and he drove his fist hard into Binford's face, sending him staggering backwards into the road, where he collapsed, moaning and bleeding.

'I can't blame you for doing that, Dewhirst,' said the sub, 'but now you really are going on compassionate leave.' He added, 'but not before you've answered to the DO.'

20

The long train journey, with its frequent stops and unscheduled interruptions, gave Ted time to reflect on the past two days. One of the ambulances had taken Binford and several casualties from the fire. The casualties were to be treated for smoke inhalation, but Binford's immediate need was for emergency dental treatment. Sub-Officer Prentice had persuaded him not to prefer criminal charges. To have three loosened teeth and two split lips was bad enough, but he'd been spared a broken nose, which would have been much more serious. In any case, he argued, a senior fireman who had maliciously jeopardised a trainee fireman's life was not in a strong position to make accusations. Ted was grateful to him for that as well as for speaking in his defence.

The District Officer took a firm line at first; striking a man of superior rank was a serious offence, but Prentice told the full story sensitively, referring to Ted's recent bereavement and his exemplary record as a fireman, and the DO quickly adopted a more reasonable attitude. Ted's misdemeanour could not be ignored, however, and the DO warned him that any repetition of the offence would be dealt with severely. Having delivered that reprimand, he offered Ted his sympathy and ordered him to take five days' compassionate leave.

Now that he had time to think about it, Ted realised his mistake in declining the sub's initial offer of leave, although the matter of Binford and Jeremy would still have remained. If he hadn't been there, who would have pulled Jeremy out of the burning tenement? He pondered that question only briefly before deciding that what-might-have-been was a pointless exercise. He continued on the journey in a more practical frame of mind.

Eileen was at school and therefore unable to meet him, so he caught the onward train to Beckworth and completed the journey on foot, finding his mother alone in the kitchen.

He'd given her only a dry and emotionless explanation for his leave, but he found her unexpectedly affected by the tragedy. After she'd accepted a kiss and held him with tears threatening, she said, 'I'll put the kettle on and make you a cup of tea.' She probably needed it as much as he did, but she would never say so.

'Thanks, Mum. I'll unpack while you're doing it.' He carried his kitbag upstairs and stowed its contents in the familiar chest of drawers. Having done that, he changed out of his uniform and into grey flannels and a fair isle jumper and went downstairs to the sitting room, where his mother was waiting with the tea things. He recognised the frown she'd worn in the past, when he'd occasionally come home with a sport injury. It was an indication of the concern she found impossible to express.

She handed him a cup of tea and asked, 'How long have you got?'

'I have to be back on Friday.'

She nodded, still wearing the frown. 'I've made rabbit pie for tonight. I thought you'd like that.'

'Oh, I shall.' He could see how she found it easier to talk about leave and rabbit pie than about Iris.

'Eileen likes rabbit pie, too.'

'Good. That's two of us who'll be suited.'

Conveniently moving the conversation on, she asked, 'What's the food like where you are?'

'In its raw state, it's probably no worse than anywhere else. It's what Olive does to it that's the problem.'

'Do London folk tend to overcook their vegetables?' She asked the question quite seriously.

'I can't comment on the majority, but Olive certainly does. What made you think of that?'

'It's just that there's not much greenery in a city like that, is there? I imagine vegetables are a bit scarce with nowhere to grow them, so people won't be used to cooking them. We saw a film at the pictures, one of those Ministry of Information films, about how to cook cabbage. I mean, who doesn't know how to cook cabbage?'

'Olive Ridley, for one. She treats greens the way cannibals treat missionaries.'

'Oh, don't, Ted. That's a horrible thing to say.'

'I haven't minded the food too much over the past few days,' he told her. 'You tend not to notice it as much when you've just lost the person you were going to marry.' He introduced the subject for his mother's benefit because, clearly, she was putting herself through torment at her inability to raise it herself.

'Oh, Ted.'

Her frown deepened, so he reached across and covered her hand with his. A rare tear fell on to his hand, prompting him to offer her his handkerchief.

'Oh, Ted,' she repeated. Her tears were flowing more freely now.

He sat on the arm of her chair, putting his arm round her. 'It's all right, Mum,' he said. 'I can cope.' He kissed her forehead. 'I'm all right,' he told her, just as she'd taught him years earlier.

'I must tidy myself up,' she said. 'Eileen and your dad will be home soon.'

'Is there anything I can do?'

'No.' Self-consciously, she stood up and straightened her skirt.

'Another cup of tea?'

'In a minute,' she said. 'You can bring one into the kitchen.'

Ted gave her time to recover and then took her a cup of tea.

'Thanks, Ted.'

He put it on the draining board and stood behind her with his arms round her waist. 'Not talking about it won't turn back the clock,' he said gently.

'I know, Ted. It's just the way I am.'

He had to agree, albeit mutely. There wasn't much else to say, so it was a relief when Eileen walked into the kitchen, although the relief was short-lived.

'Oh, Ted.' Immediately tearful, she clung to him.

'Let's go somewhere else,' he suggested.

'Yes,' said his mother, now with her composure restored, 'leave me room to work. I have to get dinner on for your dad coming home.'

Ted took Eileen into the sitting room and they sat together on the sofa.

Eventually, her sobs receded and she lifted her head from his chest. 'I've been thinking… about you all day,' she said between shudders.

'I'm all right, Eileen.'

'It was a… terrible thing… to happen.'

'I can't disagree with that, but I've no doubt I'll cope.' It was what people did, Lorna was coping, so it followed that he would.

In one of her characteristic changes of subject, Eileen asked, 'Why is… your right hand all… blue?'

'It's so that I can tell it apart from my left.'

'Don't be silly. Have… you been… fighting?'

'Not really.'

'Either you… have, or you… haven't.'

'You've got a snotty nose with crying. I'd give you my hanky but I gave it to Mum.' In truth, he didn't really want to talk about Binford and Jeremy; he didn't really want to talk about anything, but that wasn't Eileen's fault.

'I've got one.' She felt in her school bag and took out a handkerchief. After she'd blown her nose hard, she asked, 'Tell the truth, Ted. Have you been fighting?'

'Not really. I hit someone, but he didn't hit me back, so it wasn't really a fight.'

'What did he do?'

'He staggered backwards, clutching his face, and then he fell over and lay in the road, moaning.'

She finished blowing her nose. 'I meant,' she said impatiently, 'what did he do to make you hit him?'

'Something very dangerous involving another fireman. He said something that annoyed me, as well. I don't hit people without good reason, as you know.'

'No, you don't,' she agreed. With that settled, she asked, 'How long have we got you for?'

'Just until Friday.'

'It's not very long.' She considered that for a moment and said, 'You'll have to tell me what you want me to do.'

'In what sense?'

'I want to make you feel better, but I don't know how to go about it.'

He smiled sadly. 'Only time will make me feel better, Eileen. At least, I hope it will. Meanwhile, just be yourself.'

'Is that all?'

'I wouldn't want you to be anyone else.'

'Are you sure?'

'Sure as sure is sure.' He sat back and stared her in the eye. 'I wouldn't swap you for anyone else, for all your funny ways.'

'You know,' she said, 'when you're not being daft, you can be really nice.'

He was glad about that and about anything else that distracted him, however briefly, from his loss, like the news from the sub-station, when he telephoned to ask about Jeremy. To hear that he was making a full recovery and that he would most likely be discharged from hospital the next day was a huge relief. Another piece of good news was that Binford would be leaving Sub-Station 4C with immediate effect, and it was more than likely that he would be discharged from the London Fire Brigade.

———— ►◄ ————

When Ted's father arrived home, he shook his son's hand, looking him in the face briefly and said, 'A bad business, Ted. A bad business indeed.' He made no further reference to Ted's bereavement, possibly believing he'd said all that was necessary.

If dinner wasn't the luxury it might have been, it was only because everything in Ted's life was taking place in a cloud of wretchedness. For the first time since Christmas, food tasted as it should, and the rabbit pie was as good as ever. Only Ted was unable to enjoy it fully.

After dinner, Eileen was detailed to do the washing-up, so Ted got up to help her.

'You don't need to do that, Ted,' his mother told him. 'You're only here for a few days.'

'I can't sit idle while my little sister works her fingers to the bone,' he said.

'That'll be the day. I've told you before, Ted, you spoil her.'

'I'm not here all that often, so it can't do any harm.' He actually wanted to do something, anything at all, rather than join his parents in the sitting room, where he would quickly lose the thread of the BBC News, and the familiar cloak of anguish would envelope him again. He also wanted to make life a little easier for Eileen, who, with all her schoolwork, was called on to do far too much housework.

He picked up a tea towel and asked, 'Have you got much homework tonight?'

'Nothing that can't wait.'

'Aren't you seeing Geoffrey from next door?'

'Not tonight. He's only allowed out twice a week.' She stopped creating suds in the bowl to look up and say, 'I'm not the only one who gets treated like a ten-year-old.'

'It won't last forever.'

'I don't suppose it will. It just feels like it.' She concentrated on the washing-up for a while before saying, 'You used to read to me. Do you remember?'

He nodded. 'When you were little, yes, I did.'

'Not just when I was little. You read to me when I was getting over tonsilitis, and I was twelve then.'

'As old as that?'

She smacked his wrist with a wet and soapy hand. 'Don't make fun of me.'

'All right. Do you want me to read to you again?' It might be an effective distraction.

'No, I was just thinking…. Would you like me to read to you instead?'

As surprises went, it wasn't all that dramatic, but he stopped and thought about it.'Okay,' he said, 'let's give it a try.'

'We could do it in your study, where we can sit comfortably.'

'Yes.' The fourth bedroom had become his 'study' when he was preparing for Higher School Certificate. 'Do you ever use it?'

'Only when I go in there to look for a book.'

'There's no reason why you shouldn't. I mean it's no use to me when I'm in London.'

'Thanks. I'm supposed to be doing things for you, but that'll be nice.'

They finished the dishes, and Eileen began putting them away. 'I still can't reach that shelf where the dinner plates go,' she said.

'All right, pick them up one at a time. Go on.'

She picked up one dinner plate, and he put his hands round her waist and lifted her almost to the ceiling.

'You daft article,' she said.

'Well, put it away.' When she'd put the plate on the shelf, he returned her to the floor. 'Next one,' he said.

'You're as daft as a brush.' Nevertheless, she picked up another plate, and let him lift her again. 'I bet you can't do it another twice.'

'Let's see.' They continued until all the plates were in their place, which was when their mother walked in.

'I've put all the plates away,' Eileen told her.

'How did you manage that? You can't usually reach up there.'

'I've got a new system. Watch.'

Ted hoisted her as far as the top shelf to demonstrate.

'You two get dafter,' she said. Then, as Eileen wrapped her arms round her brother, she asked, 'What are you playing at now?'

'I'm giving him a "love",' she said. 'He needs it.' The word 'love' when it was used to mean 'hug' or 'cuddle' had come from Auntie Jane and Uncle George, who lived in Huddersfield. Throughout the British

Isles, people hugged, cuddled or embraced, except in Huddersfield, where they 'loved', a word that conveyed a great deal more meaning.

'You two get dafter,' she repeated. 'What are you going to do now?'

'Eileen's going to read to me,' said Ted.

His mother simply shook her head and returned to the sitting room, leaving her wayward children to their silliness.

As they climbed the stairs, Ted asked, 'What are you going to read?'

'Nothing heavy. Do you know Longfellow's poem "The Day is Done"?'

'Yes.'

' "Come, read to me some poem," ' she quoted, ' "Some simple and heartfelt lay...." '

'Eileen,' he said, 'you're speaking my language.'

'I know.' She pushed the study door open and went to the bookcase. 'Here it is,' she said. 'Take a seat and prepare to be read to.' Pulling her cardigan together because the room was colder than downstairs, she began to read.

Within seconds, Ted recognised the story his sister was reading. It was 'The Pride of the Woosters is Wounded' from *The Inimitable Jeeves* by P G Wodehouse. He closed his eyes as she read, and began to experience a kind of ease overtaking him already. Wodehouse was his favourite humorous writer, and Eileen was reading the story particularly well, but, cementing both those elements together was the knowledge that she was doing it for him simply because she wanted desperately to do something for him.

21

Back at the sub-station, Jeremy greeted him with effusive thanks. 'You've no idea how grateful I am, old chum.'

'Think nothing of it, Jeremy. It's what we're here for, as you know.'

'I'd no idea until they told me. I must have been unconscious when you found me.'

'I'd say so, Jeremy, but let's just be thankful you're safe and well. That's what matters, that and... I believe Binford's gone on his travels.'

'Yes, I'll be surprised if he survives the incident.' Jeremy shrugged, as if Binford's disgrace gave him no satisfaction, and remembered something else. 'We now have a station officer,' he said, 'Station Officer Crick. He seems all right.'

Ted met Station Officer Crick later, when Sub-Officer Prentice introduced them.

'So you're Dewhirst,' said Crick. 'You have quite a reputation.' He was a stocky man of about forty, with greying hair and a complexion that had attended many fires.

'Have I, sir?'

'All good, I have to say. We'll naturally regard that other matter as closed, now that the DO has seen you.'

'Thank you, sir.'

'Did you have a good leave?' It sounded like a genuine enquiry.

'Yes, thank you, sir.'

'Good. You naturally have my sympathy in your loss.'

'Thank you, sir.'

'Just one more thing, Dewhirst. Can you cook?'

'Oddly enough, sir, my sister taught me how to make cottage pie while I was on leave.'

'Good.' The Station Officer looked pleased. 'I think you'd better break the news, Sub.'

'Very good, sir. While you were on leave, Dewhirst, we learned that

Olive had reached retiring age for the WAFS, and she needed to take things more easily as well, so she packed her bags and went.'

'I'm sorry I missed that, Sub. I'd like to have seen her before she went.'

'Yes, that was unfortunate. It also means that, until we can find a full-time cook, everyone's lending a hand, so your cottage pie could be very welcome when the time comes.'

Having been dismissed, Ted went to the Watch Room to see Sarah and Lorna before they went off watch. As he'd expected, they were both pleased to see him.

Lorna asked, 'What did you get up to on leave, Ted?'

'Fascinating things. I learned how to make cottage pie, and I understand it could be in demand fairly soon, now that Olive's gone.'

'Cottage pie could be full of surprises,' said Sarah, 'with potatoes more plentiful than fats and flour. There's no limit to the variety of fillings that could be concocted.'

'Not soya sausages, I hope,' said Ted. 'That was too big a surprise.'

'There's a big notice up in the kitchen,' Sarah told him. 'Everyone knows about your allergy.'

'I find that very reassuring.'

Impatient to hear more, Lorna asked, 'What else did you do?'

'My little sister read to me.' Seeing their blank faces, he told them, 'It has soothing properties that could surprise you.'

———◄►———

Leave had been both necessary and a relief, but it was good to be back with friends, Albert, Jeremy and the Watch Room staff in particular. Even spud bashing was a pleasant routine in the company of genuine friends, and the general atmosphere at the sub-station was greatly improved after Binford's departure. Fire-watching was another duty made pleasanter by friendly company than it might have been, and Ted's partner the next time round was Lorna.

'I'm sorry I couldn't join you last time,' she said.

'Don't give it another thought. You sent a very capable deputy, so there was no harm done.'

'Mrs Chandler's is a safe pair of hands,' she agreed, 'whatever the occasion. I know that better than most.'

'Yes, I know.'

Anti-aircraft guns were firing to the southeast. Before long, the aircraft would be overhead.

'How are you coping, Lorna?'

'Much better, thanks.' She put her gloved hand on his. 'It gets easier, so be patient.'

'Thank you. I was actually thinking about you.'

She squeezed his hand before releasing it self-consciously.

The anti-aircraft fire had stopped, and before long, they heard the approach of a faster aircraft.

'Hopefully, that's a night fighter,' said Ted. His hunch was confirmed by the sound of machine-gun fire and the slower clatter of cannon fire. There was an explosion in the sky much bigger than a shell burst, and an aircraft spun earthward in flames.

'That's one to us,' said Ted.

Lorna was quiet.

He asked, 'Are you all right?'

'Mm.' She sounded unsure. 'I know they're the enemy, but it's not as straightforward as that for me.'

'I know what you mean. They have wives and girlfriends too.' There was the thud of magnesium alloy on slate. 'Incendiary,' he said. 'Leave it to me.' He smothered the burning fuse with sand just as another incendiary hit the roof.

'Mine,' said Lorna, also pouring sand over the fizzing thermite fuse.

Below them, a heavy unit and two trailer pumps were leaving the yard. Red Watch were in demand.

'Mrs Chandler said something funny – something a bit odd, anyway – after she'd been fire-watching with you.'

'What did she say?'

She was almost embarrassed. 'She said you gave a good hug.' She winced as a high explosive bomb went off in the direction of the docks.

'Oh, yes. A few weeks ago, when she was feeling a bit worn and weary, I gave her a squeeze. I explained that we northerners tend to be somewhat physical. I suppose I meant it by way of an apology, but she was happy enough.'

Another incendiary bounced off the roof and fell into the yard, where it ignited. Ted opened the rooftop door and shouted, 'Incendiary in the yard!' There was an answering shout, and someone ran into the yard to deal with it.

'She said you hugged her again after fire-watching,' said Lorna.

'You're determined to embarrass me, aren't you?'

'Of course not. I think it was a nice thing to do.'

'In my experience, it usually is.'

She slapped his wrist playfully. 'I meant it was a nice gesture. She thought so too.'

'She'd been very kind and supportive. It felt like the natural thing to do.'

'Incendiary. I'll do it.' The nearest equipment was a bucket of water and a stirrup pump, which Lorna used to put the fire out.

'You can come fire-watching with me again, Lorna. You're like lightning with that thing.'

'You have to be.' She resumed her place beside him, surprising him by asking, 'What did your sister read to you?'

'P G Wodehouse. It was one of the stories from *The Inimitable Jeeves.*'

'Which one?'

' "The Pride of the Woosters is Wounded".'

'I know that one.' She hesitated and said, 'That's if it's the one when Bingo Little becomes infatuated with Honoria Glossop.'

'Right in one.'

'The musclebound girl who "probably boxed for the varsity".' She smiled, presumably at some memory of the story. 'What gave your sister the idea of reading to you?'

'My turn,' said Ted on hearing the incendiary hit the slates and slide into the gutter. He plied the stirrup pump until the fuse was out, and then kicked the dead incendiary into the yard. As he sat down again, he asked, 'What were you saying when that thing landed?'

'I asked you what made your sister think of reading to you.'

'I used to read to her when she was little, and sometimes when she was older, when she'd been ill, for example. She used to enjoy it, so she thought it might help me as well.'

'She sounds like a lovely girl. How old is she? You must have told me, but I can't remember what you said.'

'Seventeen, nearly eighteen. She's grown up in a home where she's been shown no affection, except when I've been there, but she has masses of it to give.'

There was a familiar thud and clatter, and Lorna said, 'Mine.' She drenched the fuse and kicked the bomb into the yard.

Sitting down again, she asked, 'Did your sister learn about love from your aunt and uncle as well?'

He was surprised for a second, and then he remembered telling

Lorna about Auntie Jane and Uncle George. 'She must have.' He'd never really thought about it, but it made sense, and so did something else. 'When I learned that there was a baby on the way,' he said, 'I wanted a brother to play with. Then, when Eileen was born, I was so protective of her that I forgot all about boys' antics and I helped to bring her up instead. Sometimes, when she teases me, I remind her that I used to see her having her nappies changed. My mother says I spoil her, but it's not true.'

'There's spoiling and spoiling, isn't there?'

'Oh, yes.' One such case came conveniently to mind. 'Shortly before I left home to come here,' he said, 'I remember there was one night when Eileen washed her hair – she has lovely hair, dark and curly, rather like yours – and she came downstairs with a towel. She sat in front of me, and I dried her hair in front of the fire, the way I did when she was little. My mother accused me of spoiling her, but if that's spoiling, there should be more of it.'

'So that's what gave you the idea.' She put a hand on Ted's arm and then withdrew it self-consciously.

'The idea for what?'

'Drying my hair after I'd used the shower. Don't you remember?'

'I remember something. I'm afraid I'm a bit vague about that morning. We'd had the worst raid since the Blitz began, and I was so tired, I was like an automaton.'

'I was feeling hopeless and helpless, and then you came along and dried my hair so that I wouldn't catch a chill when I went outside.'

'I remember now.' He shrugged. 'I was just being sensible. My mother always used to say, "Dry yourself thoroughly before you go outside," ' Another HE exploded closer to them than before, and they both ducked instinctively. As if reluctant to be left out of the game, an incendiary landed only feet away. 'This one's on me,' said Ted, grabbing a bucket of sand and covering the fuse.

When he sat down, he said, 'They've got the job sized up now. They drop a few HE's to keep people's heads down, but they know they can do far more damage by showering the place with incendiaries.'

'They had more than eight hundred appliances at the docks last week,' said Lorna. 'They were bringing them in from outside London. It looked like one mile-long blaze.' Then, referring to the previous conversation, she said, 'And for what it's worth, you weren't being sensible.'

'No?'

'No, you were being kind.'

'The sub told me to look after you, so I did. I was only obeying orders.'

'You know, you can be infuriating.'

'Mm.' He tried to look suitably penitent. 'I'm just not used to having nice things said about me.' More seriously, he said, 'When you feel desperately sorry for someone, it's usually accompanied by a feeling of helplessness, because there's nothing you can do. On that occasion, I was lucky enough to find something to do, and it was something I was quite good at. So, you see, it helped me as well as you.' After a moment's consideration, he said, 'That's why Eileen read to me. She wanted very badly to do something for me, and it was the only thing she could think of.'

'Well, I'm glad she did.'

Ted checked the luminous dial on his watch and said, 'Our reliefs should be here soon. You know, I usually feel awkward talking about the kind of thing we've been discussing, but I've enjoyed our heart-to-heart.'

'Me too.'

—————

By the end of the month Auxiliary Firewoman Eunice Wilkins, an experienced peace-time cook, was drafted to the sub-station, and was soon recognised as a cook *par excellence*.

22

When word was passed that a newcomer had arrived at the sub-station, there was a degree of speculation and some conjecture. Only Spud Murphy had seen him, and he was now checking hydrants, so the rest of the watch had to wait.

The mystery was unravelled when the sub called Ted into his office and introduced a tall, fair-haired, elegant-looking man of forty or so. He wore his uniform smartly, and his shoes were buffed to a commendable sheen. The only defect in his otherwise immaculate appearance was a facial scar terminating in a half-closed eye.

'This is Rawlinson, Dewhirst.'

Ted offered his hand. 'How d' you do.'

'Glad to meet you.'

'He's fully trained,' said the sub, 'and quite experienced, even though he's been a part-timer until now, so he's not like Durrance. You won't need to carry him. I want you to take him to the gym to stow his gear, and then take him to meet the rest of the watch.'

'Okay, Sub.' Ted moved towards the doorway. 'As we're next door to the Watch Room, we'll start there. Follow me, Rawlinson.' He knocked on the door of the Watch Room and, hearing the voice of welcome, opened the door. 'Ladies,' he said, 'this is the new bloke. He was introduced to me as Rawlinson, but I'm sure he has another name.'

'I'm Gerald,' said Rawlinson.

'This is Mrs Chandler and Lorna, who man the civilised end of the sub-station.'

'How d' you do, ladies.' Rawlinson shook hands with them.

'While we're on the subject, my name's Ted.'

Rawlinson smiled and nodded.

'I'll show you to the gym, Gerald. It's a bit primitive, but we spend most of our time in there asleep, so it doesn't really matter. Thank you, ladies.'

Rawlinson added his thanks, a gesture that won Ted's approval.

They walked across to the gym, stopping on the way for Ted to point out the shower room.

'That's quite a refinement,' observed Gerald. 'I doubt if many stations have shower facilities.'

'This one didn't until I pinched some steel tubes and fittings from the caretaker's store.'

Gerald nodded appreciatively.

Ted asked, 'What did you do before you joined the AFS full-time?'

'I was a journalist.'

'For one of the national dailies?'

'No, freelance.'

Ted hesitated and then said, 'It's none of my business, but what made you go full-time?'

'Basically, I thought it was time I did something more useful than turning out on evenings and weekends. Do you find that as pathetic as I do?'

'It's not at all pathetic, Gerald. You did it for the best of motives, so good for you, I say.'

'Thank you, Ted.'

'Not at all.' Ted opened the door to the gym and said, 'This is where we sleep.' He pointed to a bed with a pile of folded linen and a blanket. 'That'll be your bed. Let's see if we can find you a locker.' He ran his eye down the row until he spotted a key in a lock. 'I should stow your gear in that one and take the key,' he said.

'Thank you.'

Ted watched him stow the contents of his kitbag neatly in the locker. 'I'm very impressed with your shoes,' he said. 'You'll put the rest of us to shame.'

'Oh.' Gerald laughed modestly. 'I'm an old soldier. Old habits die hard.'

'Were you in the last war?'

Gerald nodded. 'The last two years of it, anyway.'

'It seems to me you've already done your bit.'

'Well, a little more won't go amiss.'

Ted was impressed with his new colleague. He hoped the others would be.

'Ted,' said Gerald, 'how do the ladies in the Watch Room cope among so many men?'

'They can look after themselves. In any case, the blokes treat them with respect. They're both widows. I don't know when Mrs Chandler lost her husband, but Lorna's was killed just before Christmas. He was serving in the desert.'

'Oh, the poor girl.'

'Yes, it's only been a little over two months, but she's coping much better now.'

'Good.'

For purely practical reasons, he had to say, 'I'm not looking for sympathy, but you may as well know, also, that I lost my fiancée recently. She was a nurse at the London Hospital.'

'Ted, I'm so sorry.'

'That's war, isn't it? Come, and I'll introduce you to the rest of the watch. They're a good lot, but you may find their humour a trifle rough-hewn.'

'I got used to that in the trenches, Ted.'

'Of course.' It was easy to forget.

They walked to the yard, where Ted introduced the watch. There was inevitably some leg-pulling, as Ted had anticipated.

'Blimey, Gerald,' said Albert, 'You don't want to polish your shoes up like that. I can see me face in 'em, and with a face like mine, I don't want to look at it too often.'

'Don't worry,' said Gerald. 'My fire boots are as dull as anybody's.'

'Gerald's an old soldier,' Ted told them.

Spud asked, 'Were you in the last lot?'

Gerald nodded.

'Rather you than me.' Then, as an afterthought, he asked, 'Wouldn't they have you back?'

'No,' he said, indicating his damaged right eye, 'an injury at Amiens left me with less than perfect eyesight.'

'I'm sorry, mate,' said Spud hurriedly. 'As usual, I spoke without thinking.'

'Don't let it worry you.'

'I'm going to report back to the sub,' said Ted. 'If I hear a commotion out here, I'll know that Spud's put his foot in it again.'

——————

Ted went to his usual retreat after lunch, and Lorna joined him shortly afterwards.

'We're lucky to have Eunice as station cook,' she said. 'The only drawback is that we no longer get your cottage pie, and everyone agrees that it was a triumph.'

'Thank you.' It was nice to know. 'But the credit for that should go to my little sister. She's quite a cook.'

'Did your mother teach her to cook?'

'Yes, but she treats her like Cinderella. If the poor girl gets a decent Higher School Certificate, it'll be the greatest achievement, considering all the housework she has to fit in.'

Lorna surprised him by saying, 'I got an HSC.'

'Did you?'

'Yes, I left school in nineteen thirty-seven with an HSC in English Lit., Latin, French and German.'

'Good for you, but you'd have been very welcome in the women's forces with French and German, surely.'

'Probably.' She smiled wistfully. 'I was born into a loving, caring home. The only missing element was enlightenment. My father, a fair man in most respects, would never countenance his daughter joining the forces. If it comes to that, he can see no point in girls going to university either.'

'What did you do when you left school?'

'I trained as a secretary, and then I joined the WAFS. I went full-time as soon as I could.'

Looking for some atom of comfort to offer her, he said, 'I'm sure there'll be opportunities after the war. They can't ignore the fact that so many have given up their jobs and missed out on their education.'

'That depends on who wins the war.'

'Oh, tut-tut. That could be construed as spreading alarm and despondency.'

'Not if you keep it to yourself.'

'I'd never betray you, Lorna, and I'm working as hard as I can to keep the country from going up in smoke. All the same, I think you should make a commitment to complete your education after the war. What will you study at university?'

'Languages.' She put a hand to her mouth and said, 'I just made a commitment, didn't I?'

'Bravely done.' As he spoke, he heard Sub-Officer Prentice calling the watch back to work. 'See you later, Lorna.'

''Bye.'

Chatting with Lorna was always a pleasure, and their latest conversation had yielded at least one surprise. Ted also realised that, during that time, he'd not thought about his loss. It was too early to be thinking in terms of healing and recovery, but maybe he, too, was learning, albeit slowly, to cope.

———◆◄———

There were times, also, when memories of Iris and of that terrible morning returned, and he was powerless to rid himself of them.

On one occasion, the watch was called out to a daytime incident in Bethnal Green, which was awful enough, being so close to the sub-station. What made it infinitely worse for Ted, however, was that the fire was at the Athenaeum Ballroom, the place he and Iris had been obliged to leave early on two occasions, when air raids had interrupted their precious time together. He stood on the extension ladder, lost in grief and automatically training his hose on the blazing dance hall. At such times, coping seemed a long way off, if not an impossibility.

A red-letter day occurred during March, that called for celebration. Greg's wife went into labour in the early morning, and by ten o' clock, she was delivered of a girl, her seventh child. Quite unofficially, Station Officer Crick allowed Greg the day off. His absence made little difference to anyone else; his duties were shared out between the rest of the watch, and everyone was happy to discharge them. To give Greg a proper break, he was also excused his stint of fire-watching that night, so Ted wasn't surprised when the sub asked, 'Will you do Gregory's fire-watching tonight, Dewhirst?'

'Of course I will, Sub. Just as long as he names the baby after me.'

'You'll have to sort that out with him.' The sub went on his way, satisfied that Greg's fire-watching was in safe hands.

In the event, Ted had only been on the roof a few minutes, when the door opened, and Sarah came to join him.

'Hello, Sarah,' he said, 'I didn't know you were Greg's fire-watching partner.'

'Neither does Greg most of the time. Getting a few words out of him is a work of art, he's so shy. I don't usually have that effect on people.' The anti-aircraft barrage had stopped; here and there, a night fighter could be heard, but the bombers had still to arrive.

'No, it's not you, Sarah. Greg's just naturally shy, right up to the moment he switches off the bedroom light, and then there's no stopping

154

him.' The sinister beat of multiple aero engines was now distinct and growing louder.

She nudged him reprovingly. 'Don't be awful, Ted.'

'This baby is his seventh, and it's a standing joke with the watch.'

'I hope you don't tease him about it. I know the way you men treat each other when you get together.'

'Raiders overhead,' he reported. 'We're not cruel, Sarah. It's all in fun, and I think he enjoys his reputation on the quiet.'

As if to signal the bombers' presence, an incendiary hit the roof about two feet from where Sarah was sitting, causing her to leap to her feet with a cry of alarm.

'I've got it,' said Ted, seizing a bucket and covering the bomb with sand.

'I dread one of those things landing on me. It happened to one of the girls in B District. She was horribly burned.'

'Come and sit down, Sarah,' he said, realising that the incident had unnerved her. Moving his chair closer to hers, he stroked her arm and asked, 'Would you like a cup of tea?'

'No yet, thanks. I'm just a bit shaken, that's all. I'll be all right.'

He took her hands between his, much as she had done for him on a previous occasion, and he felt her shaking. He asked, 'Do you want to go below, just until you feel better? I can carry on alone.'

'No,' she said, 'just stay here with me and I'll be all right.' After a while, she stopped shaking and said, 'This is all in a day's work for you firemen, isn't it? Bombs falling and incendiaries going off?'

'We're not bomb-proof, Sarah, and there's no need to feel embarrassed about it.'

'With anyone else, I might be, but not with you. Thanks, Ted.'

He gave her a supportive squeeze and said, 'You're welcome. If you remember, the last time we did this together, you braced me up.'

'I suppose I did. How are you coping?'

He shrugged. 'Some days are better than others – you know how it is – but I'm beginning to see my way ahead.' Another incendiary fell, hitting the chimney stack a glancing blow before landing on the tiles. 'Leave it to me,' he said, smothering it with sand.

'I really will get the next one,' she said as he re-joined her.

'You don't have to.'

'Yes, I do, for my own peace of mind.'

'I'm going to have a brew,' he said, picking up the flask. 'Will you join me?'

'All right.' She took a mug from the bag beside her. 'You know,' she said, 'you remind me very much of my late husband.'

He waited for the crash of a high explosive bomb to recede and asked, 'In what way do I remind you of your husband?'

'He was a strong chap like you, but he was very gentle, just as you are.'

'Senior Fireman Binford might have disagreed with the word "gentle".'

'He might,' she agreed, 'but he was an exceptional case.' In the yard below, Red Watch were boarding Heavy Unit 1. When they were out of the gates, she said, 'My husband was a very fit man, as I said, but when they brought him back from the front, he was helpless. Gas had almost destroyed his lungs, you know. He died in hospital two weeks after he arrived home.'

'Sarah, I'm so sorry.' He'd known she was a widow, but what she'd told him made it so much worse.

'I don't know why I told you that. I hope I haven't upset you.'

'Not at all.' He gave her a squeeze. 'More tea?'

'No, thank you. Your company is better than a gallon of tea.'

There was a familiar thud, and Sarah looked around the rooftop for the bomb. 'I'll do it,' she said.

He let her deal with the incendiary, knowing how determined she was. When it was extinguished, he waited for her to come back to her seat. 'Well done,' he said.

'I'm all right now.'

'Good.'

'I've been thinking a lot about my husband lately. I'm sorry I had to burden you with it.'

'You didn't, and there's no need to be sorry.' He took her empty mug from her and held her hands again. 'You've not been having an easy time, have you?'

'What do you mean?'

'You've had to support Lorna, and then there was me. On top of all that, you have the memory of what happened to your husband. That's what I mean. It's bound to take something out of you.'

'Yes.' It was as if it had only just occurred to her.

In the light provided only by the fires of London, he could see she had something on her mind.

'Ted?'

'Mm?'

'Do you know the new chap at all well?'

'Gerald?' The sudden change of subject came as a surprise. 'I suppose I know him as well as anyone. If you remember, I had the job of settling him in.'

'How does he seem to you?'

'Do you mean, what do I think of him?'

'Yes.'

'He's a sound bloke and, as far as I know, a decent one. I think he'll fit in and be a strong member of the watch. Why do you ask?'

'Oh, just idle curiosity.'

Something in her expression, even by the flickering light of the distant fires, suggested that her curiosity was anything but idle. Ted was beginning to understand why her late husband had been so much on her mind.

23

Now relieved of Binford's bullying attentions, Jeremy continued to make good progress. He would soon be independent of his mentors and become a dependable member of the watch. In that, he was not alone. In what remained of March, Gerald confirmed Ted's impression that he was honest and trustworthy. He was also fully-trained, as the sub had pointed out, and that meant he could pull his weight. His activities were not confined to his duties, however, as Ted had half-suspected. His hunch was confirmed when he and Lorna met, as they so often did, in the Boys' Entrance after lunch.

'You'll never guess,' she said.

'Not without a hint or several,' he agreed. 'I take it this is about some*one*, rather than some*thing*? Let me guess. Is this someone Sarah Chandler, by any chance?'

'Yes. How do you know her Christian name?'

'She told me. We've been on Ted and Sarah terms ever since she did your fire-watching.'

'All right.' Lorna wore the disappointed air of someone whose imminent disclosure was about to become yesterday's headline. 'What do you know about Mrs Chandler?'

'Lots of things, but I imagine you're going to tell me something....' He hesitated. 'No, I shan't guess. Go ahead and tell me. Feed my burgeoning curiosity.'

'All right, there's no need to tease. She's seeing Gerald Rawlinson, and I'm not being sneaky, because it's not a secret. It's just that not everyone knows about it yet.' She studied his face and said, 'You knew all along, didn't you?'

'Yes,' he admitted.

'You horror. You never told me.' Changing the subject slightly, she said, 'Mrs Chandler said she had a close escape last time she was fire-watching with you.'

'What a thing to say about me. I feel wounded. I'm the very soul of propriety.'

'I didn't mean that, silly. She said an incendiary landed right beside her, and she was very shaken.'

'Oh, that. Yes, it wasn't very pleasant for her.'

'She told me all about it.'

Speaking of bombs had set him thinking. 'Surely,' he said, 'they've got to run out of bombs soon.'

'If only.' After a while, she asked, 'Do you believe in anything… you know?' She inclined her head upwards.

'Yes, I was a choirboy until my voice broke.'

'It's difficult to imagine you as a choirboy.'

'I was smaller then, I wore short trousers and I only shaved once a day. Why do you ask?'

'I believe in a great design. I have to, now that it's got me through the past three months.'

'In that case, I'm all for it,' he said.

'I think each of us was put on the planet to perform a special task. You know, the way Mr Churchill took over as Prime Minister last year, and he braced us all up and made us think positively. That was his special task, even though he had to wait more than sixty years to carry it out.'

'Have you performed your special task yet, Lorna?'

'I'm not sure. I don't think it's happened yet, although I did once save four kittens from drowning.'

'That should rank highly as a special deed. I'm sure the kittens would back me up on that, anyway.'

'I don't know. Maybe there's another, more important job waiting to be done.'

'My money's on the four kittens, but I'm a softie. My father hates them because they dig up the soil between his cauliflowers, but I rather like them.'

'Is your father a keen gardener?'

'It's his line of business. He's a market gardener.'

'How lovely it must be to do something creative like that.'

'Yes, although I doubt if he sees it that way. He's not what I'd describe as a romantic.'

After some thought, she said, 'Your *magnum opus* must be the great fire of London.'

'I think you'll find I arrived about two-and-a-half centuries late for that.'

'Not that one. I mean this one.'

'I suppose you could call it that, but there must be thousands of firemen out there,' he said, 'and many of them will have performed greater deeds than I have.'

'You know, you're either very unimaginative or very modest. I think it's the latter.'

'You could be right. I've never given it any thought.'

'What will your sister do when she leaves school, Ted?'

'She'll probably join the Wrens as soon as she can, just to get away from home, and I don't blame her.'

'Why the Wrens, particularly?'

'Oh, the smart, blue uniform, without a doubt, give or take the old ladies' hat. Of course, the black, artificial silk stockings are an irresistible inducement.'

'Stockings of any kind are precious now.'

'And it doesn't seem all that long since she was a little girl running around barefoot.'

'That's what parents say. I suppose that's what you are, really, a substitute parent, and a good one, I'd say.'

'How can you possibly know that?'

'Because you're full of love, as a parents should be. You're solid and protective and all kinds of good things, and you're not aware of most of them.' She looked thoughtful and asked, 'Did Iris know about your qualities?'

'I don't know. We didn't have all that long to get to know each other.'

'I'm sorry. I shouldn't have mentioned her.'

'That's all right. I'm not going to behave as if she never happened.'

'Of course not.' She looked at him in a way he'd come to recognise. It usually meant that she was about to divulge some personal secret. 'There are times,' she said, 'when I struggle to remember what Reg looked like. Does that sound awful?'

'Well, you did say you'd had very little time together before you were married, but surely you have a photograph of him, a wedding photo, maybe?'

'I did, and this *is* awful. I knocked it off the sideboard when I was dusting, and the glass broke, so I took it to a place where they do framing, to get it replaced.' Her expression told him the rest.

'Was the shop destroyed in the bombing?' So many had been.

She nodded. 'I felt awful about it for a long time afterwards. It was after the funeral. The two seemed to go together.'

'I can understand that, but you're not guilty of anything.'

'Except carelessness.' Leaving guilt aside, she asked, 'Have you got a photo of Iris?'

'No, we never had the time to do all that stuff.'

'What stuff?'

'Swapping photos, birthdays, birthmarks, favourite colours, superstitions, favourite dance bands and songs, favourite films and actors, likes and dislikes....'

'If it helps, neither did we, even though we were married.'

Their conversation could have continued for some time, but Sub-Officer Prentice chose that moment to bring the lunchbreak to a close.

Towards the end of the month, the police called Green Watch out to a road traffic accident in Roman Road, where a woman was apparently trapped in an overturned vehicle.

They arrived at the incident at the same time as the ambulance and found a Standard Nine lying on its side. The nearside doors, which were now uppermost, were buckled and quite obviously incapable of being opened. A policeman was interviewing the sorry-looking driver of an RAF three-ton lorry.

'It appears that the lorry came out of Globe Road and hit the car,' the police inspector told the sub hurriedly. 'The lady driver is still inside.'

'Let's have a look,' said the sub, going over to the car.

The trapped driver was pleading tearfully, 'Please get me out of here.'

The sub spoke to her through the broken windscreen. 'Don't you worry, love. We'll have you out of there in no time.' To the crew, he said more quietly, 'There's a strong smell of petrol, so I don't want to use the circular saw. Spud and Jenkins, you'll have to use crowbars to wrench this passenger door open. It'll take a while, but we've no choice. Try not to make any sparks while you're doing it.'

'Right, sub,' said Albert, opening the tool compartment and taking out two wrecking bars.

Ted went to the sun roof and used his clasp knife to cut through the waterproof layer and the lining beneath it. As he peeled the fabric away, he saw the driver's face. It was contorted with terror. She was young, possibly in her twenties, and understandably tearful.

'You won't get her out through there,' the sub told him.

'I can see that now, Sub, but maybe I can reassure her. She's going through torment inside there.'

'Good lad.' The sub walked round to the other side of the car to supervise the opening of the door.

Ted tore the rest of the fabric away and spoke to the driver. 'Hello. My name's Ted. What's yours?'

'Alison… Winthrop,' she sobbed.

'Do you mind if I call you "Alison"?'

'You can call me… anything… you like as long as you… get me out of here.'

'We've got men working on it now. It won't take much longer.' He hoped that was true. Certainly, Albert and Spud were working as fast as they could. 'Where are you injured, Alison?'

'I don't know. I can't move my… right leg.'

'Don't try to move it. Does it hurt anywhere else?'

'I got a bang… on the head, but… I don't think it's… anything awful.' Fresh tears started, and she asked, 'Is it going to take much longer?'

'You'll be out very soon.' He became conscious that a queue had formed beside him, and the reason became apparent when one of the ambulance staff said, 'There's a doctor here. He wants to speak to the patient.'

'Of course. A doctor's coming to talk to you, Alison.' He moved aside for the newcomer, who said, 'Hello in there. I'm going to ask you some questions.'

'Please get me out.'

'The firemen are working on it. Now, are you aware of any injuries?'

'I've already told the fireman I can't move my right leg.'

'In that case, don't try to move it.'

'That's what the fireman said.'

'I'm the doctor, Miss…. What is your name?'

'Alison Winthrop.'

'Right, Miss Winthrop. I'm the doctor here, not the fireman. Don't try to move your leg. In falling sideways against the door, you may have fractured your pelvis.'

'Oh heck.'

'It's nothing to worry about. Stay where you are and they'll have you out of there in no time at all.'

'Funnily enough, I wasn't thinking of going anywhere just yet.'

Straightening up again, the doctor said almost wistfully, 'In stressful situations, sarcasm often comes to the fore.'

If the doctor had encountered it before, Ted wasn't surprised. He did seem to invite it. Crouching again by the open sun roof, he said, 'Alison, it's me again, Ted, the fireman. They're very nearly there. Is your leg hurting badly?'

'Yes, it's awful.'

He extended his left arm into the car and asked, 'Can you reach my hand? Don't do it if it hurts.'

She took his hand with her left. 'No, that's all right.'

'Okay, I'll tell you what to do. 'When the pain's really bad, grip my hand as hard as you can. It'll help.'

'Are you sure?'

'Positive.' It had worked when one of the kids at school had broken his ankle at cricket and they'd had to wait for one of the staff to fetch his car and drive the lad to hospital. He waited, and felt her hand tighten on his. To distract her, he asked, 'What do you do for a living, Alison?'

'I'm an assistant manager in a food office.'

'In that case, we'll have to get you back to work or we'll all be starving.' As jokes went, it was pretty feeble, but he was only trying to give her something else to think about.

'How much longer do you think it'll take?'

'I don't know, Alison. I'll ask.' Raising his voice, he called to Albert and Spud, 'How's it going, lads?'

'Nearly there,' said Albert. 'We've got a bit of purchase now.' As if to demonstrate, there was a screech of tortured metal and a loud snapping noise, and the passenger door swung open.

'Cut through that leather strap,' said the sub, 'and then the door won't try to swing shut again while they're getting her out.'

Ted saw Spud wield his knife, and the door fell open against the car bonnet. 'There,' he said, releasing Alison's hand, 'all we have to do now is pick you up and put you into the ambulance.'

One of the ambulance women looked into the car with dismay. 'We can't lift her out of there,' she said, earning a reproachful look from her partner and prompting a fresh burst of tears from Alison.

'Don't worry,' said the sub, 'we'll lift her out. Dewhirst, you're the one with the gentle touch. Can you come round here and lift her out of her seat?'

'Right-oh, Sub.' Ted took off his helmet and leaned into the car. 'I'll need two blokes to grab my ankles and haul me out, Sub.'

'Right. Greg and Rawlinson, you two can do something useful now. Take a leg each and haul when Dewhirst tells you to.' As an afterthought, he said, 'You'd better be ready to stop when he tells you, as well.'

'Okay, Sub.'

'Right, Sub.'

Ted reached inside and asked, 'I know it's difficult, but can you move at all, Alison?'

'I don't know.' She wriggled towards him, but the action made her yelp with pain.

'Easy now. Give me your hands.' As she reached towards him, he seized her wrists. They were easier to grip than hands. 'It's bound to hurt,' he told her, but it's the only way.' Calling to Albert and Spud, he said, 'Ready, lads? Pull!'

As they hauled on his legs, he pulled Alison on to the passenger seat, causing her to shriek with pain. 'I'm sorry, Alison. We're nearly there. Put your right arm round my neck, then your left. That's right.' He grasped her upper body, thankful for the slightness of her build. 'Haul away, lads. We're nearly there. Tell the ambulance people to get a stretcher ready.'

'There's one here, Ted,' said Albert.

'Thanks, Albert. Come on, Alison love.' He slipped his left arm behind her knees to lift her bodily from the car. 'I'm sorry,' he said in response to a loud cry of pain. 'Where's the stretcher?'

'Behind you,' said Spud.

As gently as he could, he lowered Alison on to the stretcher.

'Well done,' said the more sensitive of the ambulance women.

'Don't go, Ted,' pleaded Alison.

'I can't go to the hospital with you,' he said. 'I have my duties to see to. You never know, I may have to rescue someone else.'

She asked him earnestly, 'Are you married?'

'No.'

'Neither am I. Come down here, Ted.'

'All right.' He wondered if she might want to whisper something in his ear, maybe to express her thanks. Instead, she seized his face with both hands and kissed him full on the lips, earning a loud cheer from Green Watch, the two ambulance women and the policemen who were waiting for the recovery vehicle.

'Thank you, Ted.'

'You're welcome, Alison. Take care and get well soon.' As the ambulance people carried her away, he asked, 'Where are you taking her?'

'To the London Hospital,' one of them told him. It made sense, as it was close-by.

———◆◄—

It was as well that Ted never took himself seriously, because it seemed at times that the ribbing would never end. He was called various names including 'Romeo', 'Casanova', 'Lover Boy' and 'Ladies' Pin-Up'. He was also reminded by several of his colleagues, quite unnecessarily, that firemen featured regularly in many women's erotic daydreams.

It was all good-natured banter, and there were worse ways of spending the eve of another month of nights.

24

APRIL

Possibly because of his unusual involvement with Alison when she was trapped and helpless inside the car, Ted thought of her as an acquaintance rather than simply as a casualty. Partly for that reason and out of genuine concern, he telephoned the hospital to enquire after her progress, but he was unable to learn any more than that the patient was comfortable and as well as could be expected. With that rationed information, he knew at least that she was all right, and he was pleased about that.

Meanwhile, the Blitz continued with unrelenting ferocity, which meant that Green Watch were in constant demand. With the workload as it was, its members welcomed the newcomer, drafted in from Bedford. His name was Jim Rafferty, he was friendly, and he became initially quite popular with the rest of the watch. Spud Murphy identified a somewhat dubious bonus, pointing out that the others would always be able to find Jim at an incident, because his bright red hair glowed in the dark. Jim advised him to stick to playing the piano and leave jokes to the comedians. The others agreed with that advice.

Tim's first night at the docks was a sensational introduction to the London Blitz, but he came through it with undiminished zeal, prompting Albert Jenkins to say to Ted as they came out of the shower, 'He had no fear at all.'

'Maybe he has no imagination.'

'Whatever it is,' said Albert, 'I'm glad he was behind me and not in front. He was all for going on the roof to fight the fire, and it looked bloody dicey to me.'

'He's young. Maybe he'll settle down once the newness has worn off.'

'I hope so.'

Both men were desperately tired, so the conversation was never destined to be a lengthy one. They dried themselves and went gratefully to their sleeping quarters.

———•◦•———

Having risen deliberately early, Ted walked down the road to the London Hospital for the first time since he'd learned of Iris's death. It was inevitable that it would be a poignant experience, although he found it less difficult than he'd feared. Only a month had elapsed since his previous visit, but it seemed much longer.

He followed the signs for Women's Surgical, and stood at the end of the public ward, scanning the two rows of patients.

A nurse asked, 'Who are you looking for?'

'Miss Alison Winthrop.'

'Miss Winthrop? Left-hand side, number seven. You know you've only got twenty minutes' visiting left, don't you?'

'Have I? I'm on the night watch. I've only just got out of bed.'

The nurse smiled and nodded sympathetically, no doubt having worked many a night shift herself.

'Thank you.' He set off down the ward, counting beds, but he recognised Alison by her fair hair long before he reached number seven. One of her feet seemed to be suspended from a frame above the bed. It looked most uncomfortable. He stopped at her bed and spoke to her. 'Hello, Alison.'

She recognised him immediately. 'Ted. How good of you to come.'

'I telephoned the hospital, but they only told me the usual stuff about being "as well as can be expected", so I came to see for myself. How are you?'

'I'm all right, really. At least, it's stopped hurting, but thank you for asking.'

'Not at all. When I rescue a damsel in distress, I like to know that she's living happily ever after.'

She laughed. 'So that's the reason for your visit. I don't know about "happily ever after", but I stand a better chance now than I did when I was trapped in the car.' She looked guilty for a second, remembering her manners, and asked, 'Would you like to sit down?'

'Thanks, I will. Apparently, visiting's nearly over. I got up early to come and see you, but there are limits.'

167

'What do you mean, you "got up early"?'

'I got up out of bed.' Then, realising there'd been a minor misunderstanding, he explained, 'I'm on the night watch now.'

'And you got up early to visit me? What a knight in shining armour you are.'

'Well,' he said, 'I have a steel helmet and I carry an axe. I suppose it's a start.' Looking up at the arrangement of cords and pulleys, he asked, 'What's this for?'

'It's to ease the pressure on the fracture and allow the joint to heal. I have a fractured pelvis.' She added helpfully, 'The fracture's in the hip joint.'

'And to think I pulled you out of that car like a sack of spuds.' He winced at the thought.

'I'm glad you did, Ted,' she said seriously. 'One of the ambulance women told me she'd heard the chief fireman say there was petrol leaking from the car. She said that was why they used the tools they did. She heard him tell them not to make sparks. It's quite terrifying, thinking about it now.'

'It's all over now,' he told her. Recalling the scene, he asked, 'Was that the ambulance woman who said they couldn't lift you out?'

'Yes, the same one.'

'Ah. Maybe she should take lessons in diplomacy. I'm sure distressed patients would find her more reassuring if she did.' He looked at his watch. It was almost four o'clock. 'I didn't have time to go shopping,' he said, 'or I'd have brought you some flowers.'

'That's sweet of you, Ted,' she said, smiling, 'but I think you'll find flowers hard to track down now everyone's digging for victory.'

'We can see a lot from the top of a ladder,' he said, 'but some details still elude us.'

An electric bell sounded, and a nurse announced, 'Visiting time is over.'

Ted asked, 'Do you mind if I come again?'

'Oh, please do, but I don't want you to go without sleep on my account.'

'I'm a hardened fireman,' he told her casually. 'Don't worry about me.'

A nurse stopped by the bed and said, 'Please leave the ward, sir. Visiting time is over.'

'Yes. Sorry, nurse.' Making a split-second decision, he leaned over Alison's bed and kissed her on the cheek. 'Goodbye, Alison,' he said, 'I'll see you soon.'

'Goodbye, Ted. Thank you for coming.'

He walked back to the sub-station in a state of confusion. Only five weeks had elapsed since that awful night when Iris was killed, and he'd been chatting with Alison as if she were a new girlfriend. It had seemed quite natural at the time; she was warm, friendly and attractive, all the things he would want a girl to be, but it was too early to be thinking along those lines.

He was relieved of further self-searching that night, because the watch was called out almost immediately, and inevitably, to the docks. Before long, the line of fire appliances attending the blaze stretched as far as anyone could see, and it was reported that more were on their way. Working on the pump and relaying water via numerous trailer pumps from a multiplicity of sources including water towers and portable reservoirs, Ted could only concentrate on the job he'd been given. The overview of the incident was in more senior and therefore more experienced, hands.

The night wore on, with the combined brigades and the AFS doggedly fighting fires where they could or saving buildings from the fires of those deemed inextinguishable. In the morning, when the mobile canteens arrived, Ted hung back to let those who had been on the ladders, and therefore closest to the fires have their well-deserved and much-needed tea and breathing space.

Among them was Albert Jenkins, who emerged from the queue with two mugs of tea, one of which he handed to Ted. 'Here, Ted,' he said. 'You've been working as hard as any of us.'

'Not really, but thanks, Albert.'

'I've had young Rafferty behind me most of the night, urging me on.'

'What did he want you to do?'

'I don't know. I told him I couldn't hear him because of this curtain, but I just wasn't listening. I mean, you can take just so much of that kind of thing when you're trying to concentrate, and the best thing is to ignore it. He's not talking to me now.'

'Problem solved, then.'

'Yes, it's a pity it didn't work sooner.'

A new voice demanded, 'Don't you ever listen?' It was Jim Rafferty, and he was speaking to Albert.

'Listen to what, Jim?'

'I was trying to tell you that if you turned the hose on the walls, the fire between them would be isolated.'

'Listen, Jim,' said Ted. 'Albert and I have been attending fires a lot longer than you have. We know what we're doing.'

'But it should be bloody obvious!'

Ted shrugged. 'You could try out your theory on the sub and see what he says, but don't be surprised if he agrees with us.'

Jim snorted. 'That wouldn't surprise me at all,' he said. 'He's as set in his ways as everyone else.'

———◆◆———

After a tiring night and less than six hours' sleep the previous day, Ted slept for the whole of the next. That night, the sub put Jim on the pump, so that the only conflict came from above. It was conflict enough for the fire services and everyone else concerned, but they had the fires under control by morning.

Green Watch tumbled out of the heavy unit and various towing vehicles, they spent a blissful two minutes beneath the shower and then collapsed into their beds. Even Jim Rafferty had little to say, and if he had, everyone was too tired to pay any attention to him.

Rising early again, Ted dressed and set off for the hospital. He knew his way to Women's Surgical from his last visit, and he went straight to Alison's bedside.

'Ted, how lovely to see you again,' she said. 'I hope you haven't missed too much sleep.'

'Don't worry about me. How are you?'

'I feel all right, but no one will know anything until I've been X-rayed again. Meanwhile, I have to lie flat on my back and view the world on its side. Even eating is difficult in this position.'

'That's a shame,' he said. 'In the absence of flowers, I've brought you some chocolate. I hope it won't cause you too much difficulty.' He put it on her bedside locker.

'Oh, what a lovely thing to do. Thank you, Ted.'

'It was no trouble.'

Changing the subject, she said, 'That was an awful raid last night. Did they call you out?'

He nodded. 'Yes, we made ourselves useful.' He didn't tell her they were out fighting fires every night, because he didn't want to alarm her.

'I'm going to be here for a few weeks,' she said. 'That's what they say.'

'In that case, I'll know where to find you.'

'That's right.' She looked thoughtful and said, 'My parents are travelling to London tomorrow, and they'll be visiting me then and possibly Friday and the weekend.'

'Okay, I'll give it a miss until Monday.' He added hurriedly, 'That's if you want me to come.'

'Of course I do. You're my knight in shining armour.'

'I keep forgetting that.'

Not surprisingly, considering her recent experience, the concept fascinated her. She asked, 'Have you saved many people?'

'That's my job,' he told her. 'Our first duty is to save life. After that, we put the fire out.'

'I know, but have you really saved lots of lives?'

'A few,' he admitted, 'but you're only my second damsel in distress.'

'What was the first one like?'

He thought before answering. In the end, he decided to tell the truth. 'I had difficulty in seeing her through the smoke,' he said. 'She might have been twenty-or-so at the outside, but she was completely paralysed.'

'Did she know what was happening?'

'I think so. She certainly knew she was in danger, but all she could do was cry out. She made no sense, but I knew what she was trying to say.'

Alison screwed up her eyes at the thought of it. 'It must have been awful for you,' she said.

'It sounds awful, I know, but her paralysis made it easier for me, because she couldn't struggle. People do when they panic. Instead, she just lay helpless, so I lifted her on to my shoulders and carried her to the ladder.' He smiled quickly, realising that the conversation had become very serious. 'I've always remembered it,' he said, 'because it was my first rescue.'

'Do you think you'll remember rescuing me?'

'Of course I will, if only for the kiss when I put you on the stretcher.'

The bell rang to end visiting, prompting Alison to say, 'Will you kiss me again?'

'I think so,' he said, bending to kiss her cheek.

As he did so, she turned to meet his lips with hers. 'See you soon,' she said.

'Oh, yes.'

Ted tried not to make too much of that kiss as he walked back to the sub-station. Alison was a playful person, and she probably only meant it in fun. In any case, his thoughts were still very much of Iris, although he still felt drawn, if only by friendship, to Alison's bedside.

———— ◆◄ ————

He continued to visit her for the next two weeks, during which she was no less delighted to see him. He took her his chocolate ration, and she rewarded him with almost a re-enaction of the scene by the ambulance.

'Come down here, Ted,' she said.

He bent over her, this time knowing what was about to happen, and happy to respond.

'I could get used to this,' she said. 'Could you?'

'I think so, but not with you in a hospital bed.'

'Do you think we could go on seeing each other?'

'I don't see why not.'

She seemed thoughtful and said, 'I was seeing someone before all this happened, but it wasn't going at all well, so we decided more or less to go our separate ways.'

It was his turn. 'I was almost engaged to someone, a nurse at this hospital.'

'Almost?'

'When I say "almost", I mean that we'd made the decision, but I hadn't yet met her parents, and we hadn't bought the ring.'

'What happened?'

'She was killed in an air raid.'

'Oh, Ted.' She took his hands in hers. 'When did it happen?'

'Two months ago.'

His reply seemed to take her by surprise. She said, 'It must hurt very badly.'

'Not as much as it did.'

She made no reply, but waited for him to go on.

'It's very strange,' he confessed. 'Maybe it has something to do with the work I do. I see death and destruction on a nightly basis, and it must have a desensitising effect. Also, coming here to the hospital has helped. I associate it with coming to see you, and that tends to close out any negative feelings I had about the place.'

'You know what I'm going to say, don't you?'

'Do I?'

'Come down here, Ted.'

Regardless of anyone who might be watching, he bent and kissed her, revelling in the luscious feel of her lips until, like a stern chaperone, the bell rang for the end of visiting. ''Bye, Alison,' he said. 'See you soon.'

'Very soon, I hope.'

He kissed her quickly and left before the scowling sister who was watching him could take him to task.

———◄►◄———

The last week of April continued as the month had begun, and Green Watch, now weary and looking forward to ending their month of nights, were nevertheless working fiercely to contain the fires at the docks and around the East End.

They had arrived at a brewery in Butchers' Row, and Sub-Officer Prentice called for the extension ladder. When it was in position, he directed Ted and Jim Rafferty to go up, clearly intending Ted to go first, but before he could reach the ladder, Jim was already on it.

'He meant me first,' said Ted.

'In that case, he should have said so.'

'He called my name first. That's the way it's done.'

'I know,' said Jim derisively. 'That's the way it's always been done, and that's how it has to stay. Well, I disagree.'

'Just behave yourself up there.'

'I'm not a child.'

Ted decided to save his breath. All the same, he watched Jim secure his line to the top of the ladder before hurling the rest down to the party below.

'You're supposed to warn them to stand clear,' he reminded his junior colleague.

'Let them think for themselves for a change.' Jim waited until the hose and branch were fastened, and the sub shouted, 'Ready!' He hauled it up and secured it to the top rung, finally shouting, 'Ready!'

Ted felt the water surge through the hose, and the whole thing bucked as it gushed forth.

Because the brewery backed into a yard, where no appliance could gain admission, the fire had to be fought from the front of the building, and it was necessary to aim the hose over the rooftop and into the fire, while those on the ground attempted to contain it by pumping water in through the windows.

From behind Jim, Ted shouted, 'Aim at the base of the fire!'

'I know what I'm doing.' After a short spell, he said, 'Mind the hose while I have a proper look.'

'What are you going to do?'

'Just mind the hose!' As Jim stepped on to the roof, the hose went vertical, sending the jet high into the air. Ted grabbed the branch and turned it downward to aim the jet at the base of the fire. Even so, the sub demanded angrily to be told what was happening. After another second, he bellowed to Jim, 'Get off that roof!'

Ignoring him completely, Jim shouted to Ted, 'Aim it at the far wall!'

'Bugger off!'

'Aim it at the far wall, I tell you!'

'No.'

Jim started back towards the ladder. As he came, two slates became dislodged, followed by several more, and part of the roof gave way beneath him. Ted reached out to grasp his hand, but it was beyond his reach, and Jim crashed through the tiles.

Ted shouted 'Man down! Inside the building!' There was nothing else he could do, so he continued to aim the hose at the base of the fire beyond the roof, while the sub organised two men to enter the building with breathing apparatus.

No ambulance came, and Ted could only fear the worst. When the fire was under control and he came down the ladder, he heard of Jim's fate. It seemed that he'd fallen on to a high platform that housed the huge vessels that brewed the ale, and then he'd fallen again to the floor, where his colleagues found him with his neck broken.

The watch that returned to the sub-station was quieter than usual.

Over the next few days, an internal inquest was held, presided over by the District Officer. Otherwise, there were occasional muted references to the incident, but no one was keen to say much about it. Instead, they carried on with their work. That was how they coped with disaster.

———◆◄———

Now back on days, Ted ascertained that evening visiting time at the hospital was from six-thirty p.m. until eight, and he welcomed the new freedom. At last, he could be with Alison for more than the meagre half-hour or so to which he'd been accustomed, and he set off in good spirits.

He arrived at the ward shortly after six-thirty and saw that quite a lot of visitors were already there, no doubt keen to make their visit before the air-raid warning sounded. As he approached Alison's bed, he saw that she already had a visitor, a young man with whom she was locked in what seemed to be a passionate clinch, at least as far as her incapacity allowed, and he was about to turn away, but they came apart and she saw him. Clearly embarrassed, she said something to the young man, who released her and turned to look at Ted.

'Leonard,' she said, in her discomfiture, 'this is Ted, the fireman who rescued me from the car. Ted,' she said lamely, 'this is Leonard.'

'The man you were seeing before you decided to go your separate ways?'

'Yes, I meant to speak to you, but you haven't been in lately. I suppose you've been busy.'

'I have,' he confirmed. 'We had a disaster of a different kind a few nights ago, and now we have a funeral to attend. Still, it keeps us busy.' As he turned to leave, he looked at them both, each as uncomfortable as the other, and said, 'Good luck, both of you. One way or another, you're going to need it.'

He walked home, convinced now that it had been too soon after Iris's death. He was also conscious that he'd been spared a relationship that would never have worked.

25

MAY

Curiously, his experience that night at the hospital, far from embarrassing him, seemed to have an almost therapeutic effect on his state of mind. He was able to dismiss Alison as an overgrown child, the kind who treated her playmates as expendable, and that served as a full stop as well as anything. On the other hand, he was no longer so preoccupied with Iris. He thought about her, and he would always remember her with affection, but the hurt had eased. It was difficult to understand, so he stopped trying to fathom it, although he discussed the matter with Lorna one lunchtime a few days later.

'Yes, it's very odd,' she agreed, 'but I know what you mean.'

'Have you experienced it?'

'Not exactly. Not in the same way that you have, but I did experience a kind of....' She cast around for an appropriate word and said, 'I can only call it a "release". I woke up one morning, quite recently, after a very sound sleep, and I looked around me at the familiar objects in my bedroom, and it seemed to me that the world wasn't such a bad place after all. Of course, we can all do very nicely without nightly air raids and rationing, but there are other things that are worth having. I thought about the sub-station and the people I work with.' She smiled a little bashfully. 'I thought about you because you've been so kind to me.'

'I'm flattered.'

'No, you're not. You know you've been kind to me.'

'It didn't feel like that, honestly. I was only doing what I could.'

'All right.' Sounding like an indulgent parent, she said, 'I'll allow you that. Anyway, to go on with what I was saying, I thought, all right, I'm a widow, but so are thousands more, so what makes me special?'

'Go on. What makes you special?'

176

'That's just it. Nothing. I'm like thousands of others who've received the telegram from the War Office and experienced a period of hell, but now I'm beginning to remember Reg's failings as well as his qualities. I'll always love him. At least, I think I will, but I no longer have that awful sense of my world crumbling and falling apart.'

Ted checked the time and said, 'I think we should continue this conversation on the rooftop tonight, when we're looking at the stars and....'

'Chucking sand on incendiaries. Why not? We've got to have a little fun some time.' She sounded much happier than of late.

———◄►———

At the siren's familiar wail, they emerged from the raised attic and took their places on the rooftop. Guns were firing to the southeast, which meant that the raiders would soon be overhead. It was a boring routine, only enlivened when the incendiaries began to fall. Ted checked that the buckets were filled with sand or water and took his seat beside Lorna.

'No one mentions Jim Rafferty now,' remarked Lorna, who had evidently been giving the matter some thought.

'That's the way it goes. We don't dwell on casualties, simply because it's bad for morale.'

'Did you see it happen?'

'Yes, I was right beside him when he fell through the roof.'

'How awful for you.' Then, deliberately changing the subject, she said, 'Things are going nicely between Mrs Chandler and Gerald.'

'I'm glad. I wonder if he still calls her "Mrs Chandler" or if they've progressed beyond that.'

'Don't be awful,' she said, giving his wrist a playful slap.

'No, they're two of the very best. I wish them well.'

'Mrs Chandler's been a widow for nearly twenty-five years. She told me that only recently.'

'Don't try to follow her example, Lorna. You're too good to go to waste.'

'It's sweet of you to say so, but I've no plans to change anything just yet.'

The roar of Bristol engines meant that at least one night fighter was overhead. It was always a comforting thought.

'One day,' said Lorna, 'all this will be a bad memory.'

'All of it? Does that include sitting up here with me?'

'Apart from sitting up here with you,' she conceded.

'Raiders overhead,' he reported as the rhythmic beat of Junkers engines invaded the silence. 'And guess where they're going.' As if in reply, the first explosions came from the docks. In what seemed no time at all, Red Watch poured into the yard, and a heavy unit followed by two trailer pumps left the station.

'Here goes,' said Lorna, grabbing a bucket of sand to smother an incendiary.

'Nicely done, Lorna. You know, my family – my aunt and uncle too – are completely in the dark about the Blitz down here. That's censorship for you.'

'Perhaps it's as well. They'd only worry about you. As things stand, my father worries about his only daughter consorting with ribald firemen.'

'Haven't you told him we're too busy even to give ribaldry a fleeting thought?'

'He wouldn't believe me.'

'Mind you, if I were your father, I'd worry about you.'

'If you were my father,' she told him wryly, 'you'd have cause to worry. You're only two or three years older than me.'

Ted thought about that. 'I'm twenty-five,' he said.

'I'm twenty-two.'

'I suppose I would be a little young for that.'

'Have a cup of tea instead,' she suggested, flinching as an HE burst less than half a mile away.

'Good idea.' He watched her take two mugs and fill them from the Thermos flask.

'Sandwich?' She opened the bag and offered it to him. 'It's lucky dip time again.'

'Mm,' he purred like a gourmet about to indulge in a celebrated recipe, 'Spam.'

'It's getting worse,' she said. 'The bombing, I mean.'

'Yes, they're really going for the docks.'

More and more bombers came to drop their devastating load until it seemed that almost the entire East End was ablaze.

'We may yet have to turn out and lend a hand,' said Ted.

'I hope not.'

'You'll be as safe up here on your own as you are with me around.'

'But I feel safer with you here.'

'Try to concentrate on something else,' he suggested.

'All right,' she said, taking a Spam sandwich for herself. 'You know, it's just as well they feed us at the station.'

'Well, it's been better since they gave the cook's job to Eunice, although I have to say I enjoyed the compliments about my cottage pie.' Thinking about what she'd said, he asked, 'Why is it such a good thing for you?'

Before she could answer, an incendiary fell at the other end of the roof.

'My turn,' he said, grabbing the bucket of sand. He dealt with the incendiary and returned to his seat. 'We were talking about food,' he reminded her.

'Yes, I've tried to keep the flat going, but it's difficult on my meagre wages. The rent's bad enough, but if I had to feed myself, I'd be sunk.'

In the light of so many fires, he could see the worry on her features. 'What kind of flat have you got?'

'The tiny kind. It's in Hoxton. Two bedrooms, a sitting-cum-dining room, usual offices and a scullery.' With a short and dismissive laugh, she said, 'The letting agents called it a "luxury flat" because it has its own bathroom.' She winced again when two HE's exploded in the region of Stepney.

He nodded slowly. Determined to distract her from the bombing, he asked, 'Have you thought of taking a lodger?'

'Yes, well, someone to share the rent. I can't take a lodger, as such, because I'm not the landlady.'

'What's the problem?'

'Because of my commitment here, he or she would have to be self-catering as well as trustworthy. Such people are not easy to—' She leapt up as another incendiary struck the roof.

'The stirrup pump is nearest,' he advised.

She primed the pump and drowned the fuse quickly and efficiently.

'I thought all lodgers, rent sharers or the like, needed to be trustworthy,' he said when she returned.

'I suppose they do,' she said, taking her seat. 'By that, I meant that I don't want some character coming along and trying to get too friendly. That's completely out of the question.' In competition with the noise of the raid, her voice had risen towards the end of the sentence.

'It would be safer to take a woman.'

'I could do that,' she agreed.

'Or someone you know to be trustworthy.'

'That narrows the field,' she said. 'Have you anyone in mind?'

'Let me think.' He adopted a thinking pose just as an incendiary hit the roof and self-ignited, thus claiming his immediate attention. He grabbed the stirrup pump that Lorna had just used. The fuse reacted angrily to his attentions, but it quickly succumbed to its watery end.

'I was going to say that, much as I enjoy the camaraderie of the gym, I sometimes experience a feeling of nostalgia for those pre-war days, when I had my own bedroom and I could get away from the job at the end of a watch.'

'Are you serious?'

'We're talking about your security and my peace and quiet. Of course I'm serious.'

She waited for the noise of an explosion to fade, and said 'We'll have to come to an agreement about the rent.'

He pursed his lips theatrically. 'I'll go halves with you,' he offered.

'Really?'

'Choirboys' honour.'

'I don't believe you were ever a choirboy, but you're an honourable man, so I'll accept your proposal.' They shook hands until Lorna realised the absurdity of it and withdrew her hand, laughing. 'When do you want to move in?'

'As soon as I can square things with the DO's office and become registered as living off the premises.' He added, 'That's if there's anything of London left after tonight.'

The process took less than ten minutes the next morning, so that, after supper, Lorna, Ted and his loaded kitbag caught the bus to Hoxton, signalling an end to Lorna's financial worries and allowing Ted to unpack his kitbag in his own room.

He came downstairs to find Lorna in the sitting room. 'I've been wondering,' he said, 'how we might best put the seal on our new business relationship.'

'Oh, yes?'

'I wonder if you'd allow me to buy you a drink.'

'That would be lovely. Thank you.'

'Of course, we'll have to decamp when the siren sounds.'

Lorna looked at the clock. 'It should have sounded by now.'

'Let's take advantage of Nazi inefficiency.'

'Let's.'

As Lorna locked the door behind them, Ted offered her his arm.

'My word,' she said. 'Is this going to be a regular thing?'

'Going for a drink? I hope so. I haven't travelled all this way to die of thirst.'

'It's been a long time,' she explained patiently, 'since a man offered me his arm. In fact, I can't remember the last time.'

'Think on this,' he said. 'You haven't just taken a flatmate, you've found one who's a gentleman. It's a rare bonus.'

'I always knew you were a gentleman.'

He opened the door to the Duke's Head and asked, 'What would you like to drink?'

'Oh, let me see. I haven't had a drink for so long, I can't remember what I used to like. Maybe gin, please.'

'Would you like anything with it?'

'Orange blossom if they have it. Failing that, anything, really.'

Ted pushed his way to the bar. 'Gin and orange blossom and a pint of Guinness, please.'

The landlord poured a measure of gin and added orange blossom. Leaning confidentially towards Ted, he asked, 'Is there anyfink special abaht today?'

'Nationally? I don't think so.'

'Only, we've been talkin', an' we fink there must be some'ink goin' on, on account of Jerry ain't been over yet.'

'Just enjoy it,' advised Ted. 'That's a pint of Guinness as well, please,' he reminded him.

The landlord pulled the requisite pint, repeatedly scraping off the head and adding more. 'That's a proper pint of Guinness,' he said finally.

'I can see that, and I'm honoured.'

'Maybe today's a funny religious day, but only in Germany, if you follow wha' I'm gettin' at.'

'They don't allow religion in Germany nowadays,' said Ted.

'Don't they hold with that carry-on?'

'They didn't when I was there before the war, and things can't have changed much since then.'

'Well then, it's anybody's guess, but you can bet the buggers are up to some'ink.'

'If they were going to invade,' said Ted, 'you'd expect them to intensify the bombing, rather than slackening off like this.'

'Yeah.' The landlord had evidently decided that Ted was an educated man who probably knew more than most.

'It could be Hitler's birthday,' Ted suggested darkly.

'I won't 'ave no bugger drinkin' to that in this pub.'

'Quite right,' said Ted. 'I'm with you there.'

By the time Ted was back at the table with the drinks, a crowd of regulars had taken up the theme and were voicing their disapproval of anyone unlikely enough to want to drink Hitler's birthday health. Ted explained the situation to Lorna.

'It doesn't explain why they've stayed at home tonight,' she said, adding nervously, 'if they really have.'

'Just enjoy it. That's what I told the landlord.'

Lorna looked at her wristwatch. 'It's almost eight o' clock,' she said.

'So it is. We've been bombed almost nightly for eight months, and now we're nervous because they haven't come. Make sense of that if you can.'

'You're right,' she said. 'Let's just enjoy it.' She looked around the pub and then at Ted. 'What would you be doing now,' she asked, 'if the war hadn't intervened?'

'Marking English essays, comprehension tests, grammar and punctuation exercises....' I imagine that would keep me going throughout the evening. What about you?'

'Evening classes, probably. Otherwise, I'd be reading.'

'Of course. Nineteenth century novels, if I remember correctly.'

'That's my mother. My tastes are broader than hers.'

'Good for you.'

'The last thing I read was much too spicy for her taste.' She offered the information with a glint in her eye.

'What was that?'

'Gustave Flaubert's *Madame Bovary*.'

'In French?'

'*Mais oui. Certainement.*' She laughed. 'Do I pass the test?'

'You passed that months ago.'

Eventually, they walked back to Lorna's flat and she let them in. As he passed the wall calendar, Ted noted the date. It was the 11th of May. Like the landlord at the pub, he could think of no religious occasion associated with that date, but he was too tired to think about it.

'Goodnight, Lorna,' he said.

'Goodnight, Ted. Sleep well.'

26

Incredibly, the Luftwaffe stayed at home the next night and for several nights after that, keeping everyone guessing but no less thankful for the respite. Meanwhile Ted settled into his new temporary home, his friendship with Lorna making the arrangement an easy one.

Because of the lull in air raids, they were both granted five days' leave on the understanding that, should they be required during that time, they must return forthwith. Accordingly, they set off to their respective family homes.

Ted endured a long and frequently-interrupted journey to Bradford, where he was delighted to see Eileen on the platform. He held out his arms and hugged her, lifting her off her feet in his delight at seeing her again.

When she could speak, she said, 'Thank you for my birthday present.'

'You're welcome. I'm sorry it couldn't be something more exotic.' Scarce though they were, cosmetics still seemed banal.

'It was well-received, believe me. How long have you got this time?'

'I've to go back on Wednesday,' he told her, but let's not think about that yet.' He deliberately withheld the possibility of being recalled during that time. It was no time for negative details. Instead, he asked, 'What have you been up to?'

'It's exam time, Ted. Have you forgotten?'

'I've been distracted.'

'I've already done Modern British History. Modern European's in two weeks' time, and English is shortly after that.'

As they walked outside to the Bedford, he asked, 'How was Modern British History?'

'A doddle, although it seemed odd, writing essays about Peel, Disraeli, Asquith and Co., when much greater things are happening now. Still,' she said, starting the engine, 'we have to see these things in perspective.'

'You're so right, Eileen. You know, you impress me more and more, each time I see you.'

'I told you when you came home at Christmas,' she said, blowing a kiss to the special constable on point duty, 'I have to think for myself, now you're away.'

'I should have gone away sooner.'

'No, you shouldn't. I miss you, although it means that I enjoy seeing you all the more when you come home.' She drove on, eventually asking, 'Do you feel any easier about… you know?'

'Iris? Yes, I feel much easier. I almost began a new relationship recently, but it never got off the ground.' He told her about Alison.

'The ungrateful woman! After you'd rescued her from mortal danger, too. Did you tell her and her boyfriend what was what?'

'No, I just walked away. Actually, I have to say that the experience was very good for me.'

'How?'

'It made me see things more clearly. Anyway, what about you and Geoffrey?'

'It's all over.' She punctuated the announcement by double-declutching expertly into second gear and turning into Manchester Road. 'He wanted something that wasn't on the menu, and he was such a nuisance about it that I told him we were finished.'

'Good. Is there anyone else around?'

'No, I'm concentrating on my exams for now.' She began to laugh.

'What's the joke?'

'Talking about Geoffrey and his carnal desires reminded me of something that happened last week. Mum and Dad went to the pictures, but they got the night wrong and they had to sit through an Old Mother Riley film. She sang that song "Keep Your Hand on Your Ha'penny", and Mum was disgusted. I told her there was nothing wrong with the words. It was the lewd construction she put on them, and she rounded on me, saying that, as a single young girl, I shouldn't even know what it meant.'

Ted had to smile, if only because, for all her street wisdom, his sister remained as innocent as ever.

———◆◄———

Dinner was excellent, as always, and enjoyed in the usual reserved atmosphere. Typically, neither parent made any reference to Ted's bereavement. It seemed that enough had been said already, and he was happy with that. He took care, however, to thank his mother for a magnificent meal, thereby earning her approval, at least for the time being.

He helped Eileen with the washing up, as he had during his last leave, after which their mother asked, 'What are you two going to do tonight?'

'Ted's going to help me with my revision,' said Eileen.

'Oh, well,' was all her mother could say.

Ted said nothing, as it was the first he'd heard of it.

When they reached his study and closed the door, Eileen put on her bored face and said, 'I didn't think you'd want to sit down there with them, listening to "In Town Tonight" on the wireless.'

'Thanks, Eileen. You're absolutely right.'

'What are you looking for?'

He was leafing through an old photograph album. 'I've found it. Look.' He showed her a picture of the St Barnabas choir.

'What do you want that for?'

'Nostalgia.'

She made no response, being more concerned with other things. 'I've got something to show you,' she said, opening his old desk drawer and taking out an envelope.

'I thought you were excited about something.'

'Listen to this.' She took out the letter, switched to her 'official' voice and read, ' "Dear Miss Dewhirst, Further to your application to join the Women's Royal Naval Service, you are required to attend a medical examination on Thursday, the twenty-second of May at number one, White's Terrace, Duckworth Lane, Bradford nine. Your appointment is at eleven-thirty a.m." '

'Good for you. By the time they send for you, you'll have finished with HSC's, and when you get your results, you'll be in line for rapid promotion.'

'I don't care about that. I just want them to send for me.'

'Do they need to interview you?' He had memories of some kind of interview at the RNV(W)R Training Centre.

'They did that at the recruiting office. If I pass the medical, I'll be in. Isn't it exciting?'

'It's good news,' he agreed.

Less confidently, she asked, 'What sort of thing do they do at a medical?'

'They'll test your eyesight, hearing, heart and lungs. You'll have to produce a urine sample – it's probably better to take one with you. They'll do all the usual things.' He decided not to tell her about having to touch her toes for the intimate inspection, in case the anticipation turned out to be worse than the realisation.

She considered the information before asking, 'Do you have to take all your clothes off?'

'Yes, but don't worry. If it's the same old boy at White's Terrace who examined me twice, he's seen it all before, many times.'

'Oh well, if that's what it takes, that's what I'll have to do.' The lure of the WRNS or, at least, the prospect of leaving home, made an hour's loss of dignity a price worth paying.

They chatted about school, home, the market garden, and about Ted's work in London.

'The man at the recruiting office told me it's bad in London,' she said. 'Every night, in fact.'

'He shouldn't have told you that. It has been bad,' he agreed, 'but they haven't been over since last Saturday night.'

'Why not?'

'Search me. If I knew how Hitler's mind works, I wouldn't be a fireman. They'd find something far more useful for me to do.'

'I don't really care why, as long as they stay at home.' Looking at her watch, she asked, 'Could you bear the nine o' clock news? I'm going to have a bath.'

'I should really go downstairs and be sociable,' he said.

'Okay, I'll see you later.'

Ted went downstairs to join his parents.

His father asked, 'Have you sorted her out, Ted?'

'There's no need, Dad. She's on the right track.'

'She spends hours up there,' said his mother. 'I think she does it to get out of helping with the housework.'

It was time for Ted to make an important point. 'I don't think you realise,' he said, 'how much work is involved in Higher School Certificate. For one thing, it calls for an awful lot of reading.'

'Aye, reading from morn 'til night. It beats housework.'

'It's just a shame the ugly sisters are never around when you need them, Mum. If they were, they could do their share of the work, and Eileen could leave the hearth and concentrate on her studies.'

She looked at him sharply and demanded, 'Are you trying to be funny?'

'In this house? What would be the point? I'm just saying that she's working like a galley slave to get good grades. There's nothing lazy about that.'

'Grades. Huh.'

'Yes, grades that will eventually enable her to go to university and make something of her life.'

His father had been silent until then. Now, he said, 'You went to university, and now you're riding around in fancy dress on a fire engine.'

'That's because Hitler very inconveniently sprang a war on us. I can't be held responsible for that.'

It seemed that he'd made his point, because his father disappeared again behind the *Yorkshire Post*. His mother asked, 'What's our Eileen doing?'

'She's having a bath.'

'I hope she's not using too much water.'

'I doubt it.'

'Hush,' said his father, 'it's time for the news.' They fell silent and waited, although very little seemed to have happened. Tipton, a town in the Midlands, had been bombed for the second time in six months. There were few casualties. Other than that, the war appeared to be taking a breather.

Happily, the news, such as it was, held the attention of both parents until Eileen came downstairs, rubbing her hair with a towel.

Predictably, her mother said, 'You're going to dry it yourself this time, are you?'

'Why not?'

'I thought you might get Ted to dry it for you again. He enjoys spoiling you.'

'Ted's on leave. He's earned a rest.' She sat on the floor by his chair.

'You're confusing nurturing with spoiling, Mum,' Ted told her, 'and they're not even on the same page in the dictionary. You know, all over the country, parents complain because their sons and daughters do nothing but argue and fight. Aren't you glad you haven't got that problem? Many parents would give anything to see a hint of affection between their sons and daughters.'

'We don't go in for making a big show of affection in this family, unlike some,' she told him almost proudly.

'Yes, I've noticed.' Then, to move the conversation away from home, he said, 'I dried someone else's hair quite recently. Just after Christmas, it was.'

His mother looked at him sharply, but it was Eileen who asked, 'Who was that?'

'A girl at work. Her husband had just been killed in Egypt, and she was in an awful state. As if that wasn't enough, the water company had turned off the supply to her flat, and she was reduced to using a standpipe.'

His father asked, 'Why ever did they do that?'

'Because the water main had been damaged in the bombing. It happens all the time.'

Eileen asked, 'So, how did you come to dry her hair for her?'

'She'd asked the sub-officer if she could use the shower at work when we'd finished with it, and he left me to operate it and make sure no one went near the washroom as long as she was in there.'

'I should think so,' said his mother forcefully, 'in a place full of men.'

'I did that, and she had her shower. When she came out, she was in the same yonderly state, hardly aware of anything but the terrible tragedy she'd suffered, and she sat outside the washroom with her towel on her lap, with dripping wet hair and an expression that the word "hopeless" doesn't even begin to describe, so I dried her hair so that she wouldn't catch a chill when she went outside.'

'I hope she had some clothes on,' said his mother.

'Much as I'd like to tell you that she was stark, bollock naked, because that's what you seem to want to believe, I have to tell the truth and say that she was fully clothed.'

'I'll hear no more of that kind of language.'

'No,' echoed his father, 'not in this house.'

'I plead extreme provocation.' He lifted a lock of Eileen's hair and asked, 'Are you all right down there?'

'Fine, thank you. How is she now, the girl whose hair you dried?'

'Listen to the voice of compassion,' he advised his parents, 'and feel humbled.' Lifting the lock of hair again, he said, 'She's much better, Eileen. She's coping nicely. I've been able to follow her progress because we're on fire-watching duty together.'

'They organised that here, but there was no need for it,' said his mother. 'I don't know why you bother with it down yonder.'

'Don't you? Well, I'll tell you. I'm not supposed to, but you're an extreme case. London has been bombed almost every night for eight months. Think of it. Eight months, night after night, and if that shocks you, brace yourselves for more. The Nazis come over when the tide's out, so the river is at its lowest and water is at a premium. The fires in the East End are so extensive that we sometimes have literally hundreds of appliances at an incident. In case you're wondering, an appliance is the thing you call a fire engine, one of those things I ride around on in fancy dress instead of doing something useful and sensible with my degree.' He was gratified to see that both parents were visibly shocked.

'We do fire-watching at night when we're on the day watch,' he went on. 'It involves waiting until an incendiary lands on the roof – we don't usually have to wait long – and then we smother it with sand or water before it really gets going. It's a very important task because incendiaries have been causing far more widespread damage than high explosive bombs.'

'How were we supposed to know all that?'

Ignoring his mother for the moment, he said, 'On nights, we spend the hours of darkness and beyond, rescuing terrified people from burning buildings. That's before we can start fighting the fires, Sometimes, we can't save a building, so we isolate it by drenching the adjacent properties with water.' Having reduced his mother and father to silence, he said, 'With all that hatefulness and evil being released nightly on the poor bloody East End, let's just be thankful that we human beings are also capable of decency and that we can help each other, and if I choose to dry my sister's hair because it's a cosy thing that we both remember fondly from childhood, how on earth is that going to spoil her?'

———▶◀———

If his leave had done no more good, it had enabled him to leave his parents with something to consider. As always, it had been good to see Eileen again. Goodness only knew when they would next meet; their leaves were unlikely to coincide. Otherwise, only decency dictated that he should visit his home when he could, that he had to accept that his parents were both emotionally constipated, and that his mother still resented Eileen simply because she had survived and Joseph hadn't.

27

Lorna's leave had been much quieter than Ted's, but that was only to be expected, their families being rather different in outlook. When they returned to the flat after supper, he had something to show her.

'What's this?' She took the photograph he offered her.

'Proof.'

'Proof of what? This is a choir, isn't it?'

'You didn't believe I was ever a choirboy, but there I am on the front row.'

'All right, I take it back. You looked angelic in those days,' she remarked, handing the photo back. 'Something must have gone wrong in the meantime. Anyway, how was home?'

'As anaemic as ever.' He told her about the hair-drying conversation.

'I think it was thoughtful of your mother to check that I was fully clothed,' she said. 'Bearing in mind the condition I was in, I could easily have walked out of the washroom without a stitch of clothing on me and never realised it.'

'I'd have alerted you discreetly to the fact.'

'I know you would. You're a gentleman.' She shivered. 'Do you find it cold in here?'

'Just a trifle.'

'It's because we've been away. I'm going to light the fire, if you don't mind.'

'I'll do it.' He crouched to turn on the gas tap and put a match to each of the fireclay radiants.

'Thank you. Do you mind very much if I change into my pyjamas and dressing gown?'

'Not in the least. Can I get you anything while you're changing?'

She thought for a second and asked, 'Are you any good at making cocoa?'

'I enjoy a certain reputation in that field.'

Smiling, she went to her room to change. Ted got to work in the scullery, so that by the time Lorna had returned, he was able to give her a mug of freshly-made cocoa.

'I was only joking about the cocoa,' she said.

'So was I. It was my first attempt, but it's roughly the right colour, and it should be all right when it cools down.'

'Aren't you having any?'

'No, it has an adverse effect on me.'

For a moment, she looked surprised. 'Are you allergic to cocoa as well as soya?'

'No, nothing like that. It just makes me crave my ursine namesake and a bedtime story. You'll find that behind my rugged exterior I'm an awful baby.'

'Your ursine…? Oh, you mean your teddy bear. You poor thing.' She took off her slippers and curled up at the end of the sofa with her feet tucked under her dressing gown.

'Are you still cold?'

'Just a bit. It's my feet, really. They're like ice.'

'Really?' He hadn't been so conscious of the cold.

'Come and feel them if you don't believe me.'

He joined her on the sofa.

'I was joking,' she said.

'It's hardly a joking matter. Give me your feet and let me feel how cold they are.' He held out his hands to receive them.

'Don't say I didn't warn you.' Tucking her dressing gown beneath her legs, she placed her feet in his lap.

'Ah,' he said in the erudite manner of the connoisseur, 'I'm something of an expert on cold feet, or *frigoris pedes*, as we call them.' He took one in each hand, rubbing them and cupping her toes to restore circulation and warmth. 'By that, of course, I'm not referring to the metaphorical kind most often associated with the eve of the nuptials, you understand, but the common or garden variety that function most efficiently at ninety-eight point four degrees Fahrenheit. I hope I've made that sufficiently clear.'

'Abundantly, Professor, and they feel warmer already. Thank you.'

'The sooner you drink your cocoa, the quicker the benefit will make its downward journey.'

She swung her feet over the sofa to return them to her slippers and tried her cocoa. After a trial sip, she said, 'You know, you could quite easily establish a genuine reputation as a cocoa maker.'

191

'You're too kind. How are your feet now?'

'Much warmer, thank you.' She put her mug on the hearth and said, 'So far, you've dried my hair, helped me pay the rent, made cocoa and warmed my feet.'

He nodded. 'Quite right.'

'But is it?'

'I acted always with the most honourable of motives.'

'I know you did. I mean,' she said patiently, 'you've done all that for me, and it's time I did something for you.'

'I'm not keeping a ledger.'

'Even so.'

'Have you anything particular in mind?'

'I thought you might think of something.'

He considered the question. Finally, he asked, 'How are you at bedtime stories?'

'About as experienced as you are at making cocoa, but I'm game to give it a try. Perhaps some of your beginner's luck might rub off.' She hesitated. 'I don't know where we'll find a teddy bear, but if you like to use your imagination, I don't mind standing in.'

'You'll be relieved to know,' he said, slipping his arm round her shoulders, 'that I don't suck my thumb nowadays.'

'Speaking both as flatmate and substitute teddy bear, that's quite a relief. Are you ready?'

'Yes.'

After a little thought, she began to tell her story. 'Once upon a time, there was an auxiliary firewoman who was very happy. That was until the day a telegram arrived, telling her that her husband had been killed. She was devastated, and she went about her duties in a kind of stupor, scarcely able to believe what had happened. Then, to make things worse, a wicked ogre with a silly moustache sent his airmen to bomb the water main, and the water company had to turn off the supply to her flat, so that she couldn't run a bath or wash her hair.' A tear, no doubt prompted by the memory, had formed and was poised to run down her cheek. Ted took out a handkerchief with his free hand and caught it.

'Then, the kind sub-officer offered her three wishes, but she could only think of one. She asked him if she might be allowed to use the firemen's shower. He granted her wish, and she was very grateful because she came out of the shower clean again, and she'd been able to wash her hair, a matter of great importance to her. Even then, though, she felt helpless. She sat outside the washroom in a daze, not really conscious of anything, until a handsome fireman returned from his travels and found her there. He took her towel and dried her hair.' She stopped and took Ted's handkerchief to stem the tears that had started.

'That was important to you, wasn't it?'

'Very important,' she confirmed. 'I'll never forget it.' She buried her face against his chest so that he felt her hot tears soaking through his shirt.

In the absence of anything useful he could do, he stroked her hair. 'This is bound to happen from time to time,' he said, kissing her forehead as if comforting a child. 'My shoulder is at your disposal, but I shan't intrude.'

She lifted her head to look at him. 'This isn't grief for Reg,' she said. 'I passed that milestone some time ago.' She touched his shirtfront with her fingertips. 'You're soaked through.'

'Only my shirt. The rest of me is waterproof.' Then, because he had to know, he asked, 'If it's not grief, what's really troubling you?'

'Nothing's troubling me. It's the memory of what you did for me.... It affects me like this sometimes, but I'm not unhappy.'

'Have a good blow,' he suggested, at a total loss to understand what she'd told him.

After several heroic blasts, she said, 'Excuse me for a minute,' and went to the bathroom. She was gone for several minutes, returning eventually with her face washed and her expression brightened. She asked, 'Do I look awful?'

'No, you look innocent and pure, like one of Leonardo's cherubs. He added modestly, 'I think it was Leonardo. It was one of those Renaissance blokes, anyway.'

'I don't believe you.' She surprised him by taking his arm and draping it across her shoulders again.

'You seem happy to play teddy bear,' he observed.

'For now,' she agreed, looking remarkably at ease.

'I've changed my mind about the cherub. I think you resemble a Renaissance maiden.'

'That I'm not. You have to remember I'm a widow, and whilst my experience was fleeting – "brief" barely covers it – I'm not exactly a maiden.' She looked at him directly again and asked, 'Are you thinking of kissing me?'

'The thought had crossed my mind, but I'm trying to be trustworthy.'

'Trustworthy?'

'One of the qualifications you look for in choosing a flatmate,' he reminded her.

'You're well-enough qualified to be my flatmate.'

'I am,' he confirmed, so if it's all the same to you....' He bent cautiously and kissed her softly, repeating the action with increasing boldness.

'You're not at all untrustworthy,' she said, responding freely to his attentions.

'It's not too early for this, is it?'

'No, I think your scars and mine are sufficiently healed.'

They kissed again at length until, sensing activity beneath her chin, she asked, 'What are you doing?'

Punctuating his reply with tiny kisses, he said, 'Opening... your... pyjama... jacket.'

'Why?'

'Ventil... ation'

'I suppose that makes it all right.'

Having unfastened her buttons down to her waist, he opened her pyjamas and, with a sense of exquisite discovery, buried his face between her naked breasts, emerging after a moment to favour one and then the other with kisses that, had they been able to reason for themselves, would have told them just how he felt about them.

Surprised as well as aroused, she asked, 'Is it normal for a man to do that?'

'It is for me,' he confirmed, kissing her on the lips to forestall any suggestion of favouritism. 'It depends on a man's initial emphasis. Some favour the breasts whilst some are diverted by the lower limbs. Others, I regret to say, are devoid of finesse and are more direct in their approach. I can only apologise on their behalf. I owe this information,' he explained, kissing her again, 'to assiduous theoretical research, practical opportunities being thin on the ground.'

'I'm glad you're the first kind, but I think we might be more comfortable in bed. Don't you?'

'Yes, I do. I didn't suggest it, because I didn't want to appear forward.'

'How could I possibly have thought that?'

He drew her jacket together discreetly, stood up and followed her to her bedroom. 'I don't wish to sound indelicate,' he said, but I haven't come prepared, if you know what I mean.'

'I took care of that when I freshened up,' she assured him, hanging up her dressing gown and shrugging off her pyjamas.

He undressed quickly and joined her beneath the covers.

'I'm cold again,' she said. 'Snuggle up.'

'That's just what I have in mind.' He put his arms round her and held her close, kissing her, at the same time tracing her contours ecstatically with his free hand. After a while, he reached downward to explore her lower abdomen and the wonders beyond it. It was a fascinating journey of a kind he'd not made for some time, so he allowed himself to linger until she interrupted his odyssey.

'Ted?' She sounded breathless.

'Mm?'

'Teddy says… it's time to stop playing and… come home.'

'Is it really that time already?'

'Oh yes, it is.' She confirmed it with a sudden intake of breath as she received him.

28

JUNE

The unexpected cessation in bombing continued amid widespread disbelief. The fire-watching rota still stood, although the sirens remained silent. Ted and Lorna were now on the night watch, ready as ever for action; incidents unconnected with war occurred from time to time, and the watch was called out to deal with them, but the horror of the Blitz was past, at least for the time being.

There were other distractions, including a particularly welcome letter from Eileen.

21st June, 1941.
Dear Ted,
The letter finally came, and I'm to report to a place in Mill Hill, London, to begin with, but first of all, I must tell you about the reception the letter got here. First of all, Dad went berserk. He was all set to get my job at the market garden registered as a reserved occupation so that I'd go on working for him, but now he'll have to apply for a land girl. Heaven help the poor girl! Next, Mum was apoplectic. Who did I think I was? How dare I do such a thing without telling them? Who did I think was going to help with the housework? She says I needn't expect them to pay my train fare! They needn't bother, because I've been sent an official rail warrant, and I'm going tomorrow, and Auntie Jane's sent me a postal order to help out, so knickers to them! Incidentally, if I'm using too many exclamation marks, it's their fault. Like you, I plead extreme provocation!

Don't worry about writing to me in London. It's only a depot, and I shan't be there very long before they send me on proper training. I'm going to a place in Gloucestershire to train as a telegraphist. I'll send you the address as soon as I can.

I'm glad you've got a nice girlfriend now. You never had much luck with them before. Fingers crossed, anyway.

I have to end there. I need to pack to catch the 7 o'clock tain in the morning. I've told them here that I'll get the bus to the railway station. Then I'll be free!

Take care.

Your loving sister,

Eileen XXX.

P.S. I've enclosed the English exam paper for your information. There were no horrors in it, so I'm fairly confident.

Ted showed the letter to Lorna that night. When she handed it back to him, she said, 'I didn't know about your record with girlfriends. I hope I'm not going to be a disappointment.'

'You know you're not.'

'Let's hope not. How did the exam paper strike you?'

'It's the kind of thing I'd have expected. If Eileen found it easy, it's because she prepared herself for it, and that was in spite of working on the market garden and doing more than her share of the housework.'

'Poor girl.' Lorna looked genuinely sympathetic.

'She'll be all right now. In spite of the way she's been treated, she hasn't grown up bitter and twisted. I think she'll do well in the Wrens.'

Lorna suddenly had the look of someone inspired. 'Maybe,' she said excitedly, 'that was the role you were sent here to fulfil.'

'Come again?'

'Maybe your *magnum opus* was nurturing Eileen and cushioning the girl within against the pressures without.'

He shook his head at her reasoning. 'I thought my *magnum opus* took place last month,' he said, 'when we returned from leave. Have you forgotten already?'

'Oh, that was rather splendid,' she agreed. 'I couldn't understand why you apologised for being in a hurry the first time. Then it all fell into place.'

'I was over-excited and out of practice.'

'You said so at the time, but I wasn't complaining.' She looked at her watch and said, 'I'd better get back to the Watch Room in case the Nazis do decide to join us, although they've left it a bit late.'

———◆◆◆———

There was an air of excitement when Red Watch came on in the morning, and the reason soon became known. It seemed that Hitler had launched a massive invasion of the Soviet Union. Details were still coming in, and conjecture was rife.

'No wonder they stopped bombing us,' said Sub-Officer Prentice. 'They need the planes to attack Russia.'

Greg was inclined to be cautious. 'If they invade Russia,' he said, 'what then? They'll come back and have another go at us.'

'I don't think so,' said Ted. 'The last megalomaniac who tried to invade Russia got his fingers frozen.'

'Don't you mean "burnt"?' Spud was a man of little imagination.

'No, Bonaparte stretched his supply lines too far and he was beaten by the Russian winter. The men who survived the retreat from Moscow arrived home starved, frost-bitten and exhausted, and history has an uncanny, and sometimes reassuring, way of repeating itself.'

'But it's midsummer,' protested Greg. 'Winter's months away.'

'And the Nazis have thousands of miles to cover. I'd rather be in our shoes than theirs.'

———◆———

Ted and Lorna made their way back to the flat, relieved to be off-watch and now optimistic after the morning's news.

'Isn't it strange,' said Lorna, 'that a huge lift such as we experienced this morning can leave us feeling so flat afterwards?'

'I think that owes something to being on nights.'

They undressed and went to bed, where they lay sleepily in each other's arms.

'I love you,' he said, hoping they would both stay awake long enough for him to demonstrate the fact.

'Me too.'

'I'm glad we've established that.'

'We've done our duty,' she said, stifling a yawn, 'we're off-watch, we're off the hook as far as invasion's concerned, so now we can relax with our consciences clear.'

'We could always do that, even at the height of the bombing. Remember what Mr Churchill called us last year?'

' "Heroes with grimy faces", wasn't it?'

'That was just the firemen. I mean all of us: firemen, firewomen, the wardens, rescue parties, doctors, nurses, ambulance crews, the police, the Home Guard, land girls, the Timber Corps… everyone, in fact.'

'Remind me before I fall asleep, Ted.'

'He called us "Unknown Warriors".' He spoke the words with difficulty as sleep claimed him too.

THE END